SHARDS OF SHADOW BOOK 2

THE PRISON
OF
SHADOWS

JOSEPH R. LALLO

Art commissioned by Joseph Lallo as chapter headings by viiStar.

Cover design: Deranged Doctor Designs

Published by:

Heart Ally Books, LLC
heartallybooks.com
26910 92nd Ave NW C5-406, Stanwood, WA 98292
Published on Camano Island, WA, USA

ISBN-13: 978-0-99970-819-4 (paperback)

10 9 8 7 6 5 4 3 2 1

CONTENTS

Chapter 1

A blaring tone jolted Alan roughly from sleep. He fumbled for his phone to silence it. When peace was restored, he blinked blearily at his darkened room. Alan was an early riser. He seldom had to contend with the sun, but the circumstances of the last few weeks had persuaded him to get blackout curtains. He'd become accustomed to them quite quickly. In truth, they *did* help him sleep a bit better. But that wasn't the reason he'd bought them. Judging from the potent scent of coffee filling the air, the person who'd motivated that change, and a dozen others in his life, was well into her morning routine already.

He grabbed his robe from where he'd hung it on the back of his computer chair. Though there was hardly any light, he could still see his shadow stretched out like a ribbon on the floor before him. It led under the door in a way that a proper shadow never would. He tugged the door open and marched down the short hallway from his bedroom to his kitchenette. The only light came from the dim bulb of the stove hood. It wasn't much, but it was enough to cast a shadow. That shadow *should* have led back down the hallway behind him. Instead, it bobbed up and down on the wall beside the coffeemaker, hands rubbing together expectantly. If its behavior wasn't

1

indication enough that this wasn't a run-of-the-mill shadow, a pair of white eyes blinking at him from it hammered that point home nicely.

"You're up!" she said. Her tone was a nuanced mix of excitement and impatience.

"And you're making coffee," he said thickly.

"Second pot," she said.

The silhouette shifted until it looked as though it was being cast by someone sitting on the counter. She reached out to the shadow of a coffee canister and grasped it. The canister itself obligingly rose into the air as she lifted its shadow.

"We're out of the Jamaican stuff," she said.

"We're out of..." His sleepy brain reluctantly got up to speed. "Wait, second pot? You drank an entire pot of coffee already?"

She placed a hand on her hip. "What do you expect? It's not as though I can waste four hours a day sleeping like you."

Alan rubbed his eyes. "Most people do closer to eight, Blot."

"Most people are lazy," Blot said. She reached up and pulled a cup from the cabinet, then lifted the pot to fill it for him. "Here, wake up. You've got work to do."

He accepted the cup and took a careful sip of the steamy beverage. It was hot, but that was only part of the reason to go easy on his first taste. This was *Blot's* coffee.

The concoction met his lips, and his face nearly turned inside out. She'd been experimenting with the coffeemaker with the same zeal as a mad scientist who had discovered a new element. Every day he was treated to exciting new frontiers of bitterness as she endeavored to make the strongest possible cup.

"You know, the goal of brewing coffee isn't to try to get a lethal dose of caffeine into your first sip," he muttered, giving it another try.

"This would be a lot easier if you'd just buy that espresso machine," she said. "I hear those things are *much* better at the strong stuff."

"We can't afford it right now."

"And whose fault is that?" she jabbed. "Which reminds me..."

Blot quickly filled a cup of her own and drifted around the walls of the kitchen. The cup traced the path she would have walked if she'd been a flesh-and-blood creature rather than a living shadow. She stopped at the table and "sat." Alan's laptop was set up on the table, something his sleep-deprived mind had only just been able to process. Blot grabbed the shadow of the mouse and waggled it to wake the screen.

She shuddered as the screen flicked on. Its light wasn't enough to push Blot around in the way that the ceiling light might, but it still hit her like a slap in the face. When she'd shaken it off, she pecked out a search term in the address bar. "Magnuson Scandal." It was surreal watching the keys of the keyboard clinking down on their own. He found himself slightly relieved that she wasn't a faster typist. Seeing the keys clacking away at that sort of speed would have made him feel like this was some updated version of the player piano gag in a cheesy haunted house.

The images that populated his screen were many and varied, but many were quite familiar. He'd taken most of them. Poorly framed, poorly lit, and taken at weird angles. He felt a sting of professional shame in seeing their poor quality. In his defense, he'd taken most of them while fearing for his life, but that didn't make him feel any better about the most successful images of his career being among his worst.

"Do you see what I see?" Blot asked.

"I see yet another example of Cox's willingness to sell the worst shots in the whole album to the biggest news outlets." Alan sipped the coffee again. "Jeez, Blot. You like the way Vice Versa does their coffee. Why are you boiling this stuff down like my grandmother used to? It's coffee, not stew."

"Don't change the subject." She poked the screen. "These are all recent stories again, and your pictures are all over them."

"Well sure. They make Magnuson look like a criminal, and all sorts of charges and stuff are pouring in from that case. It's like when that crazy-looking mug shot of Gary Busey was making the rounds."

"Who?"

He fought another sip down. "It was before your time."

"Whatever. How come you aren't getting paid again?"

"Because that's not how freelance photography works. I sold the pictures to Cox. He makes the money from here on out."

She crossed her arms, an odd position for a shadow, as it made them look like they'd vanished. "You need to march in there and tell him that you want more money if he's going to keep using your pictures."

"Not going to do that."

He opened the fridge to consider the issue of breakfast. Wisdom said he should make oatmeal, but the bachelor and former college student in him were making a strong case for the leftovers of last night's experiment with fried chicken. It was far too early. Wisdom never had a chance.

Alan plopped down with a drumstick and poked at his laptop with his grease-free hand.

"Alan, how are we going to get rich and powerful if you're not willing to demand more from your boss?" Blot asked.

"Photographers don't get rich and powerful, Blot."

"That's a real shame, then, because the Dawn came snooping around yesterday."

His eyes widened and he looked to her. "Really?"

She shrugged. "Them or someone else with a little more 'supernatural-ness' than cranky Ms. Levitt."

"You saw them?"

"I felt them through the door. Which is *not* a good sign. That means power, Alan."

She scooped up her cup again. It trembled slightly in the air, and her shadow huddled down, as though she'd slumped over the warmth of the cup for comfort.

"There are too many people who want us dead for us to be trusting a deadbolt and a chain to keep them out."

"We'll figure something out," Alan said, bringing up his email.

"There!" She pointed angrily at the screen. "You're not helping with that stuff either." She was indicating an email from a paranormal expert in Louisiana with the subject line "Living Shadow Legends."

"You can't keep digging about us. I've told you everything you need to know, which is that we both die if either of us dies, and now that you *know* about us, the rest of my people want both of us dead. That's on top of the Dawn, who want all my people dead already, and whoever those white-suit people are, who probably want us dead too."

"We don't know that they want us dead."

"Oh, why should they be any different? The only reason the rest of humanity doesn't want us dead is because it's impossible to prove to the normies that we even exist. So there. You've got all the info you need. That's enough to know that we should be hiding and finding a way to defend ourselves."

"I'm a photographer. It is my duty to shed light on things."

She thumped her already empty cup down. "Oh, calm down. First, it's a job, not some ancient prophecy calling you to serve antiquity. And second, I hate light getting shed on *anything* and you know it. You've got to stop acting like a hero."

"The world needs heroes sometimes, Blot."

"Uh-huh. You know *why* the world needs heroes? Because all the other ones got themselves killed."

A few minutes later, the all too often ignored voice of wisdom in Alan's mind was enjoying yet another I-told-you-so moment. Blot's "coffee" combined with the unconventional breakfast had joined forces and felt as though they were trying to claw their way out of his gut. A short, hot shower helped to make him feel a bit more human, at least. A longer one would have done a better job, but he had a schedule to worry about.

Alan bundled up, grabbed his gear, and headed for the door. "You ready?" he asked, his hand on the doorknob.

"Yeah," Blot said sullenly.

Among the dozens of little changes to his morning routine, one of the most important shifts in his thinking was giving a moment of consideration to Blot every time he was about to step out into the light. It was bad enough for her that most of the civilized world was lit brightly enough to lock her in place. The least he could do was make sure she was ready for it when it happened.

He opened the door. She darted and stretched behind him, then crept up in front of him as he turned to close and lock the door. Blot glared at the fixture overhead.

"I swear I'm going to bust that thing one of these days," she muttered. "And who is this?"

Alan glanced over his shoulder. "Oh, hi there," he said.

He turned to face a person he didn't recognize. They had a peculiar look to them. Not unattractive, but certainly atypical. They had a short blond bob framing a pale face with immaculate skin. Most of their build was obscured by a puffy white parka.

Alan blinked and shook his head, realizing to his dismay that he'd been silently staring at the newcomer for far longer than the social contract would permit. It didn't seem to bother the stranger, who simply offered a sunny smile and a friendly wave before disappearing through the doorway directly across the hall from Alan's own. The door clicking shut hit Alan like the snap of a hypnotist's fingers. His fascination and interest faded swiftly.

"I'll have to ask their name next time I see them. It's been a while since I got a new neighbor," he said, turning back to his door to ensure it was locked.

This brought him face-to-face with Blot, who had a disapproving look in her spooky white eyes.

"I don't like them."

"You don't like anybody."

"And so far I've been wrong about it exactly once. That's evidence of a good policy, if you ask me."

Aside from having a semiadversarial relationship with his shadow, the biggest change in Alan's life over the last six weeks was at work. When he'd been added to the regular freelance pool at Cox Media, the choice assignments had been given directly to a young woman named Marie-Anna Proctor, and the rest were handed out seemingly at random to the rest of the photogs on a first-come–first-serve basis. It was a ridiculous system that meant the only way to keep earning decent money was to show up early, hope there was an assignment for you, and pray it was the kind of assignment that would pay off.

These days, more often than not, his arrival was greeted with the same two words.

"Fontaine, office!" proclaimed his boss, Mr. Cox.

Cox had the sort of voice that made him seem angry regardless of his mood, though anyone who had *actually* seen him angry was treated to a whole additional spectrum of hostility. This was what Alan would classify as his "happy" voice.

Alan marched toward the hallway to Cox's office while his boss hurried the rest of the pending assignments through. Along the way, he caught eyes with Marie-Anna. She made a concerted effort to burn a hole through him with her gaze alone.

"Ha ha," Blot said mockingly as the lights caused her to swing and jump about. "The boss's favorite is getting mad at you."

"Would you shut up," Alan said through clenched teeth.

"Why? She can't hear me."

"So. Badmouthing someone behind their back is still a lousy thing to do."

She rolled her eyes. "You act like your mother is still watching everything you do."

"She always used to say we had a devil on one shoulder and an angel on the other."

"And you believed that?"

"I mean, not really. Though now that I've got someone whispering bad advice in my ear all the time, I'm starting to think she knew something I didn't."

He stepped into Cox's office and took a seat in front of his desk. It was more warmly lit than the bullpen where all the assignments were delivered. Said warmth came from an old three-way lamp, which replaced the fluorescents that kept the rest of the place lit. The lamp's shade was a putrid product of the seventies, and the whole thing was controlled by a chain dangling down. Blot grunted in exertion as she stretched toward it.

"Don't," Alan warned.

"If you get to be comfortable, I get to be comfortable."

"This isn't our office, you can't just go messing with the lights."

"If you'd start taking that advice you think is so bad, this would be *our* office in no time." She strained a bit more and managed to snag the chain. A click cast the room in darkness. "That's better."

Alan glared at the contented eyes drifting around the room and clicked the light back to its lowest level. She squinted at the glow, but didn't appear to be terribly hampered by it.

"I guess that's a compromise," she muttered. She steadied herself on the desk and looked over its contents. "What's that key-press thing to lock the screen real quick?" she asked.

He gave her a suspicious look. "Why do you need to know..."

"Never mind, I remember. It's this weird one and then the one with the *L* on it." She pecked out something on the keyboard.

"What are you doing?" he said more seriously.

"I finally managed to catch him entering his password last time. Quick, what's something worth looking up?"

"Don't! Cut that out," Alan said, glancing nervously at the door.

"He gets a lot of emails. I thought you guys were supposed to hand in your photos directly. He's got a bunch that say they're from Marie-Anna." Her eyes widened. "Oh! It's *those* kind of pictures..."

"He's coming," Alan hissed.

She hastily tapped at the mouse and the keyboard, then snapped back to where the lamp pushed her. The footsteps of his boss approached.

"I seem to remember you not being able to push past that light last week," Alan said.

"Shades get stronger the longer they're with their hosts. You should be happy about that. The better to watch our collective backs."

"I'll get right down to it, Fontaine," Cox said, marching into the room and taking a seat. "Seems like putting you front and center in our photo lineup is starting to pay off."

He opened a drawer and rummaged through it. "You wouldn't know this, because it doesn't really concern you, but we've got a standing contract with another media outlet. Insight something or other. They've got an army of writers and no media people, so when they need something that needs semipro recordings and photos, they come to us."

His voice lowered and his teeth clenched. "At least they used to. Now they just have the knucklehead interviewers snap some rotten photos with their phones half the time. Whatever happened to professionalism?!" He waved his free hand. "Regardless. I got a call from them last night. You've been requested by name."

Alan raised an eyebrow. "Really? I don't think I've ever done any work for them."

"You haven't. Not even through me. These are usually gigs for Marie."

"Then they want me based solely on the quality of my work?"

Cox stared at him flatly. "You want to quit speculating and let me get to the point?" He pulled a stack of index cards from the drawer and started shuffling through them. "*They* aren't the ones who asked for you. It was the interviewee."

"Who is it?"

"I don't know. Someone that had to do with that whole election fiasco you broke. Doesn't matter. The point is, it's an exclusive, and they're only doing it if *you* shoot it." He slapped down the index card he was looking for. "Tomorrow morning. There's the address and the name of the interviewer you'll be working with. He'll have the credentials. Meet him in the parking lot at nine fifteen a.m."

Alan took the index card. "The interview is at the prison?"

"Yeah. Don't get too fancy on this one. I want video and photos, and they're only springing for *you* on this one, so set up a stationary video so you can be free for stills. I want..."

Alan nodded through the instructions. Cox must have been paying attention in management school, because he certainly hadn't missed the lesson about telling your hired experts how to do the job you hired them to be experts in. Alan didn't mind much. It gave him the opportunity to shut his ears off for a bit and ruminate on the handwritten card. Cox had good reason to be excited about a shot at covering something related to this scandal. It was the gift that kept on giving, when it came to local news. Every couple of weeks there was a new indictment or implication. People were eating it up. No doubt Cox Media would be able to get some big bucks for Alan's photos if this turned out to be something juicy.

Things weren't so simple for Alan though. Cox didn't know what had gone down that night. All he knew was what the rest of Philadelphia knew: a would-be senator got caught meeting with some unsavory figures and making some underhanded deals, and it somehow ended up with a nut on the roof of a vandalized office building. Alan, on the other hand, knew it was part of a supernatural scheme, and that he'd been added to the enemies' list of all involved. He could only think of one reason that any of the key players would want him in a room with them, and it involved making sure he never *left* that room.

"Happy now?" Blot had obviously followed the same line of logic to its potentially ruinous conclusion. "You don't need to dig anymore. Somebody with an ax to grind has hunted *you* down."

Alan winced. The last time he'd met with any of the other shades on their terms, it had ended on the aforementioned roof while a helicopter circled. Escaping with his heart still beating had been a skin-of-the-teeth affair. He'd hoped to be a little better educated—and better armed—if they were ever to meet again.

"... And some action shots. Plenty of action shots," Cox concluded.

The odd request was enough to briefly derail his dire train of thought. "Action shots?"

"Yeah. Action shots always sell big."

"It's a prison interview, though. I'm pretty sure the guards frown on action."

"Look, I'm not telling you to goad him into anything, but if tempers start flaring, get some photos. Maybe some papers get thrown around. Maybe a chair gets flipped. Cuffs come out. He gets led away. All that good stuff. Be ready for it."

"I don't think that's going to happen, Mr. Cox."

"Probably not." He leaned forward. "Big bonus if it does, though."

Alan cleared his throat and tried to move on. "This is for tomorrow," he said. "Anything for today?"

"No. Everything else is covered. Just prepare for this."

"I'm not conducting the interview. I'm not sure I have to do anything to prepare."

He waved his hands vaguely. "Charge your cameras. Buy more storage. I don't care. I don't have any jobs for you today, so keep yourself busy and bring your A-game tomorrow. Now run along. I'm done with you."

Alan hurried out the door, index card in hand.

"You're not going to do it, are you?" Blot asked.

"Yes, I'm going to do it," he muttered.

She narrowed her eyes. "*Why* are you going to do it?"

"What does it matter?"

"Because if you're doing it for the money, I can respect that. More money, more power, more survivability. But if you're doing it because you think somehow it's the 'right' thing to do, you're a fool and you're going to get us killed."

He coughed. "I can do it for more than one reason."

"Fontaine!"

Alan turned. It was Marie-Anna. Like Cox, Marie-Anna didn't really showcase the full range of human emotion in the workplace. Whereas Cox ran the gamut between "less angry" and "more angry," Marie-Anna started at "grudgingly tolerant" and escalated to "simmering with barely suppressed rage." Right now, she was on the smoldering side of her emotional palette.

She marched up to him and gestured with her chin for him to follow as she continued into a side hallway.

"Just keep going," Blot advised.

Alan ignored the advice and followed Marie-Anna.

"Nothing good will come of this," Blot grumbled.

When they were far enough to not be overheard, Marie-Anna turned and gave Alan a withering look. "Listen, Fontaine. I don't know what you've got hanging over him in there, but you can just cut it out right now," she said.

"Hanging over who?" Alan said.

"Remington."

"... Who?"

She pointed. "Cox!"

"His name is Remington?"

"He's been signing your checks, hasn't he?"

"It's just a scribble. Are you serious? His name is Remington Cox?"

"Never mind! You've been getting some pretty choice jobs. A lot of assignments handed to you directly. And I want to know why," she said.

"I've just been doing good work for him."

"Uh-huh," she said doubtfully. "We *all* do good work for him. He doesn't invite us back if we don't. But you're the first guy to start getting all his jobs in the office. Don't act like there's not something going on."

"I really don't know what you mean, Marie-Anna. They're just assignments."

"That is a good man in there, and I won't have him blackmailed."

"Wait, what? Blackmail?"

"You ruin him, you ruin yourself, too. You realize that. And all those people out there. People like him don't *exist* anymore. Jobs like this don't exist anymore. You're threatening people's livelihoods with your extortion, and for what?"

"Extortion? Now just hold on."

"It's about me, isn't it? It's about us. I won't be responsible for him being taken down."

Blot, locked on the ground behind Marie-Anna by the bright overhead light, snickered. "Wow. She's got a whole web of intrigue spun in her head."

Alan raised his hands. "Slow down! It's not extortion. I had an exclusive, and I used it to bargain some better jobs out of him until I could get past a financial rough spot. That's it."

"Plus, it seems like her and Cox are sort of an open secret," Blot said.

"Right," Alan agreed.

"Right what?" asked Marie-Anna.

He raised his eyebrows and internally cursed at himself for losing track of the physical and metaphysical members of the conversation.

"Just tell her," Blot said.

Alan sighed. "It isn't like you and Cox are being subtle about your relationship," he said. "I don't understand what the big secret is. Cox isn't married, and I don't think you are, so it's not an affair. Even if I was the sort of person who would consider blackmail, which I absolutely am not, I don't think there's anything here to lord over anyone."

She crossed her arms. "You really are oblivious, aren't you?" she seethed.

"I'm missing something?" he said.

She turned away from him. "Just get out of here. But don't think you're off the hook. Get used to seeing this face, because I'm not going to let you slide on whatever dirty dealing you're doing."

"But I'm not—"

"You don't go from being just another face in the morning scrum to being the hotshot right-hand man of the boss for no reason. People don't change overnight," she said.

"They do if they sleep in front of the gateway tree during the eclipse," Blot observed.

Marie-Anna marched past him. Alan lingered for a moment.

"Add another one to the heap of people who have a bone to pick with you, huh?" Blot said. "Have you always accumulated enemies so easily?"

"Not before you showed up," he said. "Let's go. If I've got a free day, maybe I've got time to follow up on some of those emails. It's been a while since I called Mom and Dad, too. Oh! And maybe Jessie can help me with the last of the forensic certification studies."

"I've gotta say, you do an impressive job of filling every waking moment with work while failing to achieve any worthwhile success."

"Yeah. Around here they call that 'being a millennial.'"

A few minutes later, Alan was in the car thumbing through his phone. The life of a freelancer is usually a twenty-four–seven hustle. Multitasking is an essential skill, and every spare moment has to be spent either earning money or finding the next gig. To that end, Alan always made certain to park somewhere with good reception so he could use his car as a temporary office. Lately, some decent shade was also a requirement for a good parking spot, lest Blot be immobilized. Fortunately, he'd been able to snag his favorite spot, and was working his way through his notes trying to pick something worth spending his day researching.

"This is boring, Alan," she said.

"Good. Boring is good. The alternative is excitement, which I believe you've been very vocal about having me avoid."

"There are other alternatives to boredom than excitement. There's *fun*, isn't there?" she said.

"I enjoy research."

"That makes one of us."

She heaved heavy sigh and raised her shadowy hand. A mechanical pencil flipped into existence, followed by a memo pad.

"Did you bring those from home?" he said.

"No. I stole them from Cox's office," she said. "See?" She held out the pencil, which was a rather cheap promotional item with the Cox Media logo on it.

"*I* didn't even see you do it," he said.

"That's the idea. You're supposed to do that sort of thing when no one's looking."

She flipped through the pages of the memo pad until she found a blank one, then clicked the pencil a few times and started to sketch. "What are you researching now, anyway?" she asked.

"It's from that Louisiana guy. He's a folklore expert. I guess, uh, *intelligent* shadows are a part of a lot of cultures."

"I bet he didn't say 'intelligent.'"

"Er, no. He said 'malevolent.'"

She laughed. "That's a good word."

"Most of this seems bogus. Mumbo-jumbo type stuff. But until you, I would have said the same thing about people being twisted into monstrous shapes by their shadows."

Blot muttered something under her breath.

"What was that?"

"Nothing. I was just thinking back to when Dun was assigning specialties. I *really* wanted shape-shifting. But I didn't get it."

"What did you get assigned?"

"Observation," she said mockingly. "They ran memory drills and taught me to watch for things."

"Sounds pretty useful."

"Right up until people are trying to kill you. Then the ability to turn your host into something that can tear the throats out of your enemies would be a nice skill to have."

"What else did they teach you?"

"What do you care?"

Alan held up the phone. "I'm trying to learn more about whatever it is your people are doing here and what I can do about it. It'd help if I could cross-reference it with what you know."

"I'm already a traitor, Alan. Don't make me be the kind of traitor that gets her own people killed en masse."

"What have I said or done that would make you think that I would even consider that sort of thing?"

"Oh, it's not you. You're Mr. Helpful. It's the people who figure out you've got an inside line to the evil shades and decide to manipulate you into helping them kill everyone. Because I hate to break it to you, but Mr. Helpful is exactly the kind of person who does whatever the killer asks."

"I'm not a child. I know danger when I see it."

"We'll see. What sort of questions have you got for me that you haven't already asked?"

"How long ago was the last eclipse when your people came through?"

Her eyes shifted toward him. "One eclipse ago."

"I know that, but more specifically."

"That is exactly as specific as I can be. It's how we measure time back home. It's like if I asked you 'how long ago was last year?' The last eclipse was the last eclipse."

"Fine. Then how many of *my* years has it been?"

"No idea. For all I know, time passes at a different speed here."

"Have you ever heard of a"—he referenced his list—"stained landscape?"

"Sounds like a term your people would come up with, not mine."

"I suppose so. This guy says there are different places where the shadows tend to gather, and sometimes those places change as a result."

"Mmm..." she said. "What kind of change?"

"Uh... He says people complain of haziness in the air, cooler temperatures. Animals tend to stay away."

"Sounds like someone's making themselves at home," she said. "If that *is* a shade, can you blame them? Did you 'stain' your apartment when you hung up your photos?"

He pocketed his phone. "Fine, how about this? I know *you* came to Philadelphia because you were already linked to me, and this is where I live. But we are a *long* way away from that tree. Why did Dun show up here? Why all those others we encountered?"

She shrugged.

"You didn't have any instructions to come to Philadelphia?"

"I didn't even know what Philadelphia was. My instructions were to find a powerful host, learn as much as I could, and find a higher-ranking shade for more instructions. Dun is exactly the sort of shade I should have looked for. So I guess the reason any other shades gathered here is because Dun's the only instructor around. As for why *he's* here? Your guess is as good as mine."

Alan started the engine. A moment later his phone rang, and he shut the engine off again.

"Oh, just drive while talking," Blot moaned.

"Not if I don't have to. Distracted driving is—"

"I know, I know. By the darkness, just hurry up then."

He glanced at the screen, then answered. "Hey, Dad."

"Alan! You called?" came the voice on the other end.

"Yeah. I had a spare minute. Just checking in."

"Sorry I didn't answer. On the phone with the lawyer again."

He furrowed his brow. "Lawyer?"

"Yeah. About the land."

"What about the land? I thought it was all over but the signatures a month ago."

"So your mother didn't tell you then."

"Tell me what?"

"The buyer pulled the plug. Something about failing to meet a deadline, which is garbage, because we were done with six days to spare. The lawyers confirm it, but we can't get in touch with the guy."

"When did this happen?"

"A couple of weeks ago."

"Why am I just learning about this now?"

"Aw, you know your mother. She probably didn't want you to worry."

"Well I *am* worried. How's the money situation?"

"It is what it is."

"That's not an answer, Dad."

"Don't worry about it."

"I just told you I'm worried!"

"You're upset. Call me back when you're not so upset."

"Dad, just tell me... Dad?" He glanced at the phone. "He called me, told me the solution to their debt problem fell through, and then hung up. My parents are trying to kill me with stress."

"It beats the way everyone else is trying to kill us."

"I'm not so sure about that," he grumbled.

A few hours later, Alan was on his couch tapping at his laptop. Contrary to the name, a laptop wasn't terribly well suited to actually working on one's lap. That was why he had a desk set up in his bedroom. But these days he was in permanent hospitality mode, what with Blot looking over his shoulder all the time. Unless what he was working on was of particular interest to her, he felt bad trapping her in front of the screen with him while he worked. Thus, yet another significant shift to his routine.

"Did I miss anything?" Blot said, sliding in from the kitchen.

A pair of mugs drifted in with her. She passed one to him and nestled onto the couch beside him.

"I can pause it, remember?" he said.

"Right, right. Smart TV. I'll say this about you people. You've *really* figured out entertainment."

Alan pressed play. It had taken a little bit of trial and error to find something that Blot enjoyed. She was a ravenous consumer of new information, so to a degree, anything he put on would capture her attention. That said, most fictional stuff relied a little too heavily on the reasonable assumption that someone had grown up in a human world and had the proper context to understand why something was funny, sad, or frightening. Rather than stop what he was doing every few minutes to explain a sitcom gag, he moved away from scripted television. For a while it was documentaries, but when he'd given reality TV a try, he'd struck gold. Her latest obsession had been *The Great British Bake Off.*

"This isn't one of your nightmare concoctions is it?" he asked, sniffing the mug warily.

She shook her head. "Standard brew."

While he tapped away at his keyboard, she sat with rapt attention as someone did their level best to produce a passable chocolate roulade.

"They use just the *whites* of the eggs for this part..." she murmured with a thoughtful nod. She set her coffee down on a side table and produced a pencil and pad.

"Doing more drawing?" he asked.

"No. Taking notes."

He raised an eyebrow. "Are you planning on making a chocolate roulade?"

"You never know. Besides, it's my training. Old habits die hard."

"You know you don't *have* to do as you were taught anymore."

"Yes I do. It's the reason I'm here." She motioned toward his screen. "What are *you* working on?"

"I'm almost done with the forensic certification. It's been tough, but I really think I'm getting the hang of it. Jessie's going to be here in a few minutes to go over some stuff, remember?"

Blot grumbled a bit. "You know *you* could serve to have a little more direction hammered into you like I did."

"What do you mean?"

"One minute you're all about being a fancy photographer. The next minute you're looking for a position in the police force. Meanwhile, the only thing you *actually* do is take pictures of entertainers and the like."

"I'm a man of many passions."

"If you were a man of *one* passion, maybe you'd be closer to achieving it. Back home, they assess you and assign you."

"You don't think it's important to make your own choices in life?"

"I think it's important to make the *right* choices in life. And how do you know if they're right if you aren't told so?"

"That only works if—"

"Shh! I think this is coming out too dry. I bet it cracks when she rolls it."

Alan smirked and went back to his studies while she eagerly watched to see if this would be a good bake. A few minutes later, his phone rang.

"Jessie! You're downstairs? ... Great. I'll buzz you up."

Alan answered a knock at the door.

"Hey, study buddy," Jessie announced.

She leaned in and hugged him with one arm. The other was weighed down with a pair of reusable shopping bags. "I brought donuts," she announced.

"A cop—"

She pointed a finger in his face. "You make a cop joke and I'll kick you in the shin."

He nodded. "Duly noted."

She looked around the room as she marched inside and dropped the junk food on the table. "What's with the moody lighting, Alan?"

Alan internally gave his forehead a slap as he realized he'd not anticipated the strange looks his shade-friendly lighting choices would get from the average person.

"Sorry. It's, uh—"

"Warm lighting helps something with the pictures," Blot helpfully supplied, always quick with a lie.

"I'm trying to push cool tones, and a red tint helps make them more apparent," he said.

"Interesting. And you need to do that with tinted lights instead of just twiddling a slider in a program or something?"

"Uh. No, not really. It's more for when I'm working with printouts, but old habits, you know?"

Jessie murmured the sort of dubious sound that suggested she didn't believe him but didn't know enough to contradict him.

"You should have just stuck with it. Lies are about sticking with it," Blot said. "Stick with a lie long enough and people will start to wonder if it's true no matter how absurd it is."

Jessie flopped down on the love seat and started to rummage through the other bag.

"These should be completely up-to-date. Station specific policy stuff," she said, plopping spiral-bound manuals beside his laptop. "You won't be tested on any of it, but knowing it will get you rolling faster if you end up working with us."

She snagged what looked to be a pumpkin donut from the box and slid one book in particular over to him.

"Since you'll be a subcontractor, you won't be in the union. This sort of thing will keep you from making a mistake that'll get you fired from the gig."

Alan flicked through some of the pages. "Aren't we putting the cart before the horse on this one? I haven't even got the job yet."

"Oh, you'll get it. If not during this round, then the next one. We need good people. The guy in charge, Lieutenant Stockton, he's got an eye for quality. Not the sort to just settle with someone subpar. The crime scene photos are too important to leave in the hands of someone who'll do a mediocre job. Where were you, though? Let me see what you're working on."

He handed her a printed-out portion of a handbook. "Thanks for helping me with this, by the way."

"Oh, it's been a long time coming. I wouldn't have made it through biology without you," she said. "So let's see. Define 'chain of custody.'"

"Chain of custody is the—" Blot began.

He raised a finger and shut his eyes. "Don't tell me."

"I wasn't going to, Alan. It would kind of defeat the purpose, me being the one asking the question," she said with a snort.

"There's really no reason for all this. I can just have a copy of the stuff and tell you it if you need it," Blot muttered.

He raised his voice. "The chain of custody is the time-encoded, verified documentation associated with the handling, transfer, and... *analysis* of physical evidence."

"And?"

Alan searched his memory.

"Electronic evidence, too," Blot supplied.

"Electronic evidence," he repeated.

"That's right," she said. "What's next..."

It took eight of the twelve donuts, and three cups of coffee, but Alan slowly came to the conclusion that he was as ready as he would ever be. As his confidence became more apparent, the "studying" became less academic and more conversational.

"Oh, do you remember Deborah?" Jessie giggled, dunking her latest donut.

"Yeah, I remember Deborah," he said sternly. "She dumped me right before midterms."

"I'd ask if you're still friends with her, but I know you're not. So this'll be a juicy one for you. Guess how many kids she's got."

"... Two?"

"Seven."

He nearly spat his coffee all over her. "How?"

"Two sets of triplets, plus her dude had a kid from a previous marriage."

"Oof..."

"Are we through here?" Blot asked, eyes narrow and lips sneering. "You're talking over the big reveal on the show, and this doesn't sound like cop stuff."

"I guess we should probably wrap up. I don't want to eat your whole day off."

"Oh, don't worry about it. It's good to hang with someone besides the boys at the station. You can only do that for so long before you get sick of talking shop."

He waggled the stack of papers. "As opposed to what we're doing."

"What we're doing is kibitzing between trivia questions. Totally different."

"What kind of stuff do they talk about?"

"Thirty percent idiots they had to deal with, thirty percent times they were idiots, thirty percent attempts to gross each other out, and a smattering of heroic humblebragging."

"I'd have thought that smattering would have been the bulk of it."

"Oh, trust me, I wouldn't be able to handle it if being a cop was all heroism all the time. You'd burn out in a week."

"Tell me about it," Blot grumbled. "I've only had to be a hero once and I'm still regretting it."

"Here, wait," Jessie said, fishing out her phone. "Let me see... There, see? Look at my profile photo. See my uniform? See how I've got cuffs, and a gun down there on my belt? Never used them. But these three pens in my shirt pocket? Every day. Forget handcuffs, a nice, sturdy clicky pen should be the visual shorthand for police work."

"Oh..."

She swizzled the tepid remains of her coffee. "That sounded like disappointment. I'm not disillusioning you, am I?"

"Well, I mean. I was sort of hoping this was the thing that'd make me feel like I was doing something important for once."

"Oh, trust me. That smattering of humblebrag? It might only be a few percent, but when you *really* know you helped someone, or stopped someone who needed stopping? That's the sort of thing that'll keep you going for *years*. I'm just sore because I've been on desk duty for so long."

"Why aren't they letting you out in the field?"

She waved the question off. "Eh, long, stupid story. Mostly policy stuff." She held out her hand. "Can I have my phone back?"

He squinted at the screen, which still displayed her profile picture. He handed it back, then stood.

"Get up. Stand over there," he said.

"Why?"

"Because you look orange. The white balance is screwed up. It looks terrible."

"Oh, gee, thanks, Alan."

"No, no. I just mean I can do better. Come on. It'll take two seconds." He grabbed one of his cameras.

"Oh, come on. I'm not made up or anything," she said.

"You let me worry about that," he said.

He tipped one of the lampshades back to provide some bright light in her direction while sparing Blot the worst of it.

"Prepare yourself. You're about to be in rarefied air. This is the very camera *and* lens that caught a photo of Paul Giamatti sneezing."

She feigned a swoon. "I didn't realize I'd have my brush with history today."

"If you really nail this picture, I'll dig out the old film camera. *That* one snapped a picture of Steve Buscemi getting mustard on his shirt."

She released a genuine laugh, which he captured with practiced timing. He spun it around and showed it to her.

"There, see? Pretty good, right?"

She took the camera and zoomed in. "Oh wow... You do good work, Mr. Fontaine."

"I have just the one skill," he said. "Just trying to find some way to make it worth using."

She flicked through some of the other photos on the camera. "Well, I think you're going to get your chance. Just don't screw it up."

"I'll try. Does the forensic photographer really make that much of an impact?"

"Oh, heck yeah. Aside from DNA, pretty much all the cold-case stuff hinges on the quality of the photographic evidence. If we make mistakes, your stuff is the next line of defense."

Alan considered the words. It only felt like a few moments, but it was long enough for Jessie to coo in a manner that would have been condescending if it wasn't so genuine.

"Look at you. Your eyes are practically sparkling," she said. "How do I work this thing? I need a picture of this. The moment of idealism." She tapped a couple of buttons.

"Cut it out," he said, a blush creeping over his face as he reached for the camera.

"No, I'm serious. You're usually the one behind the camera. I bet you never get any pictures of yourself."

She managed to snap a picture. Unfortunately, in her fumbling to work out how to use the entirely too complicated professional-grade camera, she'd activated the flash. It left Alan with purple spots in his eyes, and left Blot startled and furious.

"By the void, will you get her out of here! I draw the line at random flashes!" she fumed.

"Okay, okay. Enough of that," he said, grabbing the camera from her. "You've probably got better things to do back home. I shouldn't keep you."

"Better things, nah. Laundry, though." She stood and grabbed the trash. "Same time next week?"

"Sure. That'd be great."

Blot rubbed her eyes and growled. Alan walked Jessie to the door.

"I'll send you the photo," he said.

"Send me the one I took too," she said, hugging him goodbye. "See you later."

She shut the door. Alan paced back to the couch and restored the moody lighting.

"This better not be a regular thing for very long." Blot snatched up the remote for the TV and jumped to the menu. "I have to go all the way back to the beginning of the season because you two were talking over the ingredients."

"Sorry about that. This'll probably only be until I'm done certifying."

"Mmmhmm," Blot said. "Sure it will."

Chapter 2

The prison loomed over its public parking lot as Alan approached. He cruised slowly, searching for his contact. It was a gray late-winter morning, but Alan had a feeling this place would have felt gray in the middle of spring. Some prisons were old, landmarks built at a time when every building had to have an artfulness to it. This was not one of those prisons. It was a brutal structure of cinder blocks and sorrow. The most human feature of the place was an exercise yard enclosed by a chain-link fence. But even that was ringed with razor wire. This was a warehouse for humans.

"Your prisons are a lot like ours," Blot observed, squinting from where the morning sun had pinned her behind him. "Except for the windows. And the fences. You'd never keep a shade inside a place like this. But the big thick stone walls remind me of home."

"Not a very nice thing to bring back memories of home."

"If I'd had a nice time back home, I wouldn't be here right now."

Alan rounded a corner of the parking lot for his second lap when he spotted someone climbing out of their car. He was a young man, a few years younger than Alan. At a glimpse, one could see that the raw enthusiasm of youth had yet to fade for him. He practically pranced toward Alan's car.

"Ugh. This guy is *way* too happy to be visiting a prison," Blot said.

"Mr. Fontaine?" the young man said through the still-closed driver's side window.

"Yeah, that's me." Alan rolled down his window. "You are?"

"Bill Sharr!" he said, shaking Alan's hand. "Looking forward to doing some great work?"

"Always," Alan said.

"Great! You brought ID, right? I've got mine here, and the credentials." Bill started rummaging through his bag.

"Mind if I park first?"

"Oh, right. Sure, sure." He backed away and rather theatrically directed Alan toward the nearest spot.

"This has the makings of being a very long day," Blot said.

The inside of the prison wasn't much more welcoming than the outside. Old linoleum and buzzing fluorescents put Alan in mind of his high school, as did the overabundance of stern faces glaring at him.

Bill handled all the bureaucracy. Alan would have expected him to fumble through it, but he handled it like a pro. Or, rather, he handled it like a receptionist, which was far more efficient. Most of the journalist types he'd worked with had a tendency to try to get schmoozy and chummy, which in Alan's experience only served to make suspicious people even more suspicious, and a prison seemed like a haven for the habitually suspicious. Bill just worked his way through the assorted paperwork and procedures with efficiency and a smile. He still earned hard looks and dismissive comments at times—journalists didn't tend to have positive things to report about in prisons, after all—but they didn't give him a hard time.

Before long they were marching through the halls in the lower-security portion of the prison. A thickly built, neatly uniformed guard was their guide. He dictated a lengthy rehearsed speech. The fact that it was equal parts instructions and sales pitch suggested this guard was higher up in management.

"You'll be conducting the interview just outside Cellblock 33, which is part of a pilot program in prison reorganization," he said. "You've already been searched and cleared, but this *is* a prison, so I'll ask that you not attempt to exchange anything you might have with inmates. Your interview is not with a high-risk inmate, but you should still act with appropriate care. Inmates are like weapons. Even if you're sure it isn't dangerous, it's always safest to treat one like it is."

Alan glanced at Bill. The eager interviewer had a wide smile, like he was heading to the stage for his first performance. Alan gave the bright-eyed fellow a nudge. "You might want to ask about the pilot program," he whispered.

"Oh! Right, right. What's this about the pilot program?"

"I'm happy you asked," their guide said. "On the advice of our prison psychologist, we've begun grouping certain inmates based upon psychological assessments of compatibility. It has been a bit of a hassle running the tests and repositioning the inmates, but the results are unmistakable and immediate. Ah! Speak of the devil, here is our psychologist now."

An older woman approached. She was dressed with ruthless precision. Crisp, starched clothing matched her severe, humorless face. A laminated plastic name tag labeled her Dr. Vale. A dozen other little details fell perfectly in line with the sort of mental image one might conjure of a career psychologist, but Alan's eyes had locked on to one feature that absolutely did not belong on such a person—or any person.

Her shadow had a pair of white eyes, just like Blot's. She had a shade of her own. Its eyes locked on to his, radiating displeasure and challenge.

"Instructor Driss..." Blot said, shuddering in place as the lights held her still.

She sounded frightened. And somehow, despite not knowing who this shade was, Alan could feel *why* she was so frightened. His weeks-long "partnership" with Blot had given him a feel for the faint, hard-to-define sensation of power associated with shades. Instructor Driss was oozing with the stuff.

"... Mr. Fontaine?" Vale said.

He glanced up to find some level of introduction had taken place while he was coping with the revelation. Dr. Vale's hand was extended, and her humorless face had been further drained of patience.

"Sorry. I was distracted for a moment there. Pleased to meet you, Dr. Vale," he said, shaking the offered hand.

"Mmm. Follow me please," she said, pulling her hand back and turning to the first of several security doors. She showed her badge to an attendant, who buzzed the door open. "I believe I overheard Officer Taradov begin telling you about the Cellblock 33 program."

"He did," said Bill. "Maybe you could discuss some of the finer details?"

"I am afraid not," Dr. Vale said. "It is a pilot program. I stand by the results thus far, but it is not yet ready to be publicized. Far too many people rush to the press with early victories only to take two steps back and face the disappointment of those who believed some magical cure-all had been found. When Cellblock 33's work is done, the world will be made aware. Until then, suffice it to say that we have helped to reduce stress and increase a feeling of community among our prisoners."

The doctor spoke with a crisp, clinical professionalism. She didn't sound sinister, but with her shadow staring intently at him, Alan couldn't help but find the words chilling. He wanted Blot to speak up, to tell him who this shade was and what he could expect. She wouldn't dare speak, though. With another shade around, Blot's comments were no longer private. Driss would be able to hear them, as would her host. All Alan could do was keep his eyes and ears open and hope for the best. Just in case, he casually tapped the power button for the beefy flash on his still camera. Driss's eyes narrowed at the electronic whine of the device charging.

"Do you mind if I get some photos of the halls? For establishing purposes?" Alan asked.

"You will regret it..." muttered Driss in an icy tone.

"I would prefer not. I do not want to disturb any of our inmates unnecessarily," Vale said.

Alan didn't bother pointing out that there were no prisoners in sight. Though they'd passed one security checkpoint already, this was still clearly a staff-only section of the prison. The question had done its job. If Driss didn't want a photo, Vale didn't want one. That meant Driss was calling the shots. This situation was starting to look *very* dangerous.

"Up ahead you'll find our interview room," Vale said. "Generally, interviews are conducted between mental health professionals such as myself and the inmates. However, on the occasions that law enforcement or media wish to interview an inmate, we can accommodate them here as well."

They had reached what looked to be the firm division point between the low-security "staff" section of the prison and the actual cells. A door a few paces away split the hall in half. Through the small wire-reinforced window, Alan caught a glimpse of a dimmer hallway and the suggestion of a larger, more open space beyond. To the left of the door was a small vestibule room of sorts, something of a guard station that was not presently occupied. To the right, Dr. Vale led the way to a substantial door with the same sophisticated lock as the cellblock. She tapped her badge. The door unlocked.

The room beyond was smallish and had been converted into something resembling a conference room. A folding table had been set up in the center with a chair on either side. Like the rest of the facility, the light came from fluorescent fixtures overhead. In this case only one of the bulbs was illuminated. The reinforced metal door had a small window that let in little of the light from the hallway. Once Dr. Vale shut the door, it was dim enough that both Driss and Blot could move freely. Driss rose up on the wall, staring imposingly downward at Alan and Blot. Blot stood firm beside Alan, though her posture suggested her courage was a house of cards ready to collapse at the slightest breath of wind.

"Is there something wrong with the lights?" Alan said.

"We have found that decreased illumination helps moderate inmate hostility," Dr. Vale said.

"Fascinating," Bill said without a drop of sincerity. "So our guest will be sitting there, I assume?"

"That is correct. I will fetch him," Dr. Vale said.

"Great! We'll just get our gear set up," Bill said.

"Behave," hissed Driss as Vale reopened the door and slipped from the room.

Once she was gone, both Bill and Blot started talking at once.

"I want the camera right here, right next to me. The video, that is. We don't need me in the shot, but I want a good look at his face. It's all in the expressions..." Bill yammered, spouting assorted information that would have been painfully obvious even if Alan *hadn't* been a pro.

Blot's comments were far more crucial. "Driss is an instructor. Not *my* instructor. But she visited sometimes, and I... er... crossed paths with her. She was sort of a... what around here you'd call a principal or a superintendent. She kept things running smooth and made sure people were doing what they were supposed to be doing."

"You seem scared of her," Alan said as quietly as possible.

"Come again?" Bill said.

"Oh, uh. Nothing," Alan said.

"She's the one who could boot you out of training. She's the one who would levy the more formal punishments. She wasn't the boss, so to speak, but she's the one who would make sure people did what the boss said. She, I don't know, runs things. People like *me* don't meet with people like *her* unless we've done something wrong. And when we do something wrong..."

Blot shivered and started pacing along the walls. Alan finished setting up the tripod with the video camera. He gave Blot a prompting look as he idly tapped through some camera settings.

"Look, you people have light all over the place here. Back home, light is like, um... like *guns* I guess. Not everyone is allowed to use it. *She* was. As bad as it is to have to cope with it here, at least we can anchor ourselves to things. Back home it's *painful*. It burns. Enough of it can kill. Maybe not all the light, but definitely the stuff she used. She carried this little lantern, and these little stones that would spark when she clicked them. I don't know if there was something special she did to it, but it was bad."

Bill was busy setting up his voice recorder and positioning it on the table. Alan took the opportunity to step back and whisper a little more quietly.

"But that shouldn't make a difference here, should it? Will she have any special powers here? Like the shape-shifting? Or the combat form?"

Blot clutched her fingers. "I don't *know*. Maybe, maybe not. But it doesn't matter. She *runs* things. If she's got that doctor person doing what she says, then I assure you, she's got something cooking in this place. You've got to get out of here."

"Hey, get a shot of the room like this, huh?" Bill said. "Maybe we can do a sort of narrative thing."

Alan nodded and took a shot. Blot casually slipped behind him. The flash was so bright one could almost hear the plastic lens sizzling after it fired. Blot's positioning kept it from hitting her too hard, but she still huffed a breath.

"I don't like that thing..."

"Oh! Jeez!" Bill said, rubbing his eyes. "Do you need all that flash?"

"They've got the room dark. I needed it to get a clear image and calibrate exposure."

Bill nodded knowingly. It was nonsense, of course. Alan took his gear very seriously, and this was a stationary shot. With the right lenses, aperture, and exposure times, he could take a photo by starlight. But the sooner he could justify the massive flash, the better, and he'd found that using words like "exposure" or "f-stop" in a sentence had a way of making non-pros glassy-eyed.

The electronic lock on the door bleeped. Dr. Vale opened the door and stepped through, flanked by a uniformed guard and an inmate in the traditional orange jumpsuit. He was not handcuffed, and from the meek and panic-stricken look on his face, there was a good reason for that. He, personally, didn't look like much of a threat. But Alan knew there was more to him than met the eye of the average observer.

Bill stood and extended his hand. "Leonard Castro?"

"Y-yeah," said the inmate. "Call me Lenny."

Alan tried to keep his face steady. Lenny the intern wasn't very much of a concern. He lacked integrity, but he wasn't ruthless or driven. The shadow he cast was another story entirely. Vicious white eyes gazed up at Alan. When Vale clicked the door shut, he surged up and crossed his arms. A thin white mouth sneered.

"So we meet again..." Dun rumbled.

Lenny flinched at the sound of his shadow's taunt. The former intern and current inmate looked like he was at the end of his rope. The dark bags under his eyes suggested sleep was rare and fitful. He'd lost weight, and he'd become terribly pale.

"Lenny, if you'll take a seat, I'd like to get started."

Alan raised his camera.

"If you use that flash, you will regret it," Dun barked. "No doubt you recognize that matters are more in my control than yours right now. Trust me when I say that I have been civil thus far, and I expect you to be the same."

Alan considered the words as the interview started with Lenny.

"Please, Alan," Blot said. "We don't have to make war. Shades can be civil, really! Just hear him out." She kept her voice as low as she could and huddled behind him. "I really don't want to have to fight Dun right now. I'm still tender from where that Dawn guy poked a hole through me, and I'm not eager to get any fresh holes."

Alan nodded and shifted his settings. When he snapped a picture, it was flashless.

"It is good to see you can be reasonable. That will serve you well. You may even survive."

Alan kept quiet and adjusted the camera to make sure the shot was framed properly. Dun continued.

"You have lived your life, these past few weeks. You have not been harassed. You are unharmed. Perhaps you've convinced yourself that there would be no consequence for your deeds. I intend to disabuse you of that notion."

"We've been keeping our nose out of your business, Dun. You don't need to worry about us," Blot said.

"Keeping your nose out of our business?" Dun snapped viciously.

Lenny flinched at the outburst, but attempted to continue answering whatever question Bill had asked.

"You were trained in the ways of manipulation and subterfuge, Blot. It shames me to think you would believe such a simple fallacy would be even worth uttering."

"I'm rusty. *This* one is always going on about honesty and other virtuous things," Blot said hastily.

"Regardless. I know you have been searching. I know you have been rummaging through the rumors and lies that this world has crafted about us to try to find what can be *done* about us. This world has changed a great deal from our last visit. Chief among those changes is the ease at which such digging can be done. Libraries of information, available at the mere swipe of a finger. With knowledge of just a few numbers, the voice of a loved one can be summoned..."

"The coffee is very good too, Dun. Have you tried the coffee?" Blot said, eager to placate him.

"Silence!" he snapped.

Again, Lenny flinched.

"Is there something wrong?" Bill asked.

"Yeah, no. I... ahem... I just have trouble focusing sometimes," Lenny stammered.

Dun rumbled with anger and curled down to glare at his host from the table. "You had a simple task. Conduct the conversation so that I may conduct *my* conversation. If this is too difficult for you, I can find someone else..."

"Can we start over? What was your question again?" Lenny yelped.

He was trembling like a struck puppy. Alan could only imagine the sort of hell his life had been, linked to Dun for all this time. He made a mental note to stop by Vice Versa and pick up a treat for Blot. As trying as things had been with her by his side, she wasn't dangling his life over him.

"Where was I..." Dun muttered.

"You were saying numbers can summon voices. But you don't really need the numbers, because there's a contact book, so—"

"555-548-7803," Dun recited loudly.

Alan's eyes widened.

"Your parents' phone number. Would you like me to recite their address? Or perhaps some cousins'. The elderly man who lives on one side of you. The woman who lives on the other side."

"You can kill Ms. Levitt. That would be fine by me," Blot said.

Alan's hands were shaking. His grip around his camera was white-knuckled. He opened his mouth to speak.

"Don't, Alan. Don't do *anything* that might draw attention. You were a nothing before. A faceless member of the endless multitudes of humans who sleepwalk through their days. All I ask is that you return to that life. Take your photos. Do your job. Forget any of this ever happened. It doesn't concern you. In fact, if I were you, I would run. Hide. Because you are marked. You know that we cannot be contained. You know that we are everywhere. You are alive because I have been merciful, and because I have been far too busy to trouble myself with one so meaningless."

"I've been trying to tell him that since I *met* him, Dun, but you rest assured, I'll keep telling him until he finally listens."

Dun blinked slowly and turned to Blot. "And you. You can cease your sniveling. What you have done cannot be ignored. If you wish to be returned to the fold, penitence must be paid. I would begin by abandoning this host of yours if ever you should find yourself with the strength to do so.

Leave him a withered husk and it would be, perhaps, the first step toward redemption. But your crimes are many. You assaulted me. You helped this man foil our plans. You are a turncoat. A traitor to your own kind. From this day, you are shunned. Exiled. Like Alan, you live only because there are more valuable ways to spend my time than taking your life. But your time is short. If you hope to find a home among your kind again, act quickly."

Throughout Dun's little monologue, Alan had been snapping pictures of the interview. It wasn't out of a sense of duty. He needed something to focus on besides the simmering cocktail of anger and fear that was seizing his mind.

"The message is delivered. We are through here," Dun decreed.

"No more questions!" Lenny barked midsentence.

"Well, sir, we're just getting started," Bill said quickly.

"Driss! We are through here!" Dun bellowed.

The shadow focused his eyes first on Alan, then on Blot. Bill failed to persuade Lenny to continue the interview. After a few moments, Dr. Vale arrived.

"That will be all," she said. "The inmate is visibly distressed. For his comfort and psychological well-being, I must ask you to leave."

"I... but... right. Okay," Bill said in defeat.

He started to gather his things. Lenny stood as a guard approached to lead him out.

"Just a second," Alan said.

All eyes turned to him. He raised the camera and tapped a setting.

"Say cheese," he said.

"No, don't!" Blot urged.

It was too late, he snapped the picture, complete with full-powered flash. The intense light hit both Driss and Dun like a hammer. They snapped suddenly and forcefully to the position a shadow would naturally fall during such a flash. Even without taking physical form, the blast hit them hard enough to cause the open door to rattle lightly on its hinges.

White eyes narrow with rage focused upon him from behind both Dr. Vale and Lenny. With both the guard and Bill as witnesses, Alan knew the shades wouldn't take action. They stepped into the hallway. A second guard came to escort Alan and Bill out of the building.

"Just keep walking. I'm watching your back," Blot said, her terror barely suppressed.

"Well, that was a bust," Bill said. "I don't know if I'm going to be able to use a *single* quote from that interview. Did you hear the nonsense he was saying?"

"I was a little distracted," Alan said.

"Exactly! It wasn't hard hitting. It wasn't riveting. Just a frightened guy who's never been in prison before taking full responsibility for his role in the Magnuson scandal. I mean, it's *novel* to have an interviewee admitting guilt, but it's not interesting. Where's the desperate pleas for mercy? Where's the insistence of innocence? That's what gets clicks and views."

He shook his head. "I'll have to spin it. The footage will be good, at least. A couple of stills of him looking squirrelly and spooked. Make sure you get that stuff delivered ASAP."

"Right, yeah," Alan said.

Bill held out his hand. "Good working with you."

Alan nodded numbly and shook Bill's hand. He quickened his pace once he was alone, heading for his car.

"What in the void is wrong with you?" Blot snapped. "They call you in specifically to threaten your family and you take a parting shot at them? Dun *and* Driss? *What were you thinking?*"

He clenched his fists. "I don't... I don't know. It's... he threatened my family."

"Yeah, I just said that."

"No, I mean. No one's ever threatened my family before. It's one thing to have something terrible happen to you, or to bring something on yourself. But because of something *I* did, he threatened my family." His jaw tightened. There wasn't any fear in his voice. There was only anger.

"Alan, maybe you don't understand the purpose of threats, or maybe you just need training on how to be a proper coward, but when someone says they are going to hurt your family if you do something, *don't do anything*."

"I know! I know. I couldn't help it. I just... I couldn't let that stand."

Blot flexed her shadowy fingers in frustration. "Let me get this straight. Your next-door neighbor relentlessly nitpicks everything you do and perpetually complicates your life with complaints to your landlord. You just smile and take it for years. A metaphysical entity with powers you can't even conceive of threatens *you*, you smile and take it. But he reads your mom's phone number and you come out swinging?"

"I guess we found my trigger," he said.

"And the first time you ever pulled it was to shoot yourself in the head," Blot grumbled.

Alan unlocked his car door and plopped into the driver's seat. He started the engine.

"Oh no..." Blot said.

Alan looked up quickly. "What? Where? What's wrong?"

"Next to the light pole, over by the other entrance," Blot said.

He scanned the parking lot until he spotted what she was referring to. There was a well-built man with a salt-and-pepper beard and white hair. He was bundled up in a dark blue overcoat with distinctive silver buttons. He held one hand low at his side. A gleaming pendant dangled at the end of a chain in his grip. The pendant was facing the prison and held rock solid despite the winter breeze.

"The Dawn is here," Alan said, relief in his voice.

"Try not to sound so happy," Blot said.

"Why! We've got a truce with them, and if there's one group I wouldn't mind stalking a bunch of shades who've threatened to kill me, it's a cult dedicated to *eliminating* those shades."

"You don't get it. Dun and Driss are a powder keg, and you're smiling about the guy playing with matches. Trust me. This won't end well." She huffed. "Nothing ends well..."

He pulled out his phone.

"What are you doing! We need to get out of here!" she snapped.

"I need to call my parents."

"Then call while moving! Even if we didn't just spit in the eye of one of the most influential shades around, I do *not* trust a member of the Dawn anywhere near me."

"Hello, Mom?" Alan said, phone to his ear.

Blot shuddered with anger. "Your family is a liability, Alan."

Alan shot her a look that could have curdled milk. "How is everything? Anything strange happen lately?"

"No, no. Everything's fine. Oh, listen, did your father tell you about the problem with the land? I told him not to, because—"

"Forget about the land for a minute, Mom. Has there been anyone creeping around the house or anything lately?"

"No. I don't think so. Nothing I noticed, anyway."

"Where's Dad?"

"He's working on the car."

"Can you see him?"

"Just a minute."

Sweat trickled down his brow as he heard his mother navigating their house. The jangle of unruly blinds clattered softly.

"Yeah. He's out there. Getting *oil* all over his new jeans!" She thumped the window. "What did I tell you? Work jeans for work!"

Alan breathed a sigh of relief. "Do me a favor. Don't let any strangers in the house. I don't care why they're there. Don't let anyone in. If you see someone suspicious, report them. And keep the lights on. All the lights."

"You know I don't like wasting energy."

"All the lights, Mom. All day."

"Why?"

"I've heard things that have got me nervous. I think it might be a good idea if I—"

"Don't go to their house! You'll kill them!" Blot hissed.

Alan pulled his head away from the phone and covered it. "What?"

"Dun *definitely* wants to punish us. He'd only attack your parents as a way to do that. If you show up at their house, you're just going to combine two targets into one big, fat, juicy sitting duck. *Don't* go into their house without a plan."

"Honey?" his mother said.

Alan raised the phone again. "I'm going to look into some stuff. Just need to check some things out to set my mind at ease. Just remember what I said. No strangers, lots of lights. Stay safe." He hung up and started the engine. "We're going to scope things out. Not at the house, but in the neighborhood."

"Why? Just what are you planning to do, Alan?" Blot said. "What do you think you *can* do?"

"We've clashed with shades before. We can do it again."

"We clashed with shades that had just shown up. And it was nearly the end of us. If we encounter someone today, it's likely to be a shade who's had more than a month to recover and work with their host. You haven't *seen* what we can do when we're prepared."

"Yeah, well, you haven't seen what I can do when someone threatens my family."

"I have. Just now. What you can do is make a terrible mistake motivated by emotion. So I'm sure this is going to go *great*."

If no one had been concerned about strange people in Alan's parents' neighborhood before he showed up, his arrival had taken care of that. For the better part of two hours he'd been cruising slowly through the neighborhood, eying everyone suspiciously and peering into every dark corner. He paid specific attention to the block his parents lived on. It was a nice little urban neighborhood. Houses butted right up against each other, with only the narrowest of alleys separating them. His parents' house was one of only a handful that had even the semblance of a front yard, though it was little more than a few square feet of overgrown grass with a flimsy aluminum fence around it. Newer buildings were mostly two and three stories, making older homes like theirs look out of place. It also left the home largely shrouded in shadow even at midday, much to Alan's dismay.

His finely honed paparazzi skills and a telephoto lens meant he didn't actually have to go down the block to get a good look. Even so, he knew he was missing a thousand different hiding places.

"You never notice just how many dark nooks and crannies there are in a neighborhood until you find yourself looking for someone who can hide in the shadows..." Alan muttered, zooming a bit farther.

"I am, in fact, intimately aware of such things," Blot said.

As the time crept closer to noon, the sun settled in directly overhead, shortening shadows and granting Blot a bit more freedom of motion in the car.

"Well call some out if you see me missing them."

"Fine. You've been directing all your attention at street level. Don't forget to look up."

He shifted his attention and sighed. Particularly this close to noon, the upper levels had their share of shadows. There were overhangs, fire escapes, and what passed for balconies. He scrutinized them one by one.

"You can feel when one of your own is close, right?"

"Somewhat."

"Do you feel someone?"

"Yes."

He took his eye from the viewfinder to glare at her. "For how long?"

"Since we showed up."

"Do you know *where*?"

"Vaguely."

"Why didn't you say so?!"

"Because I don't want anyone to find *you*," she said simply.

"We're supposed to be working together."

"Just because we're in this together doesn't mean we need to be working together. All I really need is to keep you alive. If that means getting cagey and sly, then so be it."

"Why did you tell me *now*?"

"Because he's close enough that you're going to see him soon regardless of my feelings on the subject."

He opened the door.

"You aren't seriously going to get *out of the car*, are you?" she said.

"Watch me."

He shut the door and checked that his camera and its potent flash were ready for rapid deployment.

"You should let me hang on to that," Blot said.

"Why? I should have it available in case I need it, shouldn't I?"

"It's dangling around your neck. All it'll take is one quick crunch of a claw and we're down to whatever I'm hiding for you anyway. And not that I think there's a chance of it, but if you don't show up with a weapon, you might not get attacked on sight."

Alan considered the advice. "That's fair."

He opened the door again and leaned in as though he were dropping the camera in the back seat. Instead, he dropped it onto Blot, who tugged it into the shadows. With the camera thus hidden, he locked the car up and marched down the street. He was a good distance from his parents' house, so they wouldn't spot him unless he was unlucky enough for them to decide to go on an errand at this precise moment. The local convenience store was to his left, and behind it, the only publicly accessible alleyway nearby. If there *was* a shade and host near enough for Blot to consider an encounter inevitable, it'd be here.

What had once been the place where a young Alan would pause to discard the wrapper for his candy bars now may as well have been a haunted mansion. The shadows seemed darker than they should have been. The air seemed colder. It could all have been in his mind, or it could have been some horrid influence of the figure lurking at the far side of the alleyway, against a chain-link fence.

"Hello?" Alan said, eyes trained on the half-visible figure waiting for him.

A pair of white eyes opened, turning a dark mote of the wall into a twisted, monstrous figure. The eyes weren't like Blot's. Rather than large and at times even friendly eyes like hers, this thing's stared at him like ragged tears in the darkness itself. They curled and fluttered as they stared. A third tear split the shadows below it, a horrid grin curling over itself like a Dr. Seuss villain.

"I think I know him," Blot said.

"Should I be worried?" Alan asked.

"Guess."

The host heaved himself away from the wall and staggered slightly. He paced toward Alan.

"You've spoken with Dun," croaked the shadow. "I assumed we'd be crossing paths. I had expected you to be too smart or too cowardly to be the one to initiate. So which is it? Are you brave, or are you a fool?"

"All that matters is I'm here to make it clear that a threat to my family will not be tolerated."

"Will not be *tolerated*. Listen, human. My name is Rive. I am the scourge of the wastes. I am the blade of Stigma. I am the architect of ruin. The sculptor of flesh. I am—"

"I'm Todd!" the human said brightly as he stepped close enough for his features to be clear.

He was an avuncular sort, if one has particularly rummy uncles. His grin was wide, friendly, and incomplete. A scraggly beard caught the breeze and waved like a greasy sea anemone. From the looks of the portion of his face not hidden by hair or a ratty sock hat, he might be in his midseventies. It wasn't clear how much of that estimate was skewed by too much sun and too much liquor. He had an unfortunate physique, with a potbelly supported by bony limbs that were barely up to the task. His breath carried the fumes of the rotgut clutched in his left hand. His right hand was extended for a shake.

"Proud to know ya," he said, waggling his hand.

"Would you be silent!" Rive snapped.

"I'm just saying hello to the nice fella."

"He is one of our targets!" Rive said.

"Is he?"

Todd tipped up his bottle and drained it. The booze was clearly selected for quantity rather than quality, and a third of the jug vanished down his throat in a single long swig. "I thought we were here for the older folks down the street," he said roughly, one eye shut tight as he endured the afterburn of his chosen libation.

"They are his parents. *He* is the reason we are after them."

"Oh. Well, one's better than two," Todd said. He tossed his bottle in a nearby trash can and limbered up. "So what's the order of the day? We rough him up or take him down?" he asked.

"Dun has instructed us to make our capabilities clear."

"Can do."

"Now wait a minute," Alan said, backing a step away.

Todd threw a punch. It missed by a good six inches. His impaired equilibrium caused his entire body to follow it, and he spilled out into the sunlight.

The intimidation and concern Alan had felt was wicking away by the moment. He gazed down at Rive, where the sun had pinned him.

"I take it you didn't have very many choices for a host?" Alan glanced to Todd. "No offense."

"None taken," Todd said. "No shame in being a drunk. At least, not enough shame to convince me to be otherwise." He tottered to his feet and into the shadows.

"As it happens, I took great care in my selection," Rive rumbled, now once again rising up in the darkness.

Todd swiped his hand out again. Alan, more concerned about the shadow than the man casting it, didn't dodge quite as quickly as he might have. The knobby fingers wrapped around his upper arm and clutched weakly. Alan grabbed him by the wrist and tried to pull him free. The grip strengthened *very* quickly.

"There are certain benefits to a mind with its will weakened by decades of drink," Rive stated.

Todd pivoted. If the drunk outweighed Alan, it wasn't by much. Nevertheless, the motion yanked him off his feet and hurled him into the trash cans. He slid to a stop and scrambled to his feet.

When he finally turned to Todd, he noted the drunk's unsteady gait was growing more unsteady, but for a very good reason. With each step, his body was shifting. Limbs were extending. Head was elongating. A monstrous shadow slid along the wall beside him, offering a chilling glimpse of the contorted mass of body horror that Todd was steadily becoming.

"I told you this would happen!" Blot hissed.

Todd stumbled against the wall. "Phew. It ain't easy to walk when your legs won't stay put. Give me a minute, will ya?"

"Camera. Camera," Alan hissed.

Blot flicked her hand, and the DSLR spiraled into being. Alan snatched it out of the air and snapped a series of pictures. Rive's shape flicked and shuddered, pushed back by the flash, but Todd's transition continued unabated.

"Stupid human," Rive taunted greasily. "One would think having joined forces with a traitor, you would know better than to use light as a weapon against a shifter."

"Oh, I do," Alan said, tensing himself in preparation for a sprint. "I just wanted some decent photos. And to keep your attention."

"I may be drunk, but I can pretty well keep my attention on someone when there's no one else around." Todd straightened up and took his first reasonably steady step toward Alan. "Now what was it again? Roughing up or killing? And how much am I getting for—"

The booze-addled bargaining was cut short by a devastating blow to the ribs. Alan's photographic distraction proved sufficient to keep both Todd and Rive focused on him while Blot gathered herself. An inky form burst from the shadow and hung in the air, Blot's twisted combat form. Unlike Rive, Blot couldn't make Alan's body conform to her shape, but if she put her mind to it, she could impose herself upon the world physically. Not for long, but for long enough to deliver a sucker punch or two. Rive tried to take a slash at her in kind, but Alan snapped another photo. Blot snapped back into a silhouette before he'd pressed the shutter. Rive was a half-second slower, and as such was returned to two-dimensions far more swiftly and violently. The brick of the wall chipped where he slipped into it.

"Get him! Get him you worthless idiot!" Rive insisted.

"Yeah... Yeah, give me a minute," Todd muttered.

His already impaired brain wasn't coping very well with the blow, but he'd grown into a gangly enough tangle of limbs that Alan wouldn't be escaping without climbing over him. That was about as safe and appealing as climbing over an overturned lawnmower. But he didn't have many options. He took a step forward.

"No. Deep breath. Now," Blot instructed him.

Alan realized what was coming and did as he was told. Blot's shadowy arms reached up once more, though rather than monstrous, they were her own dainty limbs. They pulled tight against his chest and tugged him backward. He tipped over, as though doing a trust fall. When he struck the ground, rather than thumping painfully, he continued downward. His body eased into the shadows, slipping into a silhouette held snugly in Blot's embrace. She dragged him swiftly away. He only had to cope with the disorienting experience of lacking depth for a moment before she released him and he slid back to reality on the far side of the chain-link fence.

Alan scrambled to his feet and got his bearings. Todd had finally gotten himself organized and was pulling himself to his full twisted height.

"We still after him, boss?" Todd asked. "Because I wouldn't mind giving him a taste of the ol' one-two."

One ponderous stride took him to the fence, and he reared back a gnarled fist. The blow tore through the metal links and shattered one of the support pipes. When he drew the fist back, though, the jagged metal raked across his flesh, gouging out an ugly wound.

"Oh. Blood, boss," he said, holding his injured arm up like a toddler expecting a scolding.

Rive's white maw tightened into a vicious grimace. "He's been shown the implements of torture. That is enough for now."

"All right," Todd said, his form already easing back to what it had been. "See you next time, Alan. Stay loose, because I'm hoping to go a couple rounds." He stumbled off and vanished around the corner.

"That was... close," Alan said, his heart hammering in his chest.

"It would have been worse if not for me," Blot said.

He took a step forward and snapped some pictures of the spatter Todd had left behind. "There's a lot of blood here. When shades shift a body, do they add blood?"

"No. We can boost the strength, but they only have the mass they started with. At least..." She tipped her head. "I *think*?"

He eyed the pool doubtfully. "If that's the case, then I don't think we're going to have to worry about Todd for a while..."

"Less time than you think. But good, fine. Your parents are safe for now. Let's go before you get some stupid idea like chasing him down."

They'd lingered long enough to be certain that Todd hadn't been playing possum, then made their way home. The ride was mostly silent. Alan needed time to untie his knotted nerves. Despite her abrasive nature, Blot had a good sense for when Alan needed a moment. By the time he was stepping back into his apartment building, his mind was at a more even keel.

"Okay, so, where do we hide?" Blot said as they stepped onto the elevator.

"We can't hide," Alan said.

"Yeah, obviously we have to *run* first. That's why I want to know where. We should get moving. Can you get a boat? We should get a boat. Something where we can be sure we're alone and no one can sneak up on us."

"No, I mean we can't hide. We have to do something."

"No!" she objected. "First, doing something never helps."

"We kept Dun from getting access to a senator."

"And look where that got us!"

"Let me ask you this. If we *do* run, and hide. If we *do* keep out of Dun's business, will that do the trick? Will he spare my family?"

"Yes," Blot said.

He glared at her. "Are you lying?"

"Of course I'm lying!" she raved. "It's the only way to tell you what you want to hear! Dun is ruthless, he's dedicated, he sees you as a threat, and he's got a vendetta against you. Even if you die first, your family is doomed. Never leave anyone alive who might want revenge. That's one of his axioms."

"Then how can I just run and hide in good conscience?"

"Because if something bad is going to happen no matter what you do, you do the thing that will keep you alive!" Blot struggled against the light of the elevator. "I can't believe I'm tied to the one human being who still thinks self-sacrifice is a worthwhile endeavor. Let's not forget you're not just giving your life, you're giving mine."

The elevator reached his floor. As he paced, the overhead lights nudged Blot about in a familiar pattern of motion. His hallway was empty, but that was to be expected. It was the middle of the work day for most of the people on his floor, and the retirees tended to stay indoors in the colder months. For the moment, that meant he was free to continue his conversation.

"I don't intend for anyone to give their life."

"Yeah, well, what you intend and what ends up happening aren't always the same thing."

Alan paused at his door, keys in hand. "Are you thinking what I'm thinking?" he whispered.

"I hope not, because you're clearly not in your right mind, and I'd hate to think it was spreading to me."

He put his ear to his apartment door. Blot started to question his behavior, then quietly realized his concern.

"Turn around. Put your back against the door," she instructed him.

Alan nodded and turned. Once he was as firmly against the door as he could get, he heard her grunting with effort. When he glanced down at his feet, he could see that she was inching slowly out of position and sliding lower.

"Just a bit... just a little... *there*! I'm on the other side. Looks like the room's clear," she said.

Blot snapped back in place. He turned to unlock the door and stepped into his dimly lit apartment.

"If we're going to be doing that for the foreseeable future, you've got to see about dimming those lights in the hallway. That was rough," Blot complained.

"Dun didn't send anyone to my apartment to kill me," Alan said.

"He didn't have to. You went to find the one he'd picked out to kill you."

"Even so. You said there are a lot of shades. He's only got one after me?"

"Give him time," she muttered. She held out her hand and summoned the coffee he'd bought her on the way home, then settled into the faint shadow of the love seat and started sipping at it.

"That's just it," Alan said, sitting beside her and fetching his laptop from his bag. "He *just* summoned us to let us know he wanted us out of his hair.

What better time to arrange to have me killed? To make *darn* sure he took care of us?"

"I would argue that literally any time *before* telling someone you were planning to kill them would be a better time to kill them," Blot said.

"That too!" Alan said. "I think something is up."

"You think something is up. Congratulations. That's a remarkable bit of sleuthing you've done," Blot said flatly.

"I think this is more than he can handle. I think Dun started doing something in that prison, and he *doesn't* have the resources to keep himself safe, so he preemptively tried to scare me away. He said it himself. It isn't like personal information is hard to come by these days. Just because he knows some addresses and phone numbers doesn't mean he's got an army of operatives scouring the state. I think Todd and Rive are the only ones he can deploy. I think he's vulnerable."

"As opposed to us."

"I'm going to look into things," he said, popping open a web browser."

"I am *so* sick of you looking into things..." she grumbled. "If you *must* keep investigating things, why don't you drop everything else and get that job at the police station? At least *then* they might give you a gun."

"They won't give me a gun. And besides, I don't like guns."

"Of course you don't." She shook her head. "Boy did I pick the wrong guy..."

He paused.

"What is it now?" she asked.

"When Dun was talking to you, he tried to persuade you to abandon me."

"He *would*. If this was one of his lessons and I decided to stick with you, he'd fail me."

"But could you? I seem to remember you saying once your kind were here awhile, you'd be strong enough to switch hosts. It's been weeks."

"Relax. Maybe the more powerful of us are ready for that, but I'm not there yet. I'm barely strong enough to fight against the glow of a desk lamp. If I were to tear myself off you and track down a new host, it would be a gamble. You're safe for now. Safe from *that*, anyway."

His jaw tightened. "Is that all it comes down to, though? If tomorrow, or next week, or next month you've got the strength to take a new host, what happens then?"

"What happens is you'll have to start paying more attention to my opinions on things if you don't want to end up a question mark on your friend Jessie's report from the medical examiner."

Alan looked long and hard in her direction. She swizzled her coffee and glanced back at him.

"It's a joke, Alan. Like I said. Relax. Moot point for now."

"I'm not worried about now." He shut his eyes. "Correction, I'm profoundly worried about now. But I don't want this dangling over my head. What will you do when you're strong enough for a new host?"

She paused for an uncomfortably long time. "I am a liar, Alan. You know I'm going to say whatever you want to hear. You've got the curse of being a man with very strong convictions. I've got the blessing of being a shade with very weak ones. Even if I answer honestly, I don't have the fortitude to say with any certainty that I'll be able to honor my own desires on that issue. You're a nice guy. A bit of an idealist, but that's a self-punishing problem."

"This is a disquieting amount of beating about the bush you're doing, Blot."

She huffed a sigh. "I don't intend to abandon you."

"But what you intend and what ends up happening aren't always the same thing."

"Now that's some deep wisdom. You been reading philosophers?"

His stern expression lingered.

"Free-will isn't something they valued back when they were preparing me for all this. I've got my training." She shut her eyes and shook her head. "Let's just start thinking about what we're going to do. If you're going to drag me into an ill-advised plan, I'd like to at least make sure it's not a complete disaster."

She slid a bit closer and slurped at her coffee. He reluctantly turned back to the screen and typed in his first search term.

CHAPTER 3

"Fontaine, office."

Alan had only just stepped through the door when his boss delivered the daily bellow. He didn't break stride, continuing from the doorway to the hallway. He felt a little bit of a flutter in his chest as he stepped into the office.

He idly clicked the desk lamp to its dimmest setting and slid his chair back a bit from the glow of the doorway. Blot drifted around the walls, gazing at them.

"How do you think this will go?" Blot asked, eyes drifting over the assorted photos and decorations on Cox's walls.

"I don't know. I've never pitched anything like this before. I've never pitched anything at all."

"I guess that makes me a muse, then," she said. "I show up and you start shooting for the stars."

"There's some truth to that, I guess. If you ignore the dire threat to life and limb."

"Back where I come from, dire threat to life and limb is the primary motivator." She crossed her arms and tossed her roiling hair. "For someone whose stock and trade is collecting them, this man does *not* have very good taste in photographs."

Alan turned. As many times as he'd been in the office, he'd never really taken the time to observe his boss's decorations. Cox did have quite a few photos on the wall. They were glossy prints, or in some cases the sort of colorful print onto metal that one sometimes sees in award plaques.

"They're just his biggest sales, I suspect."

"They're nothing but people. They don't even look like particularly *happy* people."

"Pictures of happy people don't usually have a big price tag. The ones that sell for the most are the pictures people don't want you to take."

Blot nodded. "But you don't take pictures like this very much."

"That's because I talked Cox into giving me the better jobs. Now my photos are a lot more legitimate."

"Do they pay more?"

"The low end is higher, but the high end is lower. And I can sleep better at night knowing I'm not regularly ruining someone's day."

Blot reached out and flicked the shadow of one of the pictures, causing it to swing.

"This one is yours. The picture of Magnuson. This is probably the *least* beautiful photograph I've seen you take, and it's the only one he hung up." She considered the image for a moment. "I never realized it, but you're not a detective like you always *act* like you are. You're a *spy*."

"I'm not a spy."

"You are! Or at least you *were*. You find people who don't want to be found and get proof about things they don't want you to know. I've even *helped* you, and I never realized it's what you are."

"I'm not a spy," he repeated, with less conviction. "I'm a paparazzo. I mean, I'm a photographer. But the kind of person who takes pictures of celebrities when they don't want their pictures taken is called a paparazzo."

"Is that better than being a spy?"

"... I guess that's a matter of opinion."

"Spies probably get paid better, I bet. And I've got some training in spying. We should find you a job as a spy. The kind of people who hire spies are the kind of people who won't want their spies to be found, so they'll help you hide. Plus, since it's so important to you, you can *probably* find someone who wants you to spy on a bad guy in order to fight crime or something."

She clapped her hands. "I just solved our problem. Come on, let's go find you a spy patron."

"We have a job to do, remember?"

She muttered under her breath. "I should know better than to expect you to recognize a great idea when you hear it."

Blot produced her notebook and pencil, slid down to a place where she wouldn't be seen by random passersby, and started scribbling again.

"What are you drawing there?" he asked.

She pivoted to keep the back of the pad toward him. "I have very little privacy. This pad is it."

He tipped his head. "Fair enough."

"Okay, Fontaine," Cox said, appearing in his doorway. "Let's make this quick. I've already sold some of your shots, and I'm itching to have the originals."

Alan fished a memory card out of his pocket and handed it over. "I thought the article was a dud," he said.

"Who cares? I'm not selling articles, I'm selling photos. And you've got to *read* the article to know it's a dud. The picture's enough to get them to the site, and did you see the look on that little guy's face? You'd think he was being interrogated. That blogger must have been a firecracker."

"Not so much. I think he was more afraid of someone looking over his shoulder," Alan said.

"Eh, regardless. Good stuff. Even these ones with the high flash and stark contrast are good. Gives the whole thing a scandalous vibe."

He checked something on his screen, then started writing out a check. "I've got you booked for some sort of an art thing. I guess one of the exhibitors for the festival a while back made a splash. It's not for a few days, but you'll be doing the standard routine. Take pictures of folks in their pretty outfits. Capture the ambiance of eggheads pretending they understand paintings. Society page stuff."

"Okay. Sure. But, uh..."

Cox looked up. "You have something for me? Something spicy?"

Ever since Alan had gotten the behind the scenes shots that had sparked the Magnuson election scandal, Cox had been not-so-gently urging him to dig up some similar dirt. The high quality of the work he'd been turning on standard assignments was enough to keep him in Cox's good graces, but another exclusive was perpetually on his boss's mind.

"No. Nothing like that. But a thought came to mind while I was shooting these images. The prison has some sort of a pilot program that's supposedly been helping with prisoner comportment."

Cox drummed his fingers on the desk. "Words like 'comportment' don't exactly take the world by storm, kid."

"I just think it might be worth getting permission to do a photo-essay. Reveal some of the conditions in the prison. We can probably pull in someone to write an accompanying article."

Cox drummed his fingers some more. "Prestige stuff," he said.

Alan suppressed a sigh. He'd had a feeling that phrase would come up. In Cox's version of photographic and video media, there were exactly two types of material. 'Prestige stuff' was what he called anything that didn't make money.

"Come to me with something a little more bread-and-butter and you'll get me more excited. Prestige stuff is good for the public image, though. Get the Cox Media watermark on something that the bleeding hearts share around and you start getting more good faith from the activist set. But prison conditions? Isn't there anything with a little more pop?"

"I really think there's some value in this."

Cox drummed his fingers a little harder. "It's going to be a hassle, you know. Prison stuff. There are going to be releases, permits. Prisons have strict rules on this stuff. Or I imagine they do. I've never thrown any time or money at one for something like this."

"Again. I think it'll pay off," Alan said. He did everything short of wink in his attempt at implying there was subtext to the comment.

"Mmm... So there *may* be something to this after all." Cox's phone rang. He glanced at the ID. "I've got to take this. Tell you what. You do the legwork on this. Come back to me when you've got the red tape worked out. I'll bankroll it, but if it fails, it's on you."

"I've never really—"

He answered the phone and slid the index card with the art show information across the desk, along with the check for the interview work. As if it didn't make it clear enough, he pointed out the door and swiveled his chair away.

Alan gathered them up and headed for the door.

"Fontaine," Cox called before he'd reached the hallway.

He turned.

"Marie-Anna's on this with you, if it happens," he said, covering the receiver with one hand.

"Why?"

"Because I'm the guy signing the checks, and that means I get to tell you what to do. Now go. I've got work to do."

The moment Cox was through addressing him, you'd think Alan had simply ceased to exist. Cox barked loudly into the phone with the spirit and calculated disrespect of someone talking to a frat brother. Alan took the hint and hurried down the hallway.

"All things considered, that went pretty well," he said.

"Did it? Because it sounded like all he did was give you permission to do more work, and warned you that he'd blame you if it doesn't work out," Blot said.

"That's usually the best you can expect out of someone high up in the corporation."

Blot swung by, pushed by the overhead lights.

"I think I like things better the way they are back home."

"Which is?"

"They tell you what to do, and if you refuse, Driss or someone like her comes with a lantern and makes you regret it."

Alan blinked. "You like that *better*?"

"At least they didn't act like they were doing me a favor. And I thought *we* were the only ones who got training in strategic dishonesty."

"Oh, no. I'm pretty sure there's whole classes about that in management school. But whatever. We've got a name behind us now. I was hoping he'd be willing to throw his weight around right from the get-go, but it's not nothing. I think we're going to be able to get into the prison with camera equipment. With any luck we'll be able to work out what Dun has planned."

"And then what?"

"We'll cross that bridge when we come to it."

"Spoken like a man a few steps away from falling in a ravine."

Alan had prided himself in knowing how to navigate bureaucracy. He was such a pathological rule follower that he'd gotten a tremendous amount of experience in getting whatever permission might be needed for any of his many projects he'd worked on privately and professionally in the past. It turned out, the prison system was a match for him. He was surprised—and as a compassionate human being, a little relieved—at how seriously the prison took the privacy of its inmates. He tried getting in contact with Bill to find out how he'd gotten permission to do his interview, but that had simply been the first round in a game of phone tag that ended in "We do not share the details of our professional interactions."

Before long, he'd gotten to the step that honestly should have been his first. He gave Jessie a call. She was a police officer who, to her chagrin, spent most of her time on desk duty. If anyone was going to know an angle that might work, it was her.

He hadn't gotten halfway through his request for help when she suggested he just come down to the station and talk it through down there. She seemed almost *too* eager to get him to come downtown.

When he stepped through the doors, he found the police station far more bustling than he was accustomed to. Phones were ringing, police were filing reports, and black-suited lawyer types were in ready supply.

"Alan! Over here!" shouted Jessie.

It was hard to miss Jessie when she was at work. She radiated an upbeat enthusiasm that seemed utterly out of place in the station. All around her, hard-boiled faces weighed down by years of serving and protecting went about the daily grind. And then there she was with a stack of paperwork under one arm, a Diet Coke in her free hand, and a smile on her face.

"Sarge! My buddy is here for a consult. I'll supervise him in the records room, 'kay?" she shouted.

A man replied with a gruffness far more in keeping with the atmosphere. It was less a word than a moderately meaningful growl. Evidently it was an affirmative, as Jessie cheerfully motioned with her head and nudged a half-door open with her foot.

"What's going on here?" Alan asked. "It seems like business is booming."

She nudged him in the ribs. "Don't you read the news?"

"I've been a little distracted."

"You've been a *lot* distracted. I wouldn't call it a crime wave, because the crime's not the weird part about it. We're having a justice wave."

"What do you mean?" Alan said.

"It's the strangest thing," she paused. "We're off the record, right?"

"I'm not a reporter."

"We're off the record, right?" she repeated more pointedly.

"Yes."

"Never hurts to confirm. After those pictures and recordings you took, the brass would probably want me to treat you like a journalist just to be on the safe side." She shrugged. "Not that it matters. It's all over the news already anyway. Get this door, would you?"

He turned the knob, and she backed into a room clearly not intended for the general public. Floor-to-ceiling filing cabinets stood in dense rows that covered the back two-thirds of the room. A wire cage separated it from the front of the room. A small table with three chairs, a bank of copy machines, and a computer crowded the rest. Poorly placed lights meant most of the room was rather dim, much to Blot's delight. She immediately took advantage of the freedom of darkness to roam about.

"There's a camera there, and a camera there," Blot said, scoping the space out.

Her time with Alan hadn't dulled her carefully trained sneakiness. All it had done was teach her what previously unknown pitfalls she'd have to avoid. Electronic surveillance was one she was quick to learn to spot.

"Wow. The station still has a lot of paper records," Alan said, eying Blot as she stretched herself down one of the rows and looked eagerly upon the assorted drawers.

"Yeah. It's one of those ridiculous regulation things, where no one wants to commit to digitizing everything, but everyone agrees that having digital records is important, so we somehow get stuck with having most of our stuff in the computer *and* in hard copy. Give me a second, I've got to log in. Do me a favor and look the other way."

Alan obliged, but Jessie may as well have rung the dinner bell for Blot. She snapped back to him and peered at the computer screen.

"Her username is 'jshearst,' and the password is big *V*, little *H*, that weird circled *A*..." Blot recited.

"Cut it out," Alan hissed.

"What?" Jessie said.

"Nothing, what were you saying?" Alan said.

"Fine, I'll just keep it to myself then," Blot said.

"Uh... What *was* I saying? Oh, right, wave of justice." She spun a chair away from the table and plopped down to start recording some information from her files.

"Here's the deal," she said without looking. "We have had an *unprecedented* number of people just coming in and confessing. Loads of them. Normally, that's great, but if anything starts happening more than it used to, people start getting worried. For a little while, criminals were just taking the most direct path to prison. There's a conga line of people remanded to prison for custody pending trial. Advocates started getting nervous that we were coercing suspects all of a sudden. So we've got a backup of people waiting to give an on-the-record confession. There just aren't enough public defenders to be on hand for all of them. It's the strangest problem."

While she spoke, Jessie periodically jotted codes down on a stack of sticky notes beside the computer. She stuck the notes to the folders to help with filing them.

"That *is* weird," Alan said, his mind starting to connect the dots. "Are they all going to Curran-Fromhold?"

"Uh... I'm not sure. That's a little further down the line than me. Depends upon the charges and a dozen other things, but more of them are than aren't, I'd wager."

"Is there anything they have in common?"

"I wouldn't know. I've been entering them all in, but it basically just goes from the page to the screen. Autopilot, you know. I don't remember any of it." She glanced over her shoulder. "Are you *sure* you're not a journalist? You're asking all the right questions for that."

"Just curious. I actually had some questions about the prison."

"Oh, right, right. What's up?"

"I want to do a photo-essay on prison conditions, and I'm having a little difficulty wrangling permission."

"Oh, yeah. You're going to have a hard time with that."

"I was hoping I could pick your brain on what I'd need to do to get in."

"Isn't that the kind of thing your boss would do?"

"This is sort of a personal project. He's just paying the bills on it."

"Ooh. Exciting. Are you shooting for an award or something with this?"

"I just feel like it's something I have to do," he said. "It kind of feels like life or death."

"*Artistes*," she said, emphasizing the pronunciation to the point of mockery. "Always so dramatic. Let's see... I'd say it's more of a sheriff's deputy thing than local police. But we work together enough. I can probably get you some names to get you started."

"Great. Anything would help. I'm sort of banging my head against a wall on this one."

"Sure thing." She closed the last of her folders and gathered up the pile. "Keep talking. I just have to stow these."

Jessie paced around to the door in the wire wall and unlocked it. She stepped through and locked it behind her. The very moment she was out of view, Blot rushed over to the computer desk. She snatched two sticky notes and stretched up to stick them over the camera lenses.

"Quick, say something so she can't hear me typing," Blot said.

"No, no, no. That's not why we're here," Alan whispered.

"We can be here for more than one thing, Alan," Blot lectured. "I have access to information, I have to learn what I can. I don't have a choice. Now talk to her."

"Alan?" Jessie called.

He weighed the pros and cons of trying to physically prevent Blot from rummaging around in the police computer. No matter what he thought of doing, all he could think of was how easy it would be for it to look like he was the one doing the hacking.

"I'm just going to start typing," Blot said.

She started to peck at the keys. Defeated, Alan raised his voice.

"This is sort of an important one for my future with Cox," he said, hoping his tone of voice didn't sound as unnaturally loud as it felt. "This is the first time I've ever spearheaded my own project. As far as I know, it's the first time *any* of the freelancers have. It's not that kind of media firm."

"Exciting."

"Keep talking," Blot said. "This isn't as easy to use as your computer. I'm trying to remember what she was clicking on and typing and such."

"It's extra stressful because I'm probably going to be working with Marie-Anna."

"Is that the lady he thinks no one knows he's dating?" Jessie said.

"Did... did I talk to you about her?" he asked.

"Sure you did."

Alan felt a wave of embarrassment at the realization that he'd let something like that just become idle chitchat. Obvious or not, it certainly wasn't his place to be airing someone else's dirty laundry. It was bad enough that's all Cox wanted him to be doing for celebrities. The last thing he wanted was to be doing it on his free time. Had this job started to warp his mind?

"Keep going," Blot urged. "I think I figured out how to open files on this thing."

"I don't think she likes me," Alan said.

"Don't judge a book by its cover on that one, Alan," Jessie said. "Are there many other lady photographers in the pool?"

"Not many."

"Yeah, take it from me, then. Sometimes you can't afford to be all smiles. Lots of guys take a smile as an invitation and then get belligerent when you set them straight. I had that problem here for a while."

"You did?"

"Yeah."

"But you *are* all smiles."

"That's why I had a problem with it. Don't worry about it. Do you have a timeline on this?"

"The sooner the better."

"I could have guessed that."

She started to pace up one of the rows. Blot and Alan looked at each other. If Jessie moved any farther up that row, she'd be able to see that the screen was active on the computer. Alan hastily paced over to block her view just as she stepped near enough for it to be a problem.

"Good job," Blot said. "You're starting to get an instinct for this spy stuff."

"Let me put it another way," Jessie continued. "Do you need to get this figured out *today*?"

"I mean, I'd like to work on it, but I was under no illusion that I'd actually manage it today."

"Good," she dropped a folder into a drawer and shut it, then paced back down the row. "Because the crime scene supervisor is upstairs, and you're going to meet him."

"Wait, really?" Alan said.

"Ask if you get a gun if you get the job," Blot said eagerly.

"Yeah. Why'd you think I wanted you in here to talk about this stuff? Come on. He's doing a review of some test shots from the current batch of internal recruits."

"But, do you think I'm ready? I didn't exactly ace that practice test."

She scoffed. "Please. You'll do fine."

Alan's chest fluttered with nervous excitement. "I didn't think I'd get another shot at this for *months*. You said 'maybe sometime this year.' When you say that sort of thing in January, that's usually a blow-off."

"This is excellent," Blot said. "Focus on getting the job. That'll eat up any time you'd have to spend shoving sticks into hornets' nests like this prison mess."

The expression on Alan's face grew more complex. "I'm sort of... I've got this essay. It's important. There's work to do, I can't really..."

She marched up the nearest row, prompting him to once again step in front of the computer. "You *do* want to be a photographic consultant for the forensic department, don't you? That *was* why I was over the other night, wasn't it?" She placed her hands on her hips. "Or was it just an excuse to get me over to your house?"

"No, no. I was serious about the studying."

"Good. Because if *that* was the reason, you could just ask."

Blot muttered something Alan didn't quite hear.

"Look," Jessie continued. "You skipped out on the first chance at a face-to-face because you were, admittedly, completely fried. You're fighting fit now, buddy."

"I'm distracted."

"It's now or never. That's not true. It's now or who-knows-when. I don't know if he just got sick of looking or if this whole justice wave has got him antsy, but the supervisor is finalizing a list of maybes in a hurry. If you're not on it, you're going to have to wait until a promotion or a retirement clears out a spot. So snap out of it."

She stepped out of sight and opened the last of the drawers. "You're going to go upstairs, you're going to answer some questions, and you either will or will not get invited back."

"Tell her you'll do it if they give you a gun," Blot urged.

"I don't want a gun," Alan hissed.

"Well, that's good, because they don't just hand out guns to consultants," Jessie said.

"Ugh. Tell her you won't do it, then. Waste of time," Blot said.

"I'll do it," Alan said.

The shadow glared at him. "Now you're just being contradictory. For that, I'm not going to tell you if I found anything." Blot locked the computer as she'd seen Jessie do and darted to the cameras to flick the sticky notes free.

"It's bothering me how good you are getting at this stuff."

The shade casually produced her stolen memo pad, summoned a pencil, and tucked herself behind Alan to start jotting down notes.

"Do you have to do that out in the open? Can't you take notes in the shadows?" he whispered.

"You've been there. Was it conducive to penmanship?" Blot asked.

"I guess not," he replied.

The wire door opened and Jessie stepped out. "You know, if we weren't friends I'd take offense to you muttering under your breath every time I'm out of earshot," she said.

"Sorry, I was—"

"About to make another silly excuse. Yes, I know. But come on. Time's up. I'm making your choice for you." She grabbed his wrist and dragged him toward the door.

"By the void, you really do let people push you around all day, don't you?" Blot mused as they slipped from the room.

The farther into the police station they got, the less distinctive it looked. Down on the first floor, it was exactly the sort of place one would envision from a police procedural. Once they got to the second floor, it looked like a run-of-the-mill office building. Desks were arrayed on the floor, mounded with varying degrees of clutter. Doors leading to small conference and meeting rooms lined the walls. Here and there a little sign on the wall indicated where the offices of the higher-ranking members of the force could be found. It wasn't romantic or exciting. It was just a job.

Oddly, this set Alan a bit at ease. Contrary to what recent events had required of him, Alan wasn't really the sort of person who enjoyed the idea of shootouts and hostage situations. He'd dreamed of his talents having some sort of value to society, but if that value could be applied without him eventually muttering about being too old for this stuff as bullets whizzed by, that would be ideal. Up here, it was easier to imagine people complaining about the declining quality of bagel Thursdays than reloading a gun and calling for cover.

"Lieutenant Stockton!" Jessie called.

The man she was addressing was a portly fellow who must have been quite near to retirement age. His hair was short and white, but it contrasted with his dark skin in a way that pushed the whole look further toward distinguished than old. His jaw was square and had the tenseness of someone whose teeth were never unclenched. The same went for his neck and shoulders. This man was a walking bundle of stress-knotted muscle.

"You're still going through the applicants for the photographer position, right?" Jessie said.

"Such as they are," Stockton said, poking at a mechanical push-button combo lock on his office door. He punched in the code, tried the handle, and trembled with frustration. "Whatever happened to keys..." he fumed.

"I hear they're going to be doing the keycards up here soon, sir."

"As though that'll be an improvement." He glanced at Alan. "You're not on the force."

"Uh, no, sir."

"I really don't want to hire outside the force," he said. Stockton thumbed in another attempt at the combo and finally opened his door.

"Two-five-one-four-three," Blot recited.

The lieutenant stepped inside. Jessie stepped in after him. Alan started to follow.

"No, Alan, you have to wait until—" Jessie whispered.

"Would you get him out of here!" Stockton barked.

Jessie maneuvered Alan out the door and turned him around.

"This is what I'm talking about," Stockton raved amid the sound of pages rustling and drawers slamming. "You get people up here without the proper protocol and they go wandering into places they don't belong, threatening to taint chain of custody and violate privacy and disclosure policies."

"Excellent first impression, Alan," Blot jabbed.

Alan stood awkwardly while the scattering of people working at their desks stared at the source of the outburst. Rather impressively, the embarrassment had managed to force his other concerns from his mind.

"Get him in here," Stockton barked.

Jessie tugged him into the room and shut the door. The office was not a large one. It had room enough for a desk, an aging desktop computer, and some filing cabinets. It didn't have much in the way of decoration or personal touches. A single photo of a notably younger version of Stockton smiling with his family and a few of certificates acknowledging various career and educational milestones broke up the otherwise featureless gray walls.

"Move over a little," Blot said. "I can't see."

Alan glanced up. Whether it was by choice or due to poor maintenance, the light diffuser was missing from the fixture in his office. Bare bulbs cast a sharper and stronger light on the room, leaving Blot pinned to the floor by the brightness. He casually stepped aside so that she could slide up the wall a bit and see what everyone was looking at.

A handful of photos was set out on the table. Bright orange tabs stuck to the corner of each identified them as "Simulated" and "For Training and Assessment Purposes Only."

"Here's what we've got," Stockton said. "The results of the last batch of in-house photographers. Trash. The lot of them."

Alan leaned forward. This cast a bit of Blot on the desk itself. She eagerly took advantage of the new perspective to look more closely at the photos.

"These are bad pictures," Blot said. "Yours are better."

The content of the pictures was about what Alan would have expected. Mostly they were small patches of pavement with this bit of evidence or that haphazardly scattered in frame. Broken glass here, a knife there. Little plastic shapes with markings to indicate scale were positioned near each. And Stockton was right. Not a single photo was what Alan would consider properly taken. Focus problems. Lighting problems. Color balance problems. They ran the gamut of amateur photography.

"Have these people had any training at all?" Alan asked.

"They've all got at least eighteen months on the force."

"No, I mean photographic training."

"How hard is it to take a photo?" Stockton asked.

"With all due respect," Alan tapped the desk, "obviously it's harder than these people thought. Have you ever done any forensic photography?"

"You're here to be assessed, not to assess me," Stockton said.

"He's always been on the interpretation side of the photos," Jessie helpfully supplied.

"So I know what makes for admissible evidence and what's going to give the defense ammunition to get photos rejected. And these are all a liability. I blame the cameras."

Alan shook his head. "No. Maybe ten years ago, but not today. You can take studio-quality photos with a mobile phone these days. It's all down to knowing how to use it."

"Pictures are pictures. You ask me, these guys who signed up just aren't interested in doing the job properly. We sent them to a seminar and everything. They should know everything they need to know about using those cameras."

"I've been taking classes and reading texts on forensic studies off and on for two years, and I know I haven't scratched the surface. I don't think it's fair to expect a single seminar to make them experts on the photographic side."

"Pictures are pictures," Stockton said. "Officer Hearst, get him out of here."

"Lieutenant, I really think getting someone in from the journalistic side of things is going to give us an insight that we're missing from inside the force," she said.

"Look. We all want to help our buddies get on the force, but how much can someone really learn about photography? Until they retired,

McMillian and Khan were both career officers who got promoted into the department, and they did excellent work."

Alan leaned a little lower. "Are these raw photos or compressed?"

Stockton blinked.

"I ask because the white balance seems off. This one should be okay because of the amount of neutral gray in frame, but that one has a definite tungsten cast to it. These three look like they were shot on full-automatic settings. Autofocus is problematic on shiny surfaces like this. It never knows what to lock on to. And the auto settings never seem to set the speed correctly either. Especially for handheld shots. You're going to get an awful lot of blur like in this one here. If you can't use a tripod or monopod, upping the light and adjusting the f-stop is probably going to be the better bet. If you've *got* to use an auto setting, shaky hands and hasty photography are better served by sport settings. I assume you're using an LED light ring and a macro lens for these detail shots?"

The flow of words was constant, like someone had opened the floodgates in his head. For the first time in too long, he felt like he wasn't out of his depth. There was nothing showy about it. He wasn't trying to impress Stockton. He just felt relieved that he actually had the expertise to properly assess the situation for once.

Stockton turned and reached into the corner. He retrieved a heavy-duty camera case and set it down atop the other photos.

"This is what they're working with. All of these shots were taken on this equipment. Show me what they should have done."

Alan opened the case. The individual elements of the camera and its accessories were each separate and tucked into cutouts in a foam organizer. He tugged the camera body from the case and inspected it. Piece by piece he assembled the camera and snapped on the accessories with military precision.

"This is a good setup. I'd recommend a battery grip. Bit light rings like this and a decent flash can kill these batteries pretty quick; and especially if you're in bad weather, it can be a problem to do a battery swap."

"To hell with critiquing the equipment. You want me to believe you know what you're talking about?" Stockton rummaged in his pocket and came up with a handful of change. He tossed it into the corner. When the nickels and dimes spun to a rest, he pointed. "There's your crime scene. I want two pictures. Show me what they did wrong, and show me what you can do right."

"It's going to take more than one photo to do it right."

"If you want to make excuses, just give me back the camera now."

"Right, sorry," Alan said.

He got down on one knee and took the first shot. All automatic, as he supposed a cop with no prior photographic experience but his eye on a higher paycheck might try. The second picture only took him a moment longer to prepare, but that moment was a busy one. It was true that modern cameras did a remarkable job at turning a single button press into a perfectly serviceable image. The further one traveled down the bottomless pit of camera know-how, the more terms started to float into one's mind. Full manual was ideal, but the halfway helper terms that were just as alien, "like aperture priority," could still work magic.

He snapped the second picture and handed the camera to Stockton. The gruff veteran grabbed it and popped out its memory card.

"Quick, move over so I can see his screen," Blot urged.

Alan resolutely remained where he was as Stockton logged on and loaded up the images. Alan and Jessie waited while he clicked back and forth between the two images, then the ones on the table. After nearly thirty seconds of clicking, zooming, and gritting his teeth, he looked up to them.

Stockton gave Alan one of the longest, hardest looks of his life. The man's gaze was penetrating, and he stared with the focused intensity of someone seeking not just to see what was right in front of him, but to see everything their peripheral vision could tell them as well. It was the definition of scrutiny.

Finally, the lieutenant snapped his gaze to Jessie. "Get him back in here for the next assessment."

"Hah! Will do!" Jessie said.

"Thank you for the opportunity, sir," Alan said.

"It's another mock crime scene. Not scheduled yet, but it'll be some time in the next few days. You'll be using the station's rig, so don't bother bringing any of your gear. But don't be late. Now get moving. I have work to do."

Alan and Jessie stepped out of the office and headed for the stairs. As they went, Jessie slapped him on the back.

"There, see? Aren't you glad I got you up here?"

"Yes. Uh, listen, about this essay I have to do."

"Oh, right. We'll talk about that, but first, I need you to say something."

"What?"

"Repeat after me. Thank you, Jessie."

He smirked. "Thank you, Jessie."

"I really appreciate you putting in the good word for me and nagging me into going through with this."

"I really do appreciate it."

"Close enough." She checked her watch. "Are you hungry? We can talk about it when you buy me lunch."

"Say no. Say you're busy," Blot said.

He gave his shadow a hard glance. "Sure, let's go."

Always the creature of habit, Alan took Jessie to the diner for lunch. He was greeted at the door by the young woman who, regardless of when he showed up, always seemed to be on shift.

"Hey, Alan. Corner booth?" the waitress asked.

"Yes please," Alan said.

She led the pair toward Alan's booth of choice, tucked in the poorly lit corner of the diner. It was farthest from the windows and farthest from the door, and Blot had persuaded Alan to surreptitiously loosen one of the two bulbs in the hanging lamp.

He took a seat. Jessie slid in opposite.

"Two coffees?" the waitress asked.

"Yes please."

She nodded and turned to Jessie. "And what'll you start with?"

Jessie cocked her head. "One of those coffees wasn't for me?"

"No, no. Double coffees for captain caffeine over here."

"I'll have one too, then."

"Sure thing. I'll be back with a menu."

The waitress walked away. Jessie gave Alan a look.

"What?" he said.

"Let's walk through it, shall we?" She counted off her points on her fingers. "You've got your own booth. It's the one booth where you can watch both the windows and the door. You've got a weirdo drink order." She placed her hands on her hips. "Have you become a cartoon mobster and didn't tell me?"

He laughed. "Nah. When business started picking up at Cox Media, I started eating at restaurants a bunch more often."

"So what's good here?" she asked.

"It's a diner. Diner stuff. Anything that comes off a griddle," he said.

She clapped her hands and rubbed them together. "Oh! Breakfast for lunch."

The waitress returned with three mugs and filled them. While she was at it, she filled two glasses with ice water. Alan strategically maneuvered one of the cups of coffee behind his ice water and stuck a stirrer in it. Blot bobbed up and sipped at it. The waitress handed the menu to Jessie, but she waved it off.

"Short stack of blueberry pancakes, two eggs looking at you, rye toast, no butter. Grape jelly," Jessie dictated.

"And for you, Alan?" the waitress said.

"What, no regular for this?" Jessie said.

"He cycles between three," the waitress joked.

"Tuna melt and tomato soup," he said.

"Number two," she said with a nod. "Okay, coming right up."

The waitress paced away. Jessie drummed on her lap. "You're big-time now, huh? I seem to remember back in college you were brown-bagging it all the time."

"Oh yeah. Now *other* people make me my grilled cheese. At least until the work dries up. So, I don't know. Another couple of weeks."

"That's the spirit."

"I need another coffee," Blot said.

Alan glanced at the empty mug. After a wary glimpse back at Jessie, he subtly swapped it for his own and mimed drinking from the cup Blot had drained so quickly.

"It's nice you're rocking and rolling, though. At least one of us is."

"Problems at the precinct?" he said. "Or is it that you're still sick of the desk work?"

"I love a man who listens."

"You said it was some policy thing?"

"Yeah. It's dumb. Substance abuse policy."

He blinked, concern flashing across his face.

She laughed. "Calm down. It's nothing crazy. I tweaked my back a while back, and during flare-ups they put me on these painkillers that are, shall we say, incompatible with field work."

"So how much longer are you sidelined?"

She reached into her pocket and revealed a prescription bottle. "Two pills a day, plus two refills if needed." She shook the bottle. "Six weeks, assuming I can convince the doctor I don't need the second refill."

"Not too much longer, then. That's good." He set his coffee down to be freshened and scratched his ear.

"Wait," she said. "Hold still." She reached across the table and angled his ear toward her. "You've got a bruise back here. Have you been fighting?"

"Oh, uh... occupational hazard," he said.

"Are you a full-contact photographer?"

"It depends on the subject."

She released a low whistle. "We've got to get you off the TMZ circuit before you get cauliflower ear."

Jessie slid her phone from her pocket. As if summoned, Blot popped up on her side of the table and watched over her shoulder as she entered her passcode. Alan gave her a dirty look. She stuck her tongue out at him—a very curious-looking expression for the white-mouthed silhouette.

For a few minutes, chitchat managed to make the whole scheme Alan was embroiled in feel far away. It was a bit of a juggling act, keeping both his mugs full without Jessie questioning just how he was drinking them so swiftly. With mysterious, supernatural forces swirling around him at all times, having an idle conversation about the good old days in college was a breath of fresh air. Before he knew it, the food had arrived. As Jessie excitedly turned to the approaching plates, a shadowy hand slipped up to the table and snatched her phone from where it had been resting. Alan gritted his teeth, but couldn't risk reprimanding her. Instead, he watched out of the corner of his eye as Blot squinted at the glowing screen, the phone floating in the air of its own accord. She tapped at the screen with her shadowy fingers, but it didn't respond.

"I need to borrow your hand," Blot said.

Before he could object, her black fingers grabbed one of his fingers and quickly smeared the phone against its tip. She managed to get the phone unlocked and got one of the messaging apps open before he could pull his hand away.

"I've got to figure out a reliable way to work these stupid touchscreens on my own," Blot said. "I'm hit-or-miss doing it myself, and needing your help and permission isn't going to work. ... Remind me to ask you what a therapist is again." She glanced down again. "She's got a lot of messages back and forth with someone labeled 'therapist.'"

The shade tossed the phone to the seat beside Jessie with precise timing, such that it landed just as the plate was being set down. Jessie glanced in its direction.

"Whoa," she said. "That was close. Must've caught my phone with my elbow." She picked it up and checked the time, then waved at the waitress. "Could you bring the check, please?" She turned to Alan. "Not to rush things, but I'm going to have to get moving pretty quick after this."

"Right, right," he said. "Hey. Not to get deep over lunch, but we've been pretty small-talky over this meal. Is everything okay... you know... in the rest of your life?"

"There's that silver tongue of yours, just smoothly sliding into the hard-hitting topics." She smeared some jelly on her rye and dipped it in the yolk. "I should have gotten it over easy. I always forget that's an option."

"Seriously, though," he said. "I don't want to pry."

"Then don't," Jessie said.

It was a blunt, direct statement, but it was delivered with the same cheerful smile and disposition as the rest of the conversation.

"Good!" Blot piped up. "Can we go?"

"Sorry," Alan said quickly. "I didn't—"

She waved him to silence. "No, no. That was weird. Listen, it's a deep well. Lots of lousy stuff happened in the last five years or so. You calling for help with this was a nice little reminder of the stuff *before* the lousy stuff. Call me selfish, but I'd rather the distraction than the heart-to-heart right now."

"Right. That's fair."

"I'll say this, though," she said, pouring some syrup over her pancakes. "And don't take this the wrong way. But all this? A rut of a routine? Cooking shows? Free time studying for certifications? It's a refreshing change of pace." She cut a bite of pancake and stuffed it in her mouth. "They say there's an ancient curse. 'May you live in interesting times,'" she continued.

"I thought that was a thing from Discworld."

"Is it? Well, regardless, it's true. I need a big dose of boring right now. So don't go getting exciting, would you?"

Blot snorted and burst into hysterics.

"I'll do my very best..." Alan said steadily before turning his attention to the soup.

Chapter 4

An hour and a half later, Alan climbed into his car. Lunch with Jessie had been a long-overdue breath of fresh air. She assured him that she'd keep working on her contacts inside the prison to see if she could find out how to give him a leg up, and that was a godsend. But more than that, she'd managed to get him to talk about something *besides* the tangle his life had tied itself into. They'd talked about sports and movies. TV and music. They'd talked about the old times. Basically, they'd talked about all the little meaningless things that it turned out were so terribly important. However brief if may have been, she'd lifted the weight from his shoulders.

But now he was alone with his thoughts again. And for the first time in hours, he realized that being alone shouldn't have been an option anymore. Blot had not said a peep since they'd left the station. He glanced down at her.

"You've been quiet," he said.

She grumbled.

"What was that?"

"Nothing," she muttered. "Did you get what you wanted out of that?"

"I think so. I got a stack of emails and phone numbers to try. I'm definitely a lot closer to getting this thing set up than I was. You were there, though. I'm sure you heard it all."

"I wasn't paying attention. This isn't going to be a regular thing is it?"

"What?"

"Lunch with Jessie."

"I don't know. I guess if we end up working together it will. Why?"

"I don't like her."

"What's not to like? Jessie's great! I've known her forever."

"It doesn't matter if Jessie is great or not. It's her or me."

"What? Wait. Is this some sort of a relationship ultimatum?"

"No. Don't flatter yourself. What we have? That's not a relationship. It's a symbiotic…"

"Relationship," Alan finished.

"Right, but key word, 'symbiotic.' I'm not a me, you're not a you. We're an us. Remember? And what's worse, I don't get to *be* me unless there's no one else around. If you're with Jessie, you can't talk to me. Which is fine. But when you're with her, you don't even act like you *hear* me."

"I couldn't respond. She'd have asked who I was talking to."

"Oh, I know *why* you don't, but it doesn't change the fact that more time with Jessie equals less time for me. And less *coffee* for me. Which is a *crime*. And it's only going to get worse, you know. She's giving you signals."

"Signals."

"You know what I mean. Signals."

"Like… *signals* signals?"

"She's going to lock lips with you the first chance she gets," Blot said bluntly.

He scrunched up his face. "You're crazy. I can't imagine I'm the kind of guy for Jessie. She's got a whole station full of guys to choose from."

"Sure. But she's got rotten taste. It's something you've got in common."

"You're making a big deal out of nothing. But point taken about the coffee. I've got an obligation to you. And even if I didn't, you're a friend. I'll try to be mindful of that sort of thing in the future."

"See that you do."

By now they'd pulled into the parking garage. Ms. Levitt had been kind enough to park like a human being for once, so they were on their way to the elevator with relatively little frustration.

"I notice you haven't asked me what I learned from the police computer."

"That's because I'd rather not rely upon information that I'd go to jail for knowing."

"What if it's a life-or-death situation?"

The elevator doors opened, and he stepped into his hallway, which was empty. "It isn't a life-or-death situation," he said.

"Not *yet*. But maybe once it *gets* to life or death, it might be too late."

"Fine. What did you learn?"

"Nothing useful."

He glared at her. "Then why did you make me ask?"

"Because you wouldn't *know* that without asking."

He fiddled with his keys in the lock. "You know, I think I prefer it when you're being manipulative to when you're being vindictive."

"If you want more manipulation, I can oblige. All you have to do is..."

Alan fought with his key a bit. The lock was not being cooperative. "All I have to do is what?" he asked.

"Never mind that... Is there something wrong with that door?"

He turned to the door opposite his. A large sign clearly labeled it as a utility closet. "What? That's just where the janitor keeps the spare garbage bags and stuff."

"Has it always been like that?" she asked.

"For as long as I've lived here." He searched his memory. "Hasn't it?"

They both gave the door a lingering look. Alan was the first one to shake it off.

"Look, we've got enough stuff to be paranoid about. Let's not waste our time worrying about utility closets, okay?"

He finally got the key to cooperate and opened the door to his apartment. He squinted and Blot grunted. The light inside was glaring. He normally shut off his lights on the way out the door, but forgetfulness alone couldn't explain this. The shades had been removed from all his lights. His curtains were open, letting the afternoon sun pour through. It was terribly bright in his apartment.

"Shut them off, Alan," Blot urged.

He shut the door and reached for the light switch beside the door to at least turn off the foyer light.

"I really wouldn't, Mr. Fontaine."

Alan's gaze shot to the hallway leading to his bedroom. A tall man with a white beard and a blue overcoat paced into view. He jingled an amulet that pointed precisely at Alan. It was a member of the Dawn. The same one he'd spotted outside the prison on the day of the interview.

"They say a little extra light can help with depression." He narrowed his eyes and pocketed the amulet. "And you've got a dark cloud hanging over you."

"What is this?" Alan switched off the foyer light. "We had a truce."

His unwelcome visitor slid his coat open, revealing a veritable bandoleer of silver daggers. A single one, no sharper than a letter opener, had nearly killed Blot. He was armed to the teeth, and they looked razor sharp.

"If we are going to be civil for this discussion, I am going to have to ask that you keep the lights on. You may trust that shadow of yours, but I don't."

"I don't need to be civil. You broke into my home! And once again, we had a truce!"

"If you'll recall, the truce required you to keep your nose clean. An argument could be made that sticking said nose into the prison matter is a violation of that agreement."

"It was part of my job!" Alan said.

"Perhaps. Or perhaps you're showing up for instruction. We know that at least one high-level shade is already inside."

Alan furrowed his brow. "I know of two. Dun and Driss."

"Don't tell him anything, Alan," Blot hissed, struggling at the bright light that kept her pinned. "They interrogated you, and they tried to kill me, which means they tried to kill you too. Get him out of here before he tries it again."

"It bothers me that you are on a first-name basis with them, my friend. Sit down. I think we need to discuss this."

"We don't need to discuss anything. Get out of my apartment before I call the cops."

"I heard about what happened in your parents' neighborhood. You took on a shifter. That's no small task. Maybe you survived because you're a scrapper. Maybe it was professional courtesy." He stepped around and took a seat in Alan's easy chair. "There was a lot of blood. But no body, and no report of one. A good shifter should be recovered from a wound with that much blood in pretty short order. Yet you're not guarding your parents' house today. It's all got me curious. Please. This isn't the venue for anything adversarial. Let's be calm about this. In fact, I have been remiss. Introductions. I know you, of course, Mr. Alan Fontaine. My name is Charles Brink."

"Pleased to meet you, Charles. Get out of my house."

Brink folded his hands. "If I were you, I would leap at this opportunity to establish my intention. You have a shade. That puts you at a significant disadvantage regarding your trustworthiness. As you may have surmised from my armaments, I'm not a member of the rank and file in the Dawn. I'm what you might call a contract man. An enforcer. They flew me in from Massachusetts to deal with what's going on. Seems Philadelphia's going to be a hot spot during this cycle. We've already shared more words than my associates would have taken the time for. They have itchier fingers than I do. But I feel that when you serve the light, you mustn't give in to the darker yearnings of the soul and leap to the blade as a solution for every problem. Maybe we can learn from one another."

Alan's nerves were taut as a guitar string, but he'd always fancied himself a man of reason. "Maybe we should listen to him..." he whispered.

"Are you out of your mind?" Blot said. "He is a member of a cult who wants to kill people like us."

"But he's making sense. And he seems reasonable."

"Making sense? He just said some of the culty-est cult stuff I've ever heard!"

Alan addressed Brink. "If we're going to be civil, that means being civil to me and Bl—"

"Don't tell him my name!" she barked.

"Why not?"

"Simple magic rules. Names have power."

"But he told me his name and he knows mine."

"That's your problem. And it's one I don't want."

"Has anyone ever told you it is rude to leave your guest out of your conversations?" Brink asked.

Alan waved his hand. "Everyone listen. If you want my cooperation, you're going to treat me *and* my shade with courtesy and respect."

Brink reached over to the side table and replaced the shade and the red cloth that had been removed from the light. "Very well. I am a reasonable man." He pointed up. "This light stays lit, but you can dim the rest."

"If you think I'm going to risk getting near him whether the lights are on or off, you are sorely mistaken," Blot said.

When lighting in the room was dim enough for Blot to have at least a modicum of mobility, Alan took a seat on the love seat. The lights maneuvered her into the spot beside him naturally, but she struggled herself into a more upright posture. Alan could swear she was even puffing her chest out, as if to intimidate the man who couldn't see her.

"There. Are we ready to talk?" Brink asked.

"Fine. Let's talk," Alan said. "I'll start. How did you get into my apartment?"

"I picked the lock. You really ought to have a word with your superintendent. These are the easiest-to-pick locks I've ever encountered. For my first question, I would like to ask just what your plans are with this photo-essay you are proposing for the prison."

"They're spying on you, Alan," Blot said. "Are you going to stand for that?"

"How do you know about the photo-essay?"

"We aren't precisely the best-equipped organization, but we have eyes and ears everywhere. Once we realized there was shade activity within the prison, we focused our attention on it. Imagine our surprise when the people we were keeping an eye on kept getting messages from you asking for permission to come inside with your camera. Now, again, what are your plans?"

"Don't tell him," Blot said.

"I'm just trying to get inside to see what's going on," Alan said.

"Am I even talking?" Blot growled. "Don't I get a say in this?"

"That's understandable," Brink said. "We're curious about that as well."

"You mean you don't know what's going on either?"

"We know the following. There is a tremendous focus of shade activity within those walls. Whoever is inside has managed to exercise a degree of influence over the workings of the prison, as multiple attempts to place one of our people inside have been thwarted. The nature of our techniques are such that it is impossible for us to know whether it is a small number of powerful shades or many weak ones like the one who has taken you as a host."

"I'm strong enough to put a claw through *you*," Blot huffed, arms crossed.

"Like I said, there's at least two. I think there might be more," Alan said. "The reason I was ever in there in the first place was because they wanted to warn me to stay away or they'd go after me and my family."

Brink stroked his beard. "And your clash in your parents' neighborhood illustrates they have the means to do so. Yet you persist with this investigation against their wishes."

"They'll come after me and my family regardless. The only way I can think of to stop them is to do it myself. And I can't do it unless I get inside." Alan leaned forward. "I don't suppose there's any way the Dawn can help protect my family?"

"We have our hands full. Stretched thin. This is a war with many fronts. We can't afford another one. Not now that the shades of this cycle are growing strong enough to switch to their next hosts. There's value in knowing where a shade will strike, though..." he mused. "I can see about having some of our people nearby, but I can't make any promises."

"I figured as much..."

Both men were silent for a time, but Brink's gaze was a measuring one.

"What's wrong?" Alan said.

"For someone marked for extermination by an arcane force, your fortification is woefully inadequate. Frankly, it shouldn't have been so easy to break in to your home in broad daylight."

"Forgive me if I don't have the know-how to turn an apartment into a bunker."

"Regardless of whether you know how or not, you haven't, and yet you are still alive."

"I guess I'm lucky, or else the shades are stretched as thin as you are and they can't afford the time and effort to keep coming after me. Dun sort of indicated I wasn't the most important thing on their agenda."

"If a shade told it to you, it is almost certainly a lie. Shades are all liars."

"I'll show you a liar," Blot said.

She snatched up a dirty mug that they'd neglected to toss in the sink before they'd left that morning and brandished it. A sparkle drew Alan's eye, and he discovered Brink had not one but two daggers in his hands.

"Whoa, whoa. Easy. I've probably already burned my damage deposit. I don't need a full brawl in my living room."

"He called me a liar! I can't let that stand," Blot said.

"You told me yourself that you were a liar."

"Yeah, but that doesn't give *him* the right to call me that. When I say it, it's wholesome and forthcoming. When he says it, it's an insult. I won't have someone coming into the only place I can even pretend to call home and calling me names."

"If you can't keep your shade in line, I don't think we can reasonably continue this truce, Mr. Fontaine," Brink said.

"It's fine. It'll be fine." Alan snatched the mug and put it down on the table. "Just calm down."

Blot glared at Brink. "Fine... But I want him out of here in five minutes, or we're going to figure out just how good of an enforcer he really is."

"Did you have a reason for insulting my friend?" Alan asked.

"Your friend?" He raised an eyebrow. "You have poor taste in friends. But the fact of the matter is, you could easily be dead right now. I assure you that shifter will be showing his face again, soon. And if I as a flesh-and-blood human being could access your apartment, that you've not woken up with twisted claws wrapped around your throat already is either a miracle, an oversight, or a collusion."

"Collusion?"

"If you were truly a liability, any shade wise and powerful enough to keep us out of the prison would have had you killed without so much as a warning. That you survived an attack could be explained as skill or luck. But receiving a warning implies you aren't a liability. Which means you may be an asset."

"I assure you, I'm not working for them."

"Not knowingly, perhaps. But the voice of their kind is in your mind. Can you even trust yourself?"

"Get him out of here, Alan," Blot spat.

"One last question before I send you on your way." Alan's expression hardened. "And you *will* be on your way after this. What would be your plan, if you were to get into that prison?"

"I would exterminate the shades."

"That's it? You wouldn't try to reason with them? You wouldn't try to save the lives of their hosts?"

"There is no reasoning with shades, and their hosts have already lost their lives."

"As a host, I can tell you that I am still very much alive."

"You are alive, certainly, but is your life still your own? You aren't what you were before. Alan Fontaine is gone. The only way forward is in an uneasy partnership with a creature who wishes to subjugate your kind, or the embrace of death. I consider the second to be preferable. And I intend to help others to that same conclusion."

"Mr. Brink, I don't know who taught you to negotiate, but seeing how I've dealt with Dun's threat should give you a pretty good idea of just how motivating I find death threats."

Blot stretched to the doorway and wrenched it open. The light that flooded in snapped her back to Alan's side.

"Leave. Now."

"As you wish."

Brink stood and marched past Alan. When he reached the doorway, he looked over his shoulder.

"If you change your mind and decide to defend the light rather than comforting the dark, give me a call. I believe you already have my information."

Alan slammed the door, locked it, and affixed the chain. After a moment of consideration, he grabbed one of the two kitchen chairs and propped it under the knob.

"So we're leaving this apartment, right?" Blot said.

"I don't know..." Alan said.

He paced around the apartment, replacing shades and dimming lights. Each renewed bit of darkness allowed Blot to more easily slide up along the walls to address him more directly.

"What do you mean you don't know? If there was one thing that lunatic was right about, it was that it is a miracle that we're still alive. This place isn't safe. You saw his pendant. I'm strong enough now that I'm not just going to be overlooked. They can find me. And if the Dawn can find me, the other shades certainly can."

"I don't have any other options. Where else am I going to stay?"

"Let's start with 'not here' and narrow it down from there. Because right now where we *will* stay isn't nearly as important as where we won't."

"Maybe I could move in with my folks. That'd help me keep an eye on them."

"Bad idea. Have you already forgotten the 'don't put all the targets in the same place' discussion we had? That's just saving them trouble."

"Jessie's apartment then? I think she has a pull-out couch."

"No!"

"Beggars can't be choosers, Blot."

"Wherever you go, you've got to be alone. First, because then there's no one else to double-cross us, and second, because then I can have something approaching a moment of autonomy from time to time."

"I didn't *ask* you to become my shadow. I try to be obliging, but let's not forget that you chose me and you sort of have to take what you get."

Blot huffed. "Fine. Fair enough. But let's not get off topic. We can't stay here. The Dawn knows we're here. The shades *must* know we're here. It's a wonder those things in the white suits haven't come knocking again."

A delicate rapping in that precise moment drew their eyes to the door.

"Don't tell me..." Blot said.

"Mr. Fontaine? May I have a word with you?" came a calm, cheerful, and particularly loud voice.

"Now is not a good time," Alan called back.

"It's a survey. Give me a few moments of your time for a survey."

He stepped toward the door. Blot stretched away from it as he opened the door. Alan kept the chain secured while inching the door wide enough to get a decent look at his visitor. The face greeting him was pleasant and rather androgynous. He quickly recognized this person as the one in the apartment across the hall. A white jumpsuit suggested some sort of role in maintenance. As they spoke, they adjusted themselves periodically, seemingly unsatisfied with the fit of the jumpsuit.

"Thank you for answering." The speaking volume was just a shade too loud to be conversational. "I have some questions. Some important and entirely ordinary survey questions regarding your satisfaction with your current abode."

"As I said, this isn't a great time."

"Answer my questions, please."

Alan's chest tightened a bit at the sound of the request. "Fine. But only if we can make it quick."

"Have you developed any concerns regarding security in and around the building?"

"Get them to leave please," Blot said, a chill in her voice.

"I've had a few break-ins, in fact," Alan said.

"If we were to offer enhanced security as an optional service, would you partake in that service?"

"If there was any way to be more secure, I'd jump at the chance. Provided I could afford it."

"What price would you consider acceptable for enhanced security, sir?"

"Please get them to leave," Blot begged.

"I don't know. Look, this really is a bad time."

"Would you consider it unacceptable if, rather than US currency, the service were to be offered as a result of a barter-type arrangement?"

"I guess... wait. Who exactly are you?"

The surveyor raised their voice. "What sort of barter would you consider acceptable? Goods, services, or information?"

Before Alan could answer, he heard a door open.

"Do you people have no decency or consideration at all?" barked Ms. Levitt, his easily agitated neighbor. She stomped into view through the crack in the door. The rims of her eyes were red, and her nose was chapped. She sniffled and continued.

"I am *trying* to recover from the flu. It is bad enough that Mr. Fontaine's friends show up and scratch away at his door. It is worse that they had such a noisy conversation once he got home. But all of that I could forgive. I'm a patient woman. I'm willing to give anyone the benefit of the doubt. But to stand here in the hallway and *yell* and *scream* without any regard for any of the good, hard-working people—"

"Thank you, ma'am. I will be quieter," the stranger said.

"*Don't you interrupt me!* That's it! Give me the name of your manager."

"I am sorry, ma'am. That will be all for you."

"I'll decide when we're through here. Now, I said give me the name of your manager, or I'll see to it that—"

"Go to sleep!" the stranger shouted.

Normally, Alan would have found such a specific and absurd statement to be puzzling. At the moment, it wasn't much of a concern for him. He was far too busy crumbling to the floor as though he'd been struck with a tranquilizer dart. He was vaguely aware of some soreness in his cheek as the chain securing his door jingled and released. The door slid open and

107

thumped his chest. Through the widened opening, he was treated to a view of Ms. Levitt. She was deeply asleep in an undignified heap in the hallway. A white boot nudged her back through her doorway and shut her door. He felt himself being lifted from the floor just as his eyes finally slid shut and sleep took him.

Alan blinked his eyes open. He was on his bed now, still dressed and sprawled on top of the covers. A sluggish turn to the right revealed the shadowy figure of Blot. Her eyes were shut and her mouth was open, a soft snore rattling with each breath. It was the first time he'd ever seen the dainty little creature asleep. In another situation it would have been adorable. At the moment, his limited brain power had other things to deal with.

The survey taker was standing in the bedroom, hands clutched behind their back as they gazed pleasantly at the miniature gallery of his photos that Alan had decorated the room with.

"What's going on?" he mumbled. "What are you doing in my house?"

"Admiring your artwork. I was told you were a fine photographer. I have never had an eye for photos, but these I like," they said.

"Huh? Hmm?" Blot snorted. "What is... Oh no..." She huddled down beside Alan. "Get it out of here," she begged.

"Look. I really think you should leave."

"You want me to stay," the visitor said.

It wasn't a question. It was a statement. And to Alan's confusion, he found he agreed with it. He tried to contradict it, because he knew a moment ago he'd felt differently.

"At least give me some room." It was the best he could muster.

"That is a very fair offer. I will stand farther back, here, by the door. Is that acceptable?"

Alan looked to Blot. She was still huddling beside him, and still staring at the stranger with a mixture of distrust and distress, but she wasn't as terrified.

"Better," Alan said.

"Good. Would you like to continue the survey?"

He stood and straightened his clothes. "I really wouldn't."

"You would like to continue the survey."

"Yes, please."

The words slipped from his lips entirely without his permission. Every time this stranger made a command, a second train of thought shoved Alan's desires and intentions aside and gave the requested response. A part of him always knew how he really felt, and what he really wanted to do, but the top layer of his mind simply obliged. His awareness of the fact seemed to weaken its effect, as he was able to interrupt the forthcoming question with a question of his own.

"Who are you?" he said.

"I am... one moment..." They reached into their pocket and retrieved a small pad. "I am... er... Angel.

"I... uh..."

"Pronouns?"

"Yeah."

"They/them, please."

"What are you doing here?"

"What a strange and silly question to ask me! I am just a curious human. Very much like you. Exactly like you, in fact. The two of us are a couple of humans, having a nice, pleasant, inquisitive conversation. Now, to continue…"

"Are you one of the white-suited people?" he said.

They flipped through the notebook again. "I neither confirm, nor deny, my allegiance to, or the existence of, the group or organization to which you have referred."

"It's one of them. I knew it!"

"Back to the matter at hand," they said, seemingly unaware of Blot's comment. "I would like to continue the survey."

"No, no. I don't know if you think you're being subtle, but you absolutely aren't."

"What have I done that has been unconvincing?"

"Where do I start? For one thing, humans don't routinely assure each other of their humanity."

"It is perfectly reasonable, when asked a question, to provide the proper context. I, a human, should therefore confirm my humanity."

"And you had to consult a notebook when I asked you your *name*!"

"I hadn't anticipated the question." Angel waggled the book. "This is simply a memory aid."

"For your *name*?"

Blot mustered herself up and reached as best she could across the room. She *just* managed to snatch the shadow of the notebook and wrench it from Angel's hands.

A flash of light filled the room. It dazzled Alan and threw Blot against the wall.

"By the *void* that hurts..." she hissed.

Alan blinked purple spots from his eyes to find Blot on the wall behind him, cradling a hand that was curled into an involuntary claw.

"My apologies. I can't quite make out your shade, or I would have warned..." Angel paused long enough to retrieve the notebook and flip to a new page. "Her. I would have warned her about the wards that protect the notebook."

They pocketed the notebook. "You really shouldn't try to take it either. The wards work on humans, too. Er. That is to say, they work on you and me. Because, as I earlier indicated, we are both humans."

"Are you okay?" Alan asked.

"I'm better than that thing is about to be," Blot said.

She reached out with one hand, then the other, grasping the shadows of the bed and dresser respectively. Then she started to haul at them. They rattled and slid an inch or two before her shadowy form emerged from the wall. It wasn't as twisted as her combat form, nor was it as imposing, but she made up for the lack of mass with the raw hostility of her posture.

It wasn't as effective as she would have liked, as Angel's expression shifted to one of genuine interest, taking in the sight of a shadow manifesting as a semidemonic figure in the room as though they'd just noticed a rainbow forming.

"Ah! Very good! I could tell she was here, but I couldn't picture her." Angel held out their hand. "Pleased to meet you!"

"Back off!" Blot spat.

The shade charged at Angel, but the strange visitor didn't even flinch. Alan stopped Blot with a hand to the shoulder.

"Everyone calm down," he urged.

"I am very calm, sir," Angel said.

"Fine. Blot, calm down."

"They assaulted both of us, Alan. And they broke and entered. I'm not the one who's out of line here."

"I am simply a surveyor with a survey for you," Angel said.

"Enough with the facade," Alan barked, finally at his limit. "If you were a run-of-the-mill human being, seeing Blot like this would have terrified you."

Angel considered the statement. "I'll grant you that was a short-coming of my performance." They cleared their throat. "You do not rememb—"

"Enough of that mind-trick stuff, too."

They sighed and flipped through the notebook some more. Blot eased back into the shadows for the sake of privacy.

"If things start to get bad, kick them into the doorway, and I'll slam it on them," Blot said.

"I haven't handled this as well as I would have liked." They glanced up at Alan. "I am new to fieldwork, you understand."

"Fieldwork," Alan repeated.

"Yes. I have been assigned to keep an eye on you."

"By the white-suits?"

"You are free to assume that, but I will not confirm it. Even if I say things which imply knowledge about them, I will not confirm that I represent them."

"Why didn't you just *say* you were here to keep an eye on me? Hell, the Dawn guy introduced himself."

"That's not how we do things."

"No. You just order people to do things and they do them."

"Right! I'm glad you understand. It is quite difficult to determine if subterfuge is effective when one can directly influence the replies to questions. I am operating at an informational handicap."

"That makes two of us. Why are you keeping an eye on me?"

"For the same reason Dina and Gabriel were. Er…" They flipped through the pages of the notebook. "They used some sort of metaphor."

"Referees or something. Trying to make sure 'the game' was being played properly."

"Right! That. I am here for that."

"Why aren't they the ones doing it?"

"Stigma has been located, and he warrants the more skilled observation."

Blot's eyes widened. "Stigma! They found Stigma!"

Her voice was thick with emotion, but it was difficult to nail down precisely what emotion she was feeling. Anxiety drenched the words, but there was the tiniest hint of what might be excitement, and even a flash of concern.

"Considering how timely you all are at arriving, one would think you could manage to keep an eye on two people."

"They can keep an eye on hundreds of people. You're low on the list. He is a threat, you are a curiosity. That's why I'm the one watching you. I deal with curiosities."

"Why?"

"I am in research, development, and record keeping. This is my first time out of the archives."

"What archives?"

"The ones which most assuredly do not exist." They flipped through the notebook. "To that end, I *am* permitted, at my discretion, to offer you valuable information or services in exchange for your cooperation."

"Don't tell them anything," Blot said.

"What sort of information, and what sort of cooperation?"

"For cooperation, I'd ask you to knock on my door periodically and keep me apprised of any significant developments."

"I'm surrounded by supernatural organizations, and somehow I'm the one everyone is coming to for information."

"You straddle two worlds in a manner with very little precedent. That *could* provide you with insight unavailable to others. An enviable position to be in."

"Lucky me."

"For information, I could provide you with... oh... the specifics of the cure for your condition."

"The cure..." Alan said steadily.

"They are offering to kill me, Alan. Get rid of them," Blot urged.

"Yes, yes. Though it is vanishingly rare that someone actually performs the necessary tasks, it *is* possible to cure your condition."

"I'm not a condition!" Blot growled.

"What would happen to Blot?" Alan asked.

"That is an *excellent* question. The sort of question that would require cooperation to have answered."

"Fine. I'm in the process of trying to get into the prison because there's something going on in there with Dun and Driss."

"Yes, that much we were aware of."

"Then what do you want from me?"

"We would very much like to know *what* is going on in there. Again, it is all a matter of threat and curiosity. Right now, we are curious. If we are threatened, then you'll likely see Dina and Gabriel again. For instance, you mention Driss. Thanks to your own exploits, we learned a bit of Dun, but Driss is an entirely new name to us. Tell me about Driss."

"She's some sort of an instructor or... um... administrator. What was it again, Blot?"

Blot glared at him. "You're going along with this? You're giving away the secrets of *my* people in exchange for a way to be rid of me?"

"I'm just trying to find out more about the cure—"

"I don't need to be cured!"

"The... separation procedure. For all we know, it'll benefit both of us."

"For all we know, it'll kill both of us. You don't say another word unless they can offer something *besides* treating the terrible infection named Blot."

Alan looked to Angel, who was pleasantly waiting for what was, from their point of view, a one-sided debate to end.

"You said you could offer services?" Alan said.

"If you prefer."

"Like what?"

They looked about the room, then leaned out into the hallway. "Based upon the difficulty you've had with... er... access control, a bit of warding might be worthwhile."

"Warding?"

"Safeguards against the supernatural. I could offer you, in exchange for more information about this Driss character..." They flipped through the pad. "A distraction ward for your apartment."

"What's that?"

"Once applied it will... oh, how to render it into layman's terms? Your apartment will be a very good hiding spot for Blot and yourself."

"Can you clarify a bit?"

Angel flipped through the pad again. "Nope!" they said brightly.

"A distraction ward might be worth something..." Blot said grudgingly.

"You know what it is?" Alan said.

"I'll explain later. If Angel can guarantee a high-quality distraction ward, you can tell them about Driss."

"A good ward for information about Driss."

"Only the finest wards! I've quite literally written the book on them," Angel said.

Alan looked to Blot.

"Fine. Repeat after me..."

Through Alan, Blot recounted a bit of Driss's history and a bit of her punishment techniques. Angel ate it up, gleefully scratching the information into their pad with a silver pen.

"Burning light as a means of discipline... interesting. Very interesting. Yes, this is valuable indeed. And you are right to want to reenter the prison to learn more. Take it from me. While the warriors and wizards get all the attention, the overseers, facilitators, and supervisors are critical operatives no less deserving of observation. This is good information. Very, very good information. I'll get that ward prepared for you as soon as possible."

"Wait…" A thought dawned on Alan. "This protective ward. Could you install it on my parents' house?"

"If you like."

"Come on, Alan. If you don't protect *us*, there's not going to be anyone to protect *them*."

"In fact, as the information has been of great value, I'd be happy to present you with a bit of information about the cure as well," Angel said.

"Never mind the cure!" Blot snapped.

"I don't need to—" Alan began.

"The first step is resecuring your original shadow. Simple and obvious, but again, often overlooked." Angel stowed their notebook. "I thank you greatly for your cooperation. It is rather important to me that I do a good job on this assignment. It *is* my first, after all, and in my line of work, one seldom recovers from a poor first impression. Good luck to you on your endeavors. I shall see myself out."

Alan followed Angel as they marched toward the door. "That's it?"

"That is plenty for now. You won't tell anyone about me or any of this."

"I won't," he replied automatically.

They opened his door and crossed the hallway to a door that, for the first time, Alan was able to perceive as both the entrance to an apartment that had always been there, and the entrance to a utility closet that *also* had always been there. The cognitive dissonance gave him a short, intense headache. His brain, possibly with some help from Angel, decided to ignore the closet version of reality and select the apartment version for now.

"Two more questions," he said as Angel lingered in front of the door.

"Of course."

"If you can just *compel* me to do things, why bargain with me?"

"Understanding of course that I do not admit to being able to compel people to do things even if I may have indicated otherwise through word or action, the fact of the matter is I cannot command you to tell me something I don't know that you know. And there *may* be some small side effects to commanding someone to offer information they lack or perform a task of which they are incapable. Not to mention, bargaining is a far more decent and respectable way to conduct business. And your second question?"

"What happened to Ms. Levitt?"

"The same thing to everyone else within earshot. She fell asleep. She's probably woken up by now, with very little memory of what occurred." Angel snapped their fingers. "And that reminds me. I simply must make a note to select such commands more carefully in the future."

Angel turned the knob and opened the door. Alan caught only a glimpse of what lay beyond, but it was enough to cause another sharp stinging pain in his head. There was a deep hallway. There were rows and rows of bookshelves. There were things far too spacious to fit within an apartment, or even the apartment building. When the door clicked shut, the pain eased away. He glanced up at the door. Like the last residue of a dream slowly slipping away, his memory of what he'd seen inside, and of the apartment number on the door, slipped and faded. Finally, he was staring at the utility closet that, of course, had always been there.

Alan slipped back into his apartment and shut the door. He rubbed the bridge of his nose. "I need coffee," he muttered.

"That much we can agree upon," Blot said.

He trudged to the kitchen and cracked open a fresh canister.

"You still need more of the Jamaican stuff," Blot reminded him.

"If you're going to be drinking it by the pot, we're switching back to the cheap stuff."

He loaded up the filter and refilled the water. As his coffee pot started heating up the much-needed stimulant, he paced about the kitchen. Blot hung on the wall beside him, watching.

"You do realize that having Angel breathing down our necks is another great reason to get out of this apartment, right?"

Alan didn't answer.

"If you're thinking about something they said, don't. The only thing they can offer us is the warding, and even *that's* going to be a stopgap."

He considered his words before speaking. "We've discussed this before. But I think we need to discuss it again. What do you know about this cure?"

"I don't know *anything* about the cure. And stop calling it a cure."

"Fine. What do you know about finding my old shadow? You tore it off. You must know what happened to it."

"Do you know what happened to the wrapper of yesterday's breakfast burrito?"

"You're talking about something that I apparently need to survive. I'll thank you not to talk about it like it's disposable. Don't think I haven't forgotten that technically this little relationship started with you attacking me in a way I didn't even know was possible."

"I can't tell you what I don't know, Alan. And I don't know what happened to your shadow. It needs an anchor, just like I do. I tore it off and it just... *went*. Like a balloon when you let go of the string."

"And you have no idea how to find it? How to get it back?"

"I only know what I was taught, and why would they teach me that? I came here expecting only enemies. As far as I knew, you may as well have been an enemy trooper. You don't learn how to treat the wounds of enemy troops."

"Yes we do. There are rules of engagement. Enemy troops get the same treatment as friendly troops."

Blot ran her fingers through her flowing hair. "I'm not so sure I believe that, but even if it's true, that's a really dumb way to run a war."

"It isn't a war if the enemy doesn't know it's fighting. It's just... I don't know... *terrorism*."

"You're really hung up on the meanings of words."

"So you expect me to believe that you don't know *anything* about this stuff? Not about the c—the treatment. Not about the white-suits. If you really came here looking to wage war, you sure as heck should have known about the white-suits. They seem like they're one of the more powerful things on the battlefield."

"I was *cannon fodder*, Alan. How many times do I have to say it? They didn't train me expecting me to survive! Most of us are just *numbers*. Just bodies to throw at the enemy. Dun always said that things might have changed here in ways that would make their lessons worthless, so no sense filling our heads with things we'd need to unlearn."

She turned her back to him. "They told us about the Dawn. They taught us how to fight, a bit, and how to learn. They taught us how to pull the strings of our host. That's it."

"Nothing about the white-suits."

"If we knew there were things like the white-suits here, I know a *lot* of us wouldn't have *come*!" she said, waving her arms in frustration.

Alan turned and focused on the coffee pot. "And if I knew about a way to stop being your host, we might never have teamed up. I might never have listened to a word you said and just found a way to be rid of you."

"Probably. It's an awfully good reason not to teach us."

He turned to her. "Maybe. Or maybe it's an awfully good thing to *pretend* they didn't teach you."

"Think! The entire point of me being here is either to make my host powerful, in which case I wouldn't want to be 'cured,' or to find a more powerful host, in which case we'd just move on. A cure is *useless* to us. But *isn't* useless to *them*. To them, the mere *suggestion* of a cure is enough to get us to fight. They're playing you, Alan. Take it from someone trained to do it."

"So you think the white-suits have something to gain by stirring us up."

"I think *they* have something to gain from it."

"Who are *they*?"

"Everyone but us! The Dawn, the white-suits, the shades. The rest of humanity. We're different now. And things that are different don't get to survive. I don't even like how much you're working with that Jessie woman."

"She's one of my oldest friends. We can trust her."

"*You* can trust her. But there isn't a you anymore. There's only us. And *we* can't trust her."

Alan took a breath. His chest felt tight. The argument could have continued. He had a thousand different concerns and angry jabs floating in his head. But for the first time in too long, he thought about what Blot was grappling with. Yes, she was the reason this was happening to him, but everything bad for him was worse for her. She was a stranger in this world. She was at his mercy when it came to where they would go and what they would do.

The coffee finished percolating. He poured himself a cup, and one for Blot.

"So what do we do?"

"Like you care," she said, snatching the cup with a calculated speed to avoid spilling a drop.

"We already know what I want to do, and how I want to do it. What do you want to do?"

"Run and hide."

"Running is running. But how do we hide? You're strong enough to be detected by the Dawn. The same goes for the rest of 'them,' doesn't it?"

"Absolutely. We need magic to hide from magic."

"And you don't know the proper magic."

"No. I don't think so. It'll take time for me to figure it out, *if* I can figure it out. I doubt we have enough time for that."

"That just leaves the white-suits."

"You're really rooting for a collaboration with the people who can directly tug your strings."

"Rooting or not, as far as we know, they're our only option."

"I suppose," she said, grudgingly.

"Do you know what sort of wards we'd need to hide?"

"I'll need to think about it. And I'll need to know what they have. But I know what I'd *like*."

"So if they come through with this warding, then maybe we can get enough to hide like you want to."

"That's a big maybe."

"It's the only maybe we've got, right?"

She sipped her coffee and nodded.

"So we need to play ball with them until we get what we need. And right now they want us to find out what's going on in the prison."

"Yeah. They've got us backed into a corner," she said through clenched teeth. "We could just fake a trip. Go in there, twiddle our thumbs, and come out with a likely story without actually checking. That might keep us from getting Dun any more motivated to kill us."

"I have a feeling the white-suits would know."

"We never know until we try."

"But we'd still have to at least get in, right?"

"Yeah."

"So we may not agree on why we need to do it, but we agree on what we need to do."

Blot nodded.

"Then I've got phone calls to make."

CHAPTER 5

T he afternoon turned to the evening as Alan and Blot worked their way through the rest of their contacts. To speed things up, Blot had been hunting and pecking her way through some emails he needed to send while he was on calls. It wasn't much—she wasn't a very fast typist—but it was something. Unfortunately, Alan still had to double-check her messages. Blot's take on negotiation didn't quite align with his own.

"'We would be willing to pay in the neighborhood of seventy thousand dollars, upon completion, for the permission to conduct this photo-essay,'" he read. "Are you crazy?"

"Too low?" she said.

"We don't have that kind of money!"

"Cox is paying for it."

"Cox is not going to pay seventy thousand dollars for a photo-essay about prison conditions."

"It *says* payment upon completion," she said.

"He won't pay it then either."

"He won't need to pay it then. We'll already have what we wanted. And besides, you could just give them a couple hundred dollars. Who's to say how big 'the neighborhood of seventy thousand' is?"

"I'm taking that line out," he said.

"Fine, but if we don't get somewhere soon, you're going to have to let me start getting creative."

He blinked some weariness from his eyes and finished revising her email, then sent it.

"What's left to be done?" he said. "I think we're scraping the bottom of the barrel here. Let's take a break."

"Suits me!" Blot said. "It's kind of tiring, having to have physical fingers for so long."

She flicked away from the computer and cast herself on the bed. A quick flick of each hand conjured a pencil and pad to start doodling again. Alan picked up his phone and thumbed through some notifications.

"Crap," he muttered.

"What is it?"

"I missed a call from Jessie like an hour ago. Stupid reception in this place."

Blot made a rude sound of dismissal as Alan tapped Jessie's contact and switched it to speaker so he could keep his hands free. She answered after barely a ring.

"Alan! Boy, do you have lousy timing," she said.

"Sorry. My phone misses calls sometimes when I—"

"Not that. I mean about this essay project of yours. I've got an answer for why you've been getting blown off."

"Oh?"

He heard her flick a piece of paper on her end of the phone. "And I quote. 'A memo to all law enforcement officials. Beginning on January eighth and continuing for the next three weeks, we will be instituting heightened security measures in and around Curran-Fromhold Correctional Facility in preparation for the visit by Senator Savage, Congressman Yaffe, and District Attorney Feldman. Access by nonessential personnel will be limited and subject to extreme vetting to ensure the safety of all involved."

Alan's weariness was such that he had to glance at his phone's display to confirm that it was indeed January eleventh, and well within the window. "The senator is visiting?" he said. "Why haven't I heard about it?"

"Because when a big shot is going to go somewhere dangerous like a prison, they keep it on the down-low until us law enforcement types have a chance to cross the *T*s and dot the *I*s. By the way, don't go spreading this around. The official press release goes out in a few hours. So, anyway. That's why you've been having so much trouble making any headway."

"Do we know anything about *why* this visit is happening?"

"Something to do with the experimental program they've been doing in one of the cellblocks."

"Cellblock 33?"

"You heard about it already?"

"It came up when I was recording an interview a couple of days ago."

"This is starting to make sense," Blot said.

He nodded at her. Considering Dun's prior scheme, something told Alan it was hardly a coincidence that he would soon be in close proximity with the senator again.

"It's good news, in a way. You're definitely going to be able to get in there to do your photos. They're probably going to do a big fat media blitz to brag about their new techniques. You'll just have to wait until after the bigwigs take their tour of the place."

"No, no. That's not going to work. I've got to get in there before."

"Why?"

"Because it would defeat the whole purpose if the senator or someone like that visited before..." He shook his head. "Never mind. You said the press release was due out in a few hours?"

"Uh, yeah. It looks like it's marked for release at six p.m. Why they wouldn't just wait until tomorrow morning is anyone's guess."

He drummed his fingers on the table. "Six p.m.... Listen, Jessie, thanks a bunch. This really helps out. I owe you one."

"We'll do lunch again soon. You can pay."

"Say no," Blot said.

"Sounds good. Sorry to rush you off the phone, but I've got to go. I think I know how I'm going to do this."

"Cool! Keep me in the loop. I'm excited for you. Oh! And keep your schedule free for January fifteenth. That's when you'll be doing your assessment for Lieutenant Stockton."

"Right. Will do. So long."

He hung up and immediately rolled through his contacts for Cox's number. It was three p.m. If he knew his boss, he'd still be in the office.

"So that's that, then. No getting in. Your friend said so," Blot said.

"No. That's just it. A visit like this is all about publicity. The senator's trying to get himself associated with this thing that looks like it's working, and the prison is looking to brag about what they've been doing. And what's a photo-essay if not publicity?"

"But they already said no."

"They said no to *me*. I'm just a photographer."

The phone rang a few times before a perpetually irritable voice answered. "Cox here."

"Mr. Cox. Alan Fontaine."

"You have any exclusives for me, Fontaine? Because if not, I've got better business to close out my day with."

"I just might. How long are you going to be in the office?"

"Until five p.m."

"I'll be there before four p.m."

"That's not how appointments work. I'm a busy man."

"Trust me, you're not going to want to be caught sleeping on this one."

The phone whistled with a frustrated sigh from Cox. "Fine. Get in here. But this better not be a waste of my time."

"It won't be."

Alan hung up and grabbed his coat. "Come on. If this is going to work, I think we might need some of those manipulation skills of yours," he said.

Blot vanished her pad and pencil and rubbed her hands together. "I thought you'd never ask."

Alan arrived at Cox Media as quickly as the traffic laws would allow. He seldom found himself at the office more than once a day. Even when he had footage or photos to turn in, he usually ended up doing it the following morning. He didn't actually know what Cox *did* past the morning assignments. The main floor was largely empty, though here and there the clack of a keyboard or a snippet of audio being edited suggested work was being done in some of the side offices. Most of the interior lights were off, leaving the hallways away from the windows increasingly shrouded in darkness. The fact was not lost on Blot.

"I like this place better like this. Why can't more places do this?"

"I think it'd probably be some sort of an OSHA violation," Alan said.

"I don't know who OSHA is, but she should calm down. A little darkness is good for the soul."

"Fontaine!" Cox called from his office. "Is that you?"

"Yes, Mr. Cox."

"Get in here and let's get this over with."

He slipped into the office. Either Cox was with Blot on the subject of the proper levels of illumination, or he'd not bothered to fix his lamp since Blot had last adjusted it, because the office was quite dim. Alan took a seat, and Blot slid along the ground to rise up on the wall behind Cox.

Cox finished typing up his current message, then glanced up to Alan. "What have you got?"

"It's about the photo-essay."

"Is that all? If you're just here to get a check to cover expenses, it could have waited until tomorrow."

"I'm not here for the money. There's something else I need help with."

"I thought I made it clear this was your baby."

Cox was clearly more irritable than usual. It could have been the un-scheduled visit, but Alan suspected there was something else to it. He glanced to Blot, who happily gazed at the screen of Cox's computer.

"It's money stuff, I think" Blot said. "Lots of red lines and a couple of green ones. Words like 'market share' and 'revenue.'"

"Right. I took full responsibility. But I've come upon some information that might motivate you to take a more direct role. In a few hours a joint press release between the senator's office and the very correctional facility we're looking into is going to announce a big tour of the prison. A tour of the very same *cellblock*, in fact, that I'm hoping to chronicle."

"Really…" He leaned forward, genuine interest dawning on his face. "And you're already signed up to do shoots?"

"Not just yet."

The approval dropped from his face as quickly as it had appeared. "Then why are you wasting my time?"

"Because I've got all the requests for permits in."

"Big deal. This one's going to go to whomever they handpick. A big tour like this probably has a PR firm attached and they'll have their own crew."

"It's only going to go to whomever they handpick once there's an official *reason* to handpick someone. But until then, it's still going to be a first-come–first-serve. And like I said, this press release isn't out yet. Now I'm sure the prison has all the important stuff hammered out already, but the people snapping pictures is going to come from the other end, and if they haven't announced it yet, maybe we've still got a chance."

"'Maybe' doesn't pay the bills, Fontaine. If you haven't been accepted yet—"

"I haven't been accepted yet because I'm a solo photographer. I'm not a media mogul like you."

Cox's waning attention turned back to his screen.

"Does D-Legacy LLC mean anything?" Blot asked.

Alan gave Blot a meaningful glance.

"He's got an article open here talking about how they're 'gaining market share at the expense of other struggling media firms,'" she said.

"I really think there's something to be gained on this one if we act fast," Alan said. "This could be an award winner."

Cox shook his head and grumbled. He clicked through to another article.

"More D-Legacy stuff," Blot said. "Tell him we're going to be directly competing with them to get this job."

"Think about it," Alan said, unwilling to give up on the current line of argument. "Another award hanging on your wall."

"I don't need awards. I need big-ticket celebrity pictures. Scandal stuff. I need something that everyone wants. If you're not making headway with this essay thing, I'm thinking of sending you up to NYC. There's a nightclub that's had *six* fist fights in the past eight months. B- and C-list celebrities, but I'd have a guaranteed buyer..." Cox continued down an unproductive line of conversation.

"Do it. Tell him D-Legacy is after the prison job," Blot said.

Alan gritted his teeth. "Yeah. It's probably for the best. It seems like D-Legacy's been sniffing around this job anyway."

Cox's eyes shot up. "D-Legacy. D-Legacy thinks they can get this gig? They think they can steal it right from under my nose? Oh, no. Oh, no no. We'll just see about that."

He picked up the phone and leaned back in his chair, eyes toward the ceiling. "This is Curran-Fromhold, right? ... That'll be Fitzy." Cox dialed a number from memory. "Fitz! You son of a gun, it's been years. ... Oh, better than you, better than you. Certainly better than you were during pledge week. ... So that was someone else puking green beer at the St. Paddy's fundraiser. ... Ha, *ha*! It may have been."

The conversation that followed was the sort of loud, crude, telling-tales-out-of-school conversation that had been one of Alan's pet peeves back in college. Blot, a self-satisfied grin on her face, drifted along the wall and subtly snaked her hands through the cracks in assorted cabinets and drawers.

Alan tried to convey with his gaze alone that she should stop whatever she was doing.

"Oh, relax," she scolded. "I'm not going to take anything he'll miss. I just want a couple of extra pads. Consider it a reward for getting this job done."

"Look, I called for a reason," Cox continued. "I've got a guy, Alan Fontaine. He's been working on getting inside for some high-brow photojournalistic crap. ... No, no, nothing hard-hitting. Basically a fluff piece. Trust me, the prison's going to come across smelling like a rose. He's had the requests in for permits for a couple of days. Probably they never made it to your desk. ... Right, right. Grunt work. What do you say you just pencil-whip the request through. ... Of course your guys will get to approve the shots. ... Yeah. Let's call it two sessions. One for initial shoots, then a couple of days later another for reshoots and replacements for anything you nix on your pass. ... Uh-huh. Whatever days work for you. I'll keep him free. ... Great. I'll get the ID and press credentials on file. ... Yeah. Oh! And before I forget, make sure you've got us down for two people. ... Yeah, I'm sending Marie-Anna down."

He gave a conspiratorial laugh. "You know it. So are we good? ... Great! See you next week, I'll buy you a scotch. So long." Cox hung up the phone. The jocular attitude dropped like a curtain.

"Let's see D-Legacy close a deal that quick." He punched the desk. "Damn, I'm good. But listen up. You better guarantee me gold on this. That man drinks like a fish, and he'll only accept green label or better."

"I assure you, this is going to be something."

"Good. You'll be getting an email with the authorized dates. Until then, I'm removing you from any assignments you've already got, and you're off the morning scrum so you can prepare. Marie-Anna gets all your jobs."

"Big surprise," Blot said.

"Now get out," Cox said. "I've still got some work to do."

"Thank you, sir."

Alan stood and hurried out the door. Blot slid up beside him on the hallway wall as he walked.

"I told you," she said.

"Fair enough," he whispered. "But don't get used to that sort of thing. Secretly spying over my boss's shoulder and tricking him into doing things with pointless rivalries he's formed isn't how I like to do business."

"But it *works*," Blot said. "And don't act like you're completely innocent."

"What have I done wrong that you didn't goad me into doing?"

"I believe Jessie's exact words were 'don't go spreading this around.' *You* just leaked the press release."

He stopped in his tracks. "... I did."

"Can't take it back. Cat's out of the bag," Blot said.

Alan squinted and slouched.

"Oh, don't give me that face. You violated your friend's trust by leaking some information just a *few* hours early, and it got you exactly what you wanted, and she's never going to find out."

"You're a bad influence," he said.

"Considering we just achieved what we were after, I'd say I'm a *superb* influence."

Chapter 6

O n the morning of his first session in the prison, Alan found himself
waiting impatiently in his car for the partner he hadn't asked for.
The morning sun would have been enough to keep Blot pinned, but as
before he'd managed to find a corner of the prison parking lot that was
shaded by the forbidding building.

"Let's go over it again," he said. "What's the plan?"

"We both keep our eyes and ears open," Blot said.

"Right. If I spot any eyes first, I'll start talking about my lens cap."

"You're not going to spot eyes before I do. Remember, I can feel the
presence of my kind."

"Even so, we've got to be prepared." He checked his camera for the fifth
time. "Flash batteries are charged. I've got my trusty Maglite in my pocket.
You've got the spare. If things go down, I snap a picture and we head for
the nearest door. We can't afford to do any fighting in there."

"We can try that, but if push comes to shove, I'm doing what it takes to
come out of this alive. How much do you think the white-suits are going
to need in order to earn some decent wards?"

"I don't know about them, but I plan to come out of this with an answer
to *exactly* what Dun's plan is."

Blot gave him a look. "You do realize it's the tour he's after, right? He wouldn't still be in the prison if he didn't want to be, and now that we know there's a tour, it can only be to try to take one of the political heavyweights as a host."

"But we're not *sure* about that."

"I'm completely sure of it."

"Fine, *I'm* not sure of it. There's too many unanswered questions. How did he get the tour booked? How does he plan to discreetly take the senator as a host. Is there more to it?"

"Uh-huh." She leaned down and slurped at her coffee. "Plus you need your pictures."

Alan took an uneasy breath. "There is that. Regardless of how this little mission turns out, I've still got to satisfy Cox."

"And that's the *only* reason," she said with a raised eyebrow. "There's *no* part of you that's legitimately excited to be doing a photo shoot that you pitched?"

He drummed his fingers on the steering wheel. "It is not lost on me that this is the first time in my life I can even *pretend* I'm a legitimate photographer, doing a shoot of my choosing. Not a paparazzi, not a hopeful hobbyist, and not a desperate pseudodetective looking for evidence. This is the kind of job I thought I'd be doing daily back when I was taking classes on composition and framing. And it's technically a facade for—"

"Another desperate bit of pseudodetective work?"

"Yeah. I don't know. It's still sort of exciting. I can almost convince myself I'm a real grown-up photojournalist."

Blot grinned. "And I'm infiltrating a human stronghold through skillful manipulation. Just like a real grown-up shade."

"We really are starting to be a pretty good team."

"Just imagine how good a team we'll be if we survive another few..." Blot slowly turned. "Oh no..."

Alan turned too. A familiar man was approaching. He was bandaged, somewhat bruised, and thoroughly unwashed.

"Broad daylight. He's getting bolder," Alan said. He opened the door and stepped out, his hand hovering over his flashlight like a cowboy ready for a quick draw.

"Hi, Alan," Todd said with his characteristic slurred chipperness. "Hi, Blot. You ready for another one of these?"

His twisted shadow flitted and shifted with snakelike motions, seemingly ready to strike. "You shouldn't *be* here, Alan," croaked the chilling voice. "You know the rules."

"If you're going to hit me again, do me a favor and don't work the ribs this time," Todd said. "He healed up my hand pretty good, but the ribs are still sore. And easy on the face. A man's got to look his best."

"There are security cameras, there are prison guards, and the sun is in the sky. You can't intimidate me here," Alan said.

"That's what I told him, but you know how he is," Todd pulled a flask from the pocket of his torn coat. "He's been *real* cranky lately. I think it bugged him that you and your shadow got a couple more hits off on him than we got on you."

Rive slid to Todd's feet and glared up at him. "Do not discuss my business, and do *not* speculate on my intentions."

"Yeah, yeah." Todd took a swig. "You just keep the booze flowing and whatever you say goes."

Rive turned to Alan and jabbed a curled finger at him. "I imagine you have great plans for this little endeavor."

The shadowy hand curled up along the front of Alan's body and flicked at the camera. Alan stepped back, and Blot slapped the claw away.

"You'll take this camera of yours. You'll snap pictures. You'll look for clues." Rive's grin curled more. "And that takes *time*, Alan. How long? An hour? Two? I can be to your parents' house in fifteen minutes."

"Oof. I hope you don't expect me to drive." Todd suppressed a burp. "I am in no shape for that."

"Your parents—" Rive continued.

"And plus there's the traffic," Todd blurted. "Everyone's trying to get to work. The buses will all be running the wrong way. Fifteen minutes, more like forty. And then there's the—"

Rive's fingers curled around the flask and shoved it into his mouth. "*Drink* if it will silence you," the shadow screeched. "Alan, you are taking the lives of your parents into your hands when you walk into that door. Tread lightly. Dun need only say a single word, and your parents will be cold before you can lift a finger to save them."

"Hey!" called a voice from behind them.

They all looked to see the bundled-up figure of Marie-Anna fighting with her camera bag as she strutted over to them.

"Buzz off, rummy," she said. "We've got work to do."

Todd glanced at his shadow, who motioned with his head that the work was done here.

"Well all right," Todd said. "You two have a good one. I'll say hi to your parents for you, if I see them." The fragrant puppet of a man staggered away.

"You can't talk to them, Alan. It only encourages them," Marie-Anna said as she fished out a cigarette. "So what's the gig? Cox just sent me down here without much in the way of instructions. He said he wanted to make sure my name was on this project."

"The gig. Right, the gig," Alan said, shakily coming down from the adrenaline of his encounter and the reality of the threats.

"They'll be safe for now," Blot assured Alan. "He won't do anything until Dun says so. Keep your mind on the task so we can get those wards and have a chance at doing something to keep us all safe long-term."

"Hey, snap out of it," Marie-Anna said. "You're the lead on this one. Give me the rundown."

Alan dug out his phone and thumbed to the proper list. "We're going to be escorted through the prison by someone named Reggie Filson. He works under Dr. Vale, the mastermind behind the Cellblock 33 project. The official reason for the visit is a photo-essay chronicling prison conditions. I hadn't structured this to include a videographer. Cox sort of thrust that upon me."

"He does that," she said simply. "So we'll do it doc-style. Audio rolling constantly. Mostly B-roll shots. Easy enough." She took a drag on the cigarette. "So what got you interested in the prison thing, anyway? Obviously, you didn't know about the bigwigs coming down to take a look before you got started. Remmy was talking about how you were gung ho about this for days before that announcement. And I *don't* think you've got an insider in the senator's offices."

Alan stumbled a bit.

"In all our planning, we never bothered to come up with a decent lie about your motivation." Blot shook her head. "That one's on me. I should have been on top of that. Just tell her it's a passion project."

"It's a passion project," he said.

She laughed. "I'm surprised anyone can hold on to their passion for this biz after working in it for a few years."

"You're not passionate about photojournalism anymore?" he said.

Marie-Anna blew out a breath of smoke. "I don't know if I ever was. But there's only so many 'clothing malfunctions' and 'makeup mishaps' you can see plastered across social media before you start to feel like the whole reason you're getting paid is to turn other people's bad days into the junk food of the internet."

"So why do you keep doing it?"

"It's the family business," she said. "If you can get a leg up on the rest of an industry, you take it."

"I didn't realize you came from a family that does this sort of thing."

She gave him a hard look. "Are you really that oblivious?"

He raised his eyebrows. "Evidently."

"Marie-Anna Proctor. My dad is Gene Proctor."

"The guy in charge of D-Legacy?"

"That's him."

"So why aren't you working for him?"

"I was, for a while. But people just treated me like the boss's daughter. It was infuriating. So I jumped ship."

"And now you're dating the boss of Cox Media."

"Makes sense to me," Blot said.

"I'm being discreet," she said. "The last thing I need is people thinking I'm dating a rival just to 'get even with Daddy.' Or to get preferential treatment."

"... But you *do* get preferential treatment. And while it's been established I'm oblivious, I had no trouble figuring out you two were an item."

She took a final drag on the cigarette and tossed it down. "I don't need to justify myself to you." She ground out the cigarette. "We just about ready?"

"Yeah."

Alan turned to the street beyond the parking lot, where Todd was standing in the sun and industriously draining his flask. His shadow grinned and cackled from the street below.

"Let's be fast but thorough. Whatever sort of photos I get in there, I'm going to want to act on them fast."

After a half hour inside, things weren't off to the most promising of starts. They were technically getting a "full" tour of the prison, but it was about as deep as a school field trip. Fascinating as it was to see the recreational facilities and hear about their educational programs, it wasn't getting him any closer to unraveling the mystery. Worse, while he'd gotten all his camera equipment through, they'd confiscated his Maglite, so he was less equipped than he would have liked for a shadowy showdown. They also had his phone. It was making him feel a bit naked.

The overall tension and defenseless feeling ratcheted up his anxiety to the point of distraction. Three times he had barely kept himself from recoiling from an imagined motion at the corner of his eye. Living in a world where the shadows might have a grudge against him made tricks of the light feel an awful lot trickier.

"Here, we have the cafeteria. It is not presently in use, as you can see, but we take the nutritional needs of our inmates very seriously..." Reggie said.

He wasn't reading from a script, but the bland and mechanical delivery suggested it wasn't the first time he'd had to deliver the speech. Alan was beginning to fear that all the work he'd put into this had been for nothing.

"I can't see anything, but I can feel something," Blot said, eyes narrow as she looked up from the floor. "It's... indistinct. It's not a vision sort of sense, but if it were, I'd call it blurry. Not natural. There's work being done to hide shades here."

"Could it be Dun's doing?" Alan whispered as quietly as he could.

"Maybe. I don't pretend to know the depths of Dun's training. Driss could be doing it too. But right now I can't tell how many there are. I know there's two, and I can't even feel that. I can tell you where it's coming from though."

He glanced down at her. She pointed to the northwest corner of the cafeteria.

"...even wholesome desserts. Next, I'd like to show you the prison workshop, where valuable trades can be learned and honed," Reggie droned and started heading for the opposite corner of the cafeteria.

"I'm sorry," Alan said. "But is any of this part of the Cellblock 33 program?"

Reggie cleared his throat. "It is all part of our holistic approach to inmate rehabilitation."

"Your spiel is pretty polished," Marie-Anna said. "Any chance you're just using us as a dress rehearsal for the senator's visit?"

The guide wrung his fingers a bit. "Does it show?"

"Oh, sure. Solid presentation," she said.

"Good, good."

"And it's very interesting, but battery and storage are both limited. My associate is shooting four-K video. I'd like to make sure she can get footage of the cellblock itself before we have to switch to lower resolution."

Marie-Anna gave him a look. She knew as well as he did that she'd have plenty of space for *hours* of additional footage. But she let it slide. And it paid off. After a quick glance at the itinerary, the guide nodded.

"I'd intended to *conclude* the tour with the cellblock. But I think we can shift the schedule somewhat. This way."

They turned in the direction Blot had indicated. From the very moment they passed through the door of the cafeteria, it was clear they were headed through some of the less visitor-friendly parts of the prison. The first serious security check awaited them at the end of the hallway. A second one followed just a few doors away. Each time, the credentials of Marie-Anna and Alan were scrutinized and their equipment was double-checked.

Things became familiar as they continued on. They weren't far from where the interview with Dun had taken place. Finally, they reached the door for Cellblock 33.

"The first thing you'll notice upon entering Cellblock 33 is the reduced illumination. One of a handful of simple quality-of-life adjustments that our own Dr. Vale is experimenting with. Prisoners surveyed have given a ninety-seven percent approval to the change. They report feeling overall reductions in anxiety and irritability. For that reason, I'll ask you to keep your flash photography and video lighting to a minimum."

Marie-Anna fiddled with the settings of her video camera, hoping to tease some better low-light performance out of it. Blot slid up to the wall beside Alan.

"Look," she hissed.

She darted up along the wall and stretched across the ceiling. Her little fingers pointed eagerly at what at first blush appeared to be graffiti. Alan stopped and snapped a picture.

"I don't think we're here for the architecture," Marie-Anna whispered. "Stay focused, this is just starting to hit the right topic."

"I'm getting a shot of—" Alan began.

"It's shadow marking," Blot said hurriedly. "She can't see it."

"... a flat surface to check my exposure settings. Give me a second," Alan said, then to Filson, "You can keep giving the speech. I just need to do something." He stopped and turned, pretending to fight with his camera to adjust various settings. "What are shadow markings?" he said under his breath.

"When I talk about warding, that's the sort of thing I'm talking about. It's *years* beyond me in terms of strength and skill, but some of the highly trained mystics that we sent through can sort of... *smear* a bit of themselves to form written spells. It's like writing with your own blood. I can't read it, but I'd bet a double shot of espresso that this is why I can't get a clean feeling about the people on the other side of that doorway."

He snapped another picture. "Okay, I think we're ready," he said.

Despite his instruction, the guide waited until Alan was paying attention again to continue talking. They approached a steel mesh doorway leading into the heart of the cellblock. Guards stood on either side of the door.

"Another aspect of the project that we are presently studying is the cellblock itself. While we pride ourselves on modernization, this is one of the older sections of the prison. We are hoping to determine what if any aspects of this older prison layout may have been beneficial without our knowledge."

The guide nodded to both guards, and they unlocked the door and escorted them forward. Sure enough, cells beyond had much more in common with classic Hollywood's interpretation of prison. A large open space dominated the wing of the prison. Metal tables with integrated benches were spaced in a wide grid along the floor, bolted down. Two levels of cell doors lined three of the walls. The opposite wall had a row of barred windows, but heavy drapes had been pulled across them. Whereas the cells in the rest of the facility were mostly solid with reinforced glass windows, here there were good old-fashioned bars. A handful of orange-jumpsuited inmates looked at the newcomers from their seats in the common area.

Alan's fingers tightened around his camera. The relatively dim cellblock meant the sharp, high-contrast shadows that made it so simple to determine whether someone was host to a shade or not were absent. It didn't matter. In the darkness beneath tables and staring out from between the bars of every filled cell were pairs of white eyes. There were easily forty prisoners in the block.

They *all* had shades.

"Good morning, everyone!" Reggie announced, ignoring the fact that they already had the inmates' full attention. "As I believe you were alerted during this morning's announcements, today you are being visited by the first of a short list of very important people. Mr. Fontaine and Ms. Proctor are here to document the improvement to your conditions. I expect you all to be on your best behavior. Making a good impression with the media will help direct additional funding to the program and further improve your time here."

Every eye in the place was focused on Alan or Blot. His shadow slid behind him.

"This is bad, Alan. This is worse than I thought..." she said.

Alan took slow, steady steps forward. The voice of the guide was a half-heard buzzing in his ears. The shades watched him like a pride of lions judging their prey.

"Among the many other adjustments we have made to Cellblock 33 was a careful psychological screening, the intent being to match disposition in a complementary way to promote harmony. An eclectic mix of different types of inmates are present here. Violent crime, fraud. Offenses of all kinds are present here thanks to their compatible dispositions."

"Compatible dispositions..." Alan repeated, eyes focused on the nearest cluster of shades.

"Those bars mean nothing," Blot said. "Any shade powerful enough to survive this long in your world will be able to pull its host in the shadows and slip through. They're only here because they *want* to be here."

The shadows shifted as he approached. Alan may as well have been some sort of inverse lantern, drawing shadows toward him as he got closer. The shapes of the shadows became more twisted, more sinister as they reached for him. Blot shifted and slid to avoid casually swiping claws. They couldn't attack Alan openly. Not while a normal human or two were nearby. But they could harass Blot without being seen. As they reached for her, they spat insults and threats.

"Traitor."

"Light lover."

"Turncoat."

"You will curl like paper in a flame."

Blot huddled as small and close to Alan as she could. "This isn't a prison, Alan," she said. "It's a fortress. They can leave anytime they want, but no one else can get to them. By the darkness, it's perfect. They have their pick of the most vicious, most toxic people your world has to offer. And getting in is as simple as committing a crime. That's what the crime wave has been. They're consolidating their power. The senator isn't the plan. *This* is the plan. They've got a stronghold, now. The senator is just the *beginning*."

Alan snapped photos on autopilot, the reality of the situation sinking deeper into his mind. He'd known there were plenty of shades in the world. Blot implied their numbers were massive, dizzying. But until now he'd been able to convince himself that the dark creatures were as out-numbered and thinly stretched as the Dawn. A peppering of creatures without the capacity to coordinate in any meaningful way. Alan had encountered a group of shades only once before, and he'd barely escaped with his life. The office building had barely a fraction of the shades present here now. What could he do? This wouldn't be as simple as foiling Dun. He shuddered to think of what would become of this place if the shades decided to make their move. *When* they decided to make their move.

"I'm sorry, but I'm not going to get any usable footage if I don't turn on some light," Marie-Anna said.

She clicked on the large light panel affixed to the top of her camera. It wasn't as potent as the monstrous flash that had saved Alan's life on more than one occasion, but it was more than enough to shove the shades around. A chorus of angry, chilling voices rose up, followed swiftly by the shouts of the inmates who served as their hosts. Alan stepped behind Marie-Anna to keep the light from shoving Blot into the fray where she would surely be clawed to within an inch of her life.

She dialed the light down, but even at the lowest useful setting it was easily the brightest thing in the room.

"Please. Be respectful of our new policies," Reggie said.

"Just trying to reach a compromise," Marie-Anna said.

Alan could feel the eyes of the inmates, the shades, the guards, and the guide fixed upon them. Marie-Anna disregarded their agitation. The constant low-level entitlement that defined Marie-Anna's professional interactions had inured her to the sort of discomfort that Alan would have felt in her position, breaking a rule in a *prison*. From his point of view, it was practically a super power. Whether she knew it or not, Marie-Anna's light provided a small safe harbor for them both, nudging the shades away as they turned and pivoted about.

The air filled with the horrid voices of the shades as they screeched ever louder.

"Huddle behind your precious light," one of them jabbed.

"You are dead to your kind. A stain on us all," hissed another.

The voices blended into a general din of anger. Twisting arms swept out with lashing claws. They came near enough to stir the rippling rags dangling from Blot's form. They whisked past her hair, trying to grab her and drag her into the fray.

"We have to go. We have to go," Blot said, huddling smaller and smaller at Alan's feet.

"Marie-Anna," Alan said.

His voice startled her, as well as the guide and guards. He'd raised it to be heard over the screeching of the sea of shades, which, of course, the others couldn't hear.

"What?" she whispered.

"I want to get a good wide shot. In the corner, by the windows."

She nodded and paced over for the proper vantage. He hurried behind her, shuffling through the wake she created in the stretching silhouettes. When she reached the corner, she turned. The light in front and the wall behind kept the shades at bay. Blot slid into the corner and watched with terrified eyes as shades attempted to curl along the wall to get to her. The guards kept the inmates distant, and the shades couldn't quite contort themselves properly around the light to easily reach her.

"Keep it rolling," Alan suggested.

She nodded. "This'll be a good background for some lengthy narration."

Reggie continued his speech. Blot swatted at any claws that came too near.

"Get back!" she shouted. "That camera is rolling. You touch me, you drag me away, and it'll be on camera."

One of the shades slashed at her, barely catching her arm.

"Ouch! Did you hear me? It'll be all over the news. Unexplained death at the prison. People will come and investigate."

Alan took a side step behind Marie-Anna just quickly enough to keep Blot from receiving another slash.

"The Dawn will get in here if you do this. You'll draw attention to yourself, and the Dawn will come and wipe you out!" she raved, her voice bordering on panic.

"Enough," came a decree from above.

The shades instantly fell into line. They withdrew, and grew silent. This seemed to calm the inmates as well. Those who had been bold enough to step closer to give their shades a better angle returned to their tables. The guards relaxed. Something resembling order was restored.

Alan and Blot looked up. The voice came from the far corner of the upper level. As Marie-Anna followed one of the guards to do a sweeping shot of the floor, Alan returned to taking photos. He zoomed in on the upper level and snapped picture after picture. The closer he got to the source of the voice, the denser the roiling mass of shades on the upper level became. One cell was completely black with them. A horrifying, inky void with a galaxy of white eyes blinking from within. And in the center, practically adrift in the sea of darkness, was Lenny. All but one pair of eyes were turned in the same direction, honoring what could have only been Dun. Dun alone stared down at Alan.

"No sense threatening what we have here," Dun instructed them. "He knows what he has set in motion by showing his face here."

Dun narrowed his eyes. "Rive is one of my best warriors, Alan. But a shifter is only as good as his host. Rive would have made it quick. But the drunkard he rides? That man will be slow and sloppy in dealing with your family. They will suffer. What you have done here has already made the decision. It will happen. Now it remains for you to decide when. Make a scene? Cut it short? Do *anything* to disrupt this place? I'll see to it they're killed as soon as possible. Behave yourself and I'll let you see them alive one last time."

A horrid white grin split the shadow. "Enjoy the rest of the tour..."

Not long after that, the tour moved on. It was a testament to his experience as a photographer that he got any additional shots worth getting, because it was entirely mechanical. He and Blot were silent, their minds racing with the implications and consequences of the day's revelations. He didn't speak again until he and Marie-Anna were back in the parking lot.

"Not too bad," she said. "All things considered, I think this'll cut together into a nice fluff piece."

He nodded numbly and found his eyes wandering over to where Todd had been standing when he stepped inside.

She tipped her head to the side to try to meet his gaze. "What was your deal in there, by the way? You seemed a little out of it. Spooked."

"Mmm?" Alan said, as if just remembering that Marie-Anna was even there. "Oh. Sorry. Just... distracted."

"Yeah. I guess I'd have been distracted too. You ever been in a prison before?" she asked, lighting another cigarette.

"Just when I did the shoot for the interview the first time."

"I've been in a few. I had a cousin who couldn't keep his nose clean. We'd visit him. There's a certain vibe in a place like that." She shook her head. "Not like this one, though. Things felt different."

"Yeah," he said. "Different."

"Do you believe that spiel they gave? About people of all sorts of criminal backgrounds being put into Cellblock 33 as a part of this program?"

"What's not to believe?"

"I've seen those looks before. Predators. Those are birds of a feather, and they're all birds of prey." She shivered a bit and pulled her coat tighter. "I'd have expected them to all be giving me the eye. A bunch of guys locked up. But they didn't. Maybe it's because so many of them are new in here. Haven't been inside long enough to get pent up. But they were giving *you* the eye pretty hard."

He nodded again.

"I can't put my finger on it, but there was something off about all of it. I could see this little pilot program of theirs going south *real* fast."

They reached her car. She unlocked the trunk with her key fob and started loading her gear.

"I take it you don't really need me on this assignment," she said.

"You were a big help, but it was definitely Cox's idea."

"Right. Well, I'm having him take me off it. I'm content with the coverage I got on this pass. And I really don't want to take another spin through that cellblock. Those people are asking for trouble, and it doesn't take a psychologist to know it."

"Yeah. That place is bad news," Alan said, hoping the degree of his understatement wasn't immediately obvious.

"You going back in? I can't imagine you're going to get any shots the second time through that'll make it worth being dangled in front of those inmates like a steak."

"I don't know yet... I think I have to."

"No one *has* to do anything. You're not a secret service agent. No one's paying you to dive in front of a bullet. Cox'll get his money from this thing. Quit while you're ahead." She slammed the trunk and tugged open the driver's side door. "Or ignore me. It's your life. What do I care?"

She climbed in and started the car. Alan watched her go, then looked down at Blot. She was pinned to the ground by the midmorning sun.

"What are you looking at me for?" Blot asked. "You're the one who wanted to get in there. I was *just* as happy not knowing all that."

"We agreed we needed to get in there!" he said, heading for his own car. "We agreed we needed to know this stuff so we could report it to Angel and get their help."

He twitched and snapped his head aside as a dark form shuddered in the corner of his vision along with the sharp skitter of claws. When he turned, there was nothing but a french fry container jostling back and forth in the wind.

"You need to calm down. You're seeing things."

"So says one of the things I'm seeing," he muttered.

"This is what you get for subjecting yourself to that prison again. We *could* have just gone through the motions and lied to them," Blot said. "You are constantly underestimating the value of a good lie."

He found his way to his own car and loaded his stuff into the trunk. "They would have known."

"Probably, but we'll never know for sure because *you* didn't want to try it. You're always *so* adventurous when it comes to exposing ourselves to people who want to kill us, but you're never willing to experiment on simple, logical dishonesty."

"They show up whenever—" Alan's phone rang. He fumbled for it. "It's an unknown number."

"If this is Angel calling you, I'm going to scream."

He answered. "Hello?"

"Alan! Guess who," came a familiar, slurred voice.

"Todd…"

"Right! Rive says you're done in there. He says you saw what he didn't want you to see."

"How would he know already?"

"I dunno," Todd said. "Maybe they got… what's that stuff… radar love?"

Alan's creeping terror was briefly sidelined by confusion. "…Like the song?"

"She sends her… something something from above. Don't need no letter at all!" Todd crooned.

"Where are you right now, Todd?"

"I'm still on the bus. I told Rive you'd be done in there before we got to your folks' house."

The ghostly half-heard voice piped up. "Alan," it croaked. "You were warned."

"You listen to me. If you lay a hand on my parents, I promise you, this isn't over. I haven't done a thing to harm you and your kind, but if you give me a reason, so help me, I'll find a way to make you pay."

"You don't have it in you. I looked in your eyes. I saw fear."

"You saw fear because I had something to lose. You take that away from me and there is no limit to what I will do. I know the truth about you. This *will* end. It's up to you to decide if we can find a way to end it peacefully or if it ends in slaughter."

"It will end in slaughter, Alan. It always ends in slaughter. Call your parents. You might not get another chance."

Todd spoke up. "Are we really going to do this? Because I'm losing my buzz, and I'm going to need a bracer if I'm going to be getting all bent out of shape again. We should stop at—"

The call ended. Alan took the phone away from his head. The case creaked in his white-knuckled grip. He looked down to Blot, his breath a vicious, terrified hiss. There was agony in her eyes as well. She looked to the sun. It had cast her as a long form stretching to the west.

"We can get there," she said. "But it's not going to be fun. And I can't promise either of us will be in any condition to do something when we get there."

"Whatever it takes."

"Get to the shadows."

He didn't have to go far. The sun had only barely shifted enough to expose his car since he'd parked it. But he used the moments wisely. He tapped his parents' contact on his phone. His mother answered after a single ring.

"Alan! Good to hear from you," she said.

"Mom! Is Dad with you?" he said.

"No, he's out picking up some fish cakes for lunch. Do you want to come down? I can get him to grab some more."

"No! Mom, listen—"

"I'll tell him to get some. We'll freeze them if you don't come."

"*Mom!* Listen, I need you to keep the doors shut, okay? Lock the doors, lock the windows. Pull the shades down."

"Why?"

"Just do it. Don't let anyone in. I'll be there as soon as I can, but I just need you to keep safe until then."

He'd hurried as near to the wall that was casting the shade as he could. He couldn't quite make it against the wall itself. This being a prison, the architects weren't satisfied with just one layer of walls separating the inmates from the outside world. The forbidding cement wall was a few yards away, with a chain-link fence between it and the parking lot.

"The clock is ticking, Alan," Blot said.

"I love you, Mom. See you soon," he said. He hung up and pocketed the phone.

"This is going to be bad. But you've got to trust me. I think I can make it," Blot said.

"Wait, you *think*?"

"It's the best I can offer."

He squeezed his eyes shut. "Fine. Do it."

Alan didn't have much time to steady himself for what happened next. A heartbeat after he was ready and in position, he felt the strangely cold hands of his shadow rise up and clutch his chest. She pulled back. He stumbled against the icy links of the fence and then simply fell through. It was a terrifying sensation, feeling frozen wires passing through him. He struck the ground and continued as though the solid blacktop of the parking lot was nothing more than the surface of a lake. The only things that felt solid were the shadowy arms wrapped around him.

For a second or two, Blot held him still. He thought perhaps she was giving him a chance to adjust to the strange sensations of being little more than a shadow adrift in the world. To call it unsettling was a profound understatement. His senses didn't know what to make of it. A mind ill-equipped to the lack of hot or cold registered the dark echo of the world as utterly frigid. He wanted to take a breath, but there was no air. Every part of his body was quivering and revolting with varying degrees of panic.

When they moved into the sunlight, it became clear. The pause was not for his benefit, it was for hers. The sun hit them not as a source of warmth, but as a force. It was a gale-force wind, one that was irresistible. He opened his eyes and tried to comprehend the world streaking by him. Any sense of perspective was gone, but there was no doubt that they were moving. They ripped along, due west, riding a tidal wave of light. Each time they flitted through a bit of shade, the force propelling them dropped away, but their momentum carried them forward. They streaked across rooftops. They rippled over curbs. His chest started to heave as his body, unwilling to conceive that it was a simple silhouette, demanded he take a breath. Blot must have felt it, because when they slid into a shaded alleyway, she took one arm away from him and dug her fingers into the surrounding darkness to slow them, then released him with the other arm.

Despite her efforts to take the edge off the motion, he launched back to three dimensions at a near sprint and went sprawling into a pile of trash bags waiting to be hauled out. He took a few gasping breaths and crawled to his feet.

"Are you okay?" Blot asked, also breathless.

He leaned against the wall for a moment, then took some unsteady steps toward the street. "How long were we in the shadows?" he asked.

"About thirty seconds."

He squinted at the nearest street sign. "We're fifteen blocks away from the prison. You guys can move incredibly fast."

"Only with light pushing us, and only *away* from the light. But yeah. How do you think we got so far away from the tree after the eclipse?"

"Why don't you all travel like this all the time?"

"For a lot of very good reasons that we're going to hope we don't run into. Now come on, deep breath."

The pair fell into a tense but tolerable rhythm. For the space of a breath, they let the sun shove them along. Then they would grind to a stop in this shadow or that. If they weren't spotted slipping into or out of a shadow along the way, it was a miracle, but there was little danger of anyone reporting what they'd seen. No sane mind would suspect that a man was emerging from the darkness itself.

For better or worse, his parents didn't live due west of the prison, so as they drew nearer, Alan spent more and more time sprinting north between shadowy jaunts. The neighborhoods became more familiar. They were close. But so was something else. Blot didn't need to tell him. When they ducked into the shadows again, he could feel it too. It was something subtle, something he couldn't quite place. While many of his senses became useless in the shadows, he gained something else, some sense that existed *only* in the shadows. His mind didn't know what to make of it, so it bridged the other senses in brain-bending ways. It was a silent sound. It was a cold warmth. It had intensity, and direction, but beyond that he could only tell that it was *there*. It was Rive. It had to be. This was what Blot felt when she said she could sense others of her kind.

He swept his eyes across the rapidly advancing landscape. He was mere blocks away from his parents' house and could already see the housing projects down the block. Dead ahead, was the curling, fluid shape of the shifter. Unlike himself and Blot, Rive was rock-solid, anchored to Todd and holding his ground.

"I've got to find someplace to emerge," Blot said.

Alan saw the images flash through his mind. He saw them slipping past and into the nearest convenient shadow. He saw himself sprinting to the open door. He saw the grim workings already done.

"No. Here," he said.

He didn't know how he'd done it—he couldn't *breathe* here—but somehow he'd spoken. Perhaps that was the secret. Perhaps he just had to accept that it was impossible and do it anyway.

"Are you sure? It won't be pleasant."

"Now!"

She released him. He popped back to reality with all the velocity he'd accumulated while lacking substance. It was as though he'd been catapulted. Todd turned and cocked a confused eyebrow. Even without a mind rendered sluggish by his latest dose of booze, he wouldn't have had time to react. Alan struck him hard. The pair went tumbling across the sidewalk and out into the street.

"Damn, son," Todd said, shaking his head as they started to untangle themselves. "You hit like a truck."

Despite the impact being his idea, Alan wasn't ready for it. He didn't seem to have any broken bones, but the world was spinning. This gave Todd the advantage, as his world had been spinning for the last few decades.

"You stay away from my family," Alan said.

"I'm just following orders, son," he said, staggering to his feet.

"Get him out of the open. I want a piece of him," Rive rumbled.

"Sure thing, boss."

Todd grabbed Alan by the neck of his jacket and hauled him to his feet. Alan tried to pull himself away, but the fingers gripping him started to grow twisted and gnarled. As Rive shifted his body, his strength grew until it felt like Alan's arm was in a vice.

"Alan, do something," Blot said.

He looked to her. For the moment, both Blot and Rive were at the mercy of the sun. She'd thrown her arms around the neck of the twisted monstrosity attached to Todd, but it was no use. She'd gotten stronger since she'd shown up, but she was hopelessly outclassed. And the threat of discovery was the only thing keeping Rive from turning Todd into a body-horror. Alan fought against Todd and patted his sides for his self-defense gear, but it was all in the trunk of his car, half a city away.

Todd threw him into the shadowy courtyard of the housing project and stepped forward. With the chill of winter still in the air, the windows were all shut tight. Whatever happened here would be entirely unobserved. Rive took full advantage.

"Oh," Todd muttered, his neck starting to shift and crackle. "This is going to be a big one."

His shadow stretched and curled into a ghoulish, gangling form. Bit by bit, Todd's body began to take on the terrifying shape necessary to cast such a shadow. His arms extended from his sleeves. He grew taller until his doughy midriff was stretched into a gaunt but rock-solid bit of sinew. The mass of his body was redistributed into the most monstrous configuration Rive could envision.

Alan backed away. The slow, disorienting process gave him a second or two to gather himself, but with Todd and Rive blocking the entrance to the courtyard, escape wasn't likely.

"Pull me back into the shadows. Maybe we can slip through the gate," Alan said.

"You don't want that. Rive can hit us twice as hard in the shadows as Todd can in the light, and I don't want to think about what happens if he injures you while you're like that."

Todd took a ponderous swing at Alan. He half dodged, half stumbled and managed to turn what would have been a punishing blow into a raking slash that exposed the insulation of his jacket.

"Hold still," Todd muttered, curling his scarecrow fingers into a wiry fist. "It's been a few years since my golden gloves days."

Alan backed away until he was pressed against the cold brick of the opposite side of the courtyard. Todd wound up and delivered a punch. Alan dove aside and slid across the ground as the blow fractured some of the brick.

"Gah!" he yelped, cradling his freshly healed hand.

He raised his foot to thump it down on Alan, but Blot heaved herself against Rive with all her might. Keeping Todd in his gruesome form took a great deal of concentration. She bounced off him with little sign that the attack had done much good, but it was enough to cause Todd to falter. He stumbled back.

"Blot, the flashlight!" Alan called, eying the exit to the courtyard.

"But it won't do any good on a shifter!" Blot said.

He dodged another swipe. Todd was clearly adjusting to his new shape, because the speed and accuracy of the attacks were increasing. Blot slid aside and produced the hefty, black, aluminum three-D-battery monstrosity. She tossed it to him. Alan clicked it on and shined it in Todd's face. He squinted, but otherwise shrugged off the beam.

"Useless," Rive cackled from the shadows.

Todd rose to his full height and balled his fists. "Again, no offense, son," he said.

With his arms raised, the un-shifted clothes that barely held to Todd's contorted body slid up. They revealed an ugly purple blotch of a bruise covering half his chest. It was what Alan was waiting for. He rushed forward and hammered the heavy flashlight into the bruise.

"Gah!" Todd roared, doubling over. "I said go easy on the ribs!"

Alan hammered them a second time. Todd's wiry form stumbled aside, and Alan dashed for the opening of the courtyard. Rive slashed at Blot, but Alan spun on his heels and shined the flashlight at the still-recovering Todd. It may not have been enough to rob him of his grotesque new form, but it was certainly enough to shove Rive out of range and keep Blot safe.

He stumbled out into the light and walked backward, his eyes focused on Todd. The gangling form lingered in the shadow of the building, unwilling to reveal himself in his full horror in the broad light of day.

"What's going on out there!"

Alan turned to see someone rushing around the corner of the housing project. From his outfit and the specific brand of indignation he we showcasing, he was one of the building's staff, responding to complaints raised by the commotion Alan and Todd had caused. He gave Alan a hard look, then turned to the courtyard. What he saw was a bewildered vagabond with oddly twisted and ill-fitting clothes. Suddenly shifting back to a proper human shape, combined with the general level of inebriation that Todd maintained, had been enough to leave him disoriented and on the cusp of losing his lunch.

"Come on, come on, move along," the building's staffer barked.

As someone with about as much combat experience and authority as a grammar school hall monitor bum-rushed a veritable demon, Alan huffed a breath and turned off the flashlight. He subtly dropped it to Blot where the sun had pinned her. She managed to "catch" it, the flashlight vanishing into the shadow until it existed only as a shape in a hand mimicking his own position.

"That was a pretty inventive use for a flashlight."

"Nah," Alan said. "My dad always said lots of fights can be ended in a hurry if you can find a common language. And everyone speaks Maglite." He turned to his parents' house and hurried to the door. "It looks intact," he said quietly. "The door isn't busted down. I think we did it."

"Huh. We did, didn't we," Blot said. "That's *twice* we tangled with a top-class shifter and walked away. I'm starting to think we've got good... what do you call it? Synergy. Better together than apart."

"I think you're right." He hurried up the front steps and rang the doorbell, murmuring, "Please be okay..."

After a few moments too long, the knob turned and his father opened the door. "Alan! Good to have you home!" he crowed.

Recently retired from what folks today would call a "customer-facing" job as a security guard for a bank, Alan's father had not yet adjusted to the relative solitude of spending his days with his wife. He was always happy for a visitor, and *extra* happy to see his son. Though the thinning salt-and-pepper hair and thick glasses made it clear he wasn't a spring chicken, he had a stature and build that made it clear why he'd been hired as a guard in the first place. Alan had always lamented the fact that he'd not inherited those particular traits, particularly now that he found himself so frequently fighting for his life.

"Don't just stand there, come on in!"

He gave Alan a slap on the back, prompting a wince of pain. His dad raised an eyebrow, then leaned forward.

"You're looking a little disheveled there. Something happen?" he said, the first whispers of concern in his voice.

"It's fine. I tripped."

His father adjusted his glasses. "What, down a flight of stairs?"

"I'm fine, Dad. Where's Mom?"

"In the kitchen. Where else would she be once she found out company was coming?" He marched along beside his son. "You've got a bit of a limp there. You need Epsom salts?"

"No one needs Epsom salts, Dad."

He paced through the house where he'd grown up. It had an awkward layout. Whoever designed the place must not have liked hallways, because getting from point A to point B in the house tended to take you through a couple of extra rooms. His parents' design sensibilities didn't help much, either. Alan had a big family, and his parents had the biggest house *in* the family, so they'd spent a fair amount of their time entertaining. Though everyone had spread out since Alan's youth and get-togethers were few and far between, the house still had the preponderance of chairs and couches and the extralong dining room table that made a dozen people feel at home during the holidays. It made for a lot of sidling and squeezing to get from here to there.

"Your mother tells me you called in a tizzy. Worried about home invasion or something."

"Yeah. There's been a crime wave, you know. I'm just trying to look out for you."

"Parents look out for their kids, not the other way around," he said.

As they approached the kitchen, Alan smelled the enticing scent of hot oil. "Is Mom frying something?"

"Yeah. Frying up some fish cakes. An early lunch. We bought plenty. A good thing, too. You didn't mention that your friend was coming over."

"... My friend?"

He finally reached the doorway to the kitchen. It had a small table of its own, directly behind the oven where his mother was happily engaging in her favorite activity: cooking too much food. The table was set with assorted salads. Mayonnaise-based deli-salads, not the "rabbit food" that his dad was so fond of mocking. And seated at the table, with nice big heap of food, was a familiar face.

"Angel..." Alan said.

Chapter 7

"Hello, Alan," Angel said, delicately slicing off a piece of the fish cake on their plate.

"What are you doing here?" Alan said, accusation in his tone.

"Alan. That's no way to talk to an old friend from... I'm sorry, where did you say you knew Alan from?" his mother said, sliding a still-sizzling fish cake onto a fresh plate.

"I am a professional friend. You remember me," Angel reminded, or rather, instructed them.

"Right, right," Alan's father said with a wooden nod. "From work."

"Mr. and Mrs. Fontaine, go inside and enjoy some television while I have a word with your son, please."

His father turned and paced away. His mother, even through the supernatural influence, managed to linger long enough to scoop a double helping of coleslaw onto the plate and push it in front of Alan.

"There's iced tea in the fridge," she said on the way out the door.

"Ask for coffee," Blot said.

It was too late for that, though. Both parents had wandered off as directed. Alan reached over and shut off the light, giving Blot a bit more freedom.

"Oh! They have one of those weird pod machines," Blot said. "That's fine, I'll make my own then."

As his shadow popped open cabinets in search of mugs, Alan took a seat across from Angel.

They had seemingly taken special care to more closely match the dress code of the other members of the bizarre white-suited faction they belonged to. Rather than the white jumpsuit, Angel wore a white polo shirt and white slacks. A long white coat hung on a hook by the door. It wasn't the kind of white-on-white suit that Gabriel and Dina wore. It was more of a business-casual version of the attire.

"I believe you requested that I apply the wards you'd earned from us to your parents' house. I did so."

"... This house is warded now?"

"Yes! Both doors. I took special care in preparing the wards, so all the windows, first *and* second floor, should be covered as well." They finally ate the bite of food on the fork. "This is very good, you know! A name like 'fish cake' conjures some sort of seafood pastry. This is *much* more appetizing than that."

"There we are," Blot said. A handful of little plastic pods drifted out of a cabinet. "What's Kona blend?" she asked. "Is that like Jamaican?"

"It's Hawaiian," Alan said irritably.

"What does that mean?"

"It's an island. It's good coffee. Do you mind? I've got a situation here," he said.

"Fine, then you're not getting any," Blot said.

"Your friend certainly makes herself at home, doesn't she?" Angel said.

"*She* makes herself at home. I come here to find you in my parents' house! Eating their food!"

They scooped up some macaroni salad. "It was offered."

"That much I can believe. The grim reaper wouldn't be able to take Mom without getting a pile of potato salad out of the deal." He took a breath. "But okay, fine. Tell me about this ward you used."

Blot drifted over while the coffee was prepared. "I want to hear this too."

"It is a rather simple but effective ward. As I said last time, a distraction ward. Your enemies, upon reaching the house, will find themselves unable to recall the identity of the person within, and as such will be sapped of the motivation to intrude."

"*I* knew who was here. And Blot."

"Of course you did. You are not an enemy of yourself or your parents." They took another forkful of the macaroni salad. "Which is admirable, may I observe. Many people down here have an *extremely* adversarial relationship with their parents."

"So your spell can tell someone's *intent*?" Alan said.

"Ward. And of course. You've dealt with us before. We are rather skilled at determining and influencing the intentions and desires of individuals."

"And by 'we,' you're talking about..."

"A particular group or organization which shall at this time remain unnamed, and whose existence, even in theory, shall not be confirmed."

"They're supernatural lawyers," Blot muttered.

"Fine. But what *is* the spell?"

"Mr. Fontaine, please. It is a ward. Terminology is important."

"What's the difference?"

"A spell is a spell and a ward is a ward. All you really need to know is that there *is* a difference." They reached down and lifted a small attaché case and opened it up. "This is a ward."

What they held was anything but what Alan would have called mystical. It was just a slip of cream-colored paper, about the size and shape of a cash register receipt. Both sides were covered with writing, though the meaning or even appearance of the writing eluded Alan. As he tried to focus on it, the letters seemed to flicker and shift. Each eye may as well have been looking at a different slip of paper, each sending conflicting information about what precisely he was seeing. Closing one eye or the other didn't help matters.

"Let me see," Blot said.

She reached out to snatch it from Alan's hand, but as her hand approached its shadow, the thing fluttered and flicked out of Alan's grip. It whisked away as Blot pursued it, like a pair of magnets repelling one another. Eventually, Angel deftly snatched it from the air and tucked it back into the attaché case.

"What was that about?" both Blot and Alan asked at the same time.

"That was a barrier ward, intended to keep shades away." They clicked the case shut and set it down.

"And just why do they have one of those?" Blot asked.

"Why do you have something to bar shades?" Alan asked.

"Because shades are the most direct threat to your life, at present."

"They say that, but *they* are the one who got into your parent's house even after you warned your parents to keep people out." Blot pulled the finished coffee from the machine.

Alan gave Blot a knowing look, but decided that now might not be the best time to further assault Angel with accusations and suspicions. There were more questions to be answered.

"How did you install this? Do you burn it like incense or something?"

"Don't be so paranormal-minded," Angel said with a chuckle. "There's a step stool there. Open the door and take a look at the top."

Alan did as he was told. He tried to pretend he was doing it simply because he wanted to rather than because he'd been instructed to. Once he had the door open a crack, causing the curtains to flutter with the icy breeze, he climbed up and looked at the top of the door. There, laminated to the wood with simple packing tape, was another of the wards.

"All you have to do is tape it to the door?" Alan said.

"Of course. The trick is making the ward. After that it must simply be installed in a location. That ward operates on entry points, so a door is ideal. Why? Does that surprise you?"

Alan climbed down and shut the door. "I didn't think I had any preconceptions about magic, but it never would have dawned on me that applying mystical protections would involve a roll of tape and a step stool."

"We endeavor to remain contemporary in our methods. A goal that I understand shades lack."

"Never mind what we do and don't do," Blot said.

"How do I know it actually works?" Alan asked.

"I am afraid I can offer only my assurance. The specific effect is subtle enough that it is difficult to witness in action beyond the general failure of an enemy to successfully enter the home."

"Convenient." Blot sipped her coffee. "Alan, your mom is better at shopping for coffee than you are."

"You'd think that, but it's just whatever she gets coupons for," he said. "Angel, tell me this. How long has the ward been installed?"

"About an hour."

"So it was in place before Rive and Todd showed up."

"Those would be the duo you just battled, correct?"

"Yes."

"Most certainly."

"So I just risked my life, and Blot's, for no good reason."

"I imagine it was cathartic to be able to clash successfully with a foe. That should be its own reward. But as fascinating as it is to discuss my own area of expertise, the nature of our interactions is *intended* to be informational. You've just come from the prison." They glanced at the clock. "Rather expediently, at that."

"That's *right*," Blot said with a cocky grin.

"I trust you learned something?"

"Plenty."

"And just what did you learn?"

Alan glanced to the other room, where an innocuous show about home renovation was playing just a bit too loud.

"I'd really rather not discuss it in earshot of my parents."

"I could easily request that they forget anything they shouldn't overhear."

"I'd also rather not have you reshaping the thoughts of my parents like a handful of clay."

Angel frowned a bit, but nodded. "I suppose that is reasonable. Your own home then?"

"As soon as we can get there. My car is..." He slapped his forehead. "My car is still at the prison."

"I'll give you a ride there. I have a van down the block."

"You drive?"

"Of course. How do you *suppose* I get around?"

"I sort of imagined you just appeared places. You certainly always seem to be right where you need to be, right *when* you need to be."

"Punctuality is not a supernatural trait."

Alan stood. "Then let's go."

Angel gave him a disapproving look. "Alan, really. Your plate is still full, as is mine. It would be rude to turn down the hospitality of our host. We will go once we have both eaten and cleaned our dishes."

He glanced down at his barely touched food, then shook his head and grabbed the iced tea from the fridge. A part of him, he would like to imagine the *largest* part of him, was doing it as an excuse to stick around to be sure the so-called ward worked. There was very little reason to suppose that a lucky shot to the ribs would be enough to keep Todd at bay forever, and the guy from the apartment complex sure didn't have the authority or capacity to take care of the situation in any lasting way.

The truth was a good deal less heroic. He felt tired. Worn out. A body quite unaccustomed to the sort of warrior's high that came from bashing into one's foe was crashing hard. More than that, he felt an odd coldness and weakness that went a lot deeper than his body. Spending a couple of minutes somewhere safe, eating his mom's cooking, was the sort of break he badly needed. He took a seat. Blot sat beside him. The unlikely trio quietly sipped their drinks and ate their food.

After a big plate of food and an unwanted second helping passed without interruption from a shape-shifting drunkard, Alan decided it was time to go. He gave each of his parents a longer than average hug and climbed into Angel's van.

As expected, like everything else associated with Angel and their ilk, the van was pristine white. It had the distinctive boxiness of a package delivery truck, and though it had a huge cargo area in the back, Angel was unwilling to open it to reveal the contents. The ride was relatively uneventful beyond the fact that the glaring white interior and midday sun made for a frustratingly bright environment. Blot was at the mercy of the shifting rays of the sun for the entire ride. Angel was not chatty. Driving was clearly a recent addition to their skill set and required all their concentration.

"Here we are," Angel said, pulling up in front of the parking lot. "The prison. I will meet you at your house to further discuss matters. For your sake I will wait *inside* your house."

Alan lingered outside the door of the van. "You're going to *break in to my house* for *my* sake?"

"Certainly! Now that your parents are safe from Todd and Rive, it is reasonable to assume that your own home will become a target. I am confident my presence will prevent anything untoward from happening. See you soon."

Alan shut the door and they drove off. When Angel's van was completely out of sight, Blot spoke up.

"Did you ever explicitly tell them Todd and Rive's names?" she asked.

"I don't think so," Alan said.

"Do you think they have an explanation for how they know that?"

"I don't even think they'll bother making up an excuse.."

"Neither do I. Lousy white-suits."

He turned to the prison. At the first glimpse of the ominous building, the events of that morning leaped back to mind. He felt a chill, and though he may have been imagining it, he also experienced a hint of that unique feeling that had curdled his soul while he was whisking through the shadows with Blot.

"We never really talked about what's going on in the prison, you and me," Alan said.

"Let's not," Blot said. "Just get in the car and drive. I only want to talk about this once more, and that's to report it to Angel so we can get the tools necessary to hunker down and ride out the coming storm."

"But we—"

"I don't want to think about it, Alan!" Blot barked.

He climbed into his car and started the trip back to his apartment. He did his best to avoid driving in direct sun so that Blot could linger in the passenger seat.

"That was a hell of a trip we took to get to my folks' house," Alan said.

"It was, wasn't it?" she said with a grin. "I didn't know if I had it in me."

"You really are getting stronger."

"You never know what you're capable of until push comes to shove." She flipped her pad and pencil into reality and started doodling.

He gave her a glance. "If you'd pulled off some of the things we've done together back where you come from, how would that have changed things?"

"Most of them couldn't have happened back home. There's no real sunlight to surf, so that stunt wouldn't have worked. And most of the rest of what I've been doing has just been fighting dirty or exploiting technology that we didn't know you people had."

"But if you'd shown this aptitude, what would have been different?"

"I wouldn't have been cannon fodder, that's for sure. I'd have been a proper soldier, like a couple of the ones we saw in that prison that I'm absolutely not going to let you trick me into discussing."

"Would that have been better? Would you have preferred that?"

"Now, or then?"

"Both."

"Back then, for sure, I would have been beside myself with joy. Crossing over and fighting the good fight is as high an achievement as someone like me could ever hope for back home. I'd have been *thrilled* to be one of the ones with more of the answers. One of the ones handing out assignments rather than waiting to get an assignment. Now? I don't know. You're a pain, Alan, but having you as a host is almost like having my own life. Almost. When you're not dragging me into these pointless, near-suicidal crusades. In the in-between times, when things are quiet? Those are nice. We go to coffee shops. We take pictures. We see things that are new to me. We talk. If I was better at what they *wanted* me to be good at, things would have been a constant tug-of-war. You'd be cowering at the sound of my voice like Lenny, or you'd be this half-functional puppet waiting for me to pull your strings like Todd. There wouldn't be Jamaican coffee and goofing off on the internet."

"Considering the fact that infiltrating and overturning our world was your childhood dream, I'd think these 'suicidal crusades' would be the sort of thing you'd be eager to do."

"The fighting wasn't what I was after. I just wanted to be something more than I was, and the fighting was the only way to do it."

"What if there had been another way?"

"What do you mean?"

"We've spoken about what you would like to do. About how you'd like to travel and all that. But if there *had* been other ways to move upward, or move forward. If you *had* been given a choice. What would you have done?"

"Why are you asking me this?" Blot said, a flutter of frustration in her voice.

"Because now that you mention it, I'm not too keen on dwelling upon what's in that prison or the other madness that's happened today, so I'm just trying to fill the silence. The alternative is music."

"Ugh. Thanks but no thanks. You have *terrible* taste in music."

"So?"

Blot muttered under her breath and flipped through the pages of the pad. "This."

She dropped the pad on what would have been her lap if she were three-dimensional. The four-by-six page of the stolen memo-book was covered in a stark, angular sketch of a creature, something like a more twisted and subtly more predatory version of a horse. The rendering wasn't spectacular in its realism, but there was an undeniable style and skill to it.

When Alan came to a stoplight, he reached down and flicked through a few more pages. Some showed shorthand in a language he didn't recognize. Most were similar sketches. Some were of animals that didn't exist on Earth. Others were innocuous objects. A mailbox drawn in blue ballpoint. A coffee cup sitting on a diner table. Alan himself, asleep in bed.

"You want to be an artist?"

"I don't know. I guess. Back home I didn't really think of art as an end upon itself. Art was a way of stretching the mind in new directions, which would help stretch the *body* in new directions. It was seen as a precursor of learning to be a shifter. But I never had the opportunity to move on, so I just practiced this bit over and over." She snatched the book up. "It is stupid. I didn't have the ability to *become* these things. I could only imagine them. I couldn't experience them, I could just envision them. It's like... I don't know... being a composer, but not being able to hear what you're composing. Stupid."

Alan gave her a look, then tugged his phone from his pocket. He was still driving, and still enough of a Goody Two-shoes to not want to do something as simple as using his phone while driving, but he dropped the phone on the console and tapped the screen.

"Play 'Ode to Joy,'" he said.

The phone spun its wheels for a few seconds, then a triumphant orchestration began to blare from it. Blot shut her eyes and listened for a time.

"It's nice. It's closer to what I'd call real music. But why are you playing it?"

"It's from Beethoven's Ninth Symphony. There are people who would call it one of the finest musical compositions of all time. And it was written by Beethoven when he was almost completely deaf."

"Ah. So this is supposed to be inspirational then? As in 'Look, the thing you said it's dumb to want to do is possible here.'"

"That's the general idea, yeah."

"Let me ask you this. Was Beethoven a sentient shadow, outcast from his own kind and hidden—with good reason—from the world that had become his new home?"

"No."

"Then it's not really much of a comparison, is it?" She flipped her pad back to the pages of shorthand, hiding the drawings. "I'm a realist, even if most people wouldn't consider me to actually *be* real. I'm not going to be an artist any more than I'll be a gifted shifter or a fiendish mastermind. The odds are against me even surviving in this world much longer. All I can do is follow what little of my training still applies. Follow the rules. Do what I'm told. What I *want* to do was never in the equation."

"You don't know that."

"I *do* know that. And there's no value in deluding yourself about it, either. I'm content to just continue living. So let's keep our eyes on *that* prize, because unless things are much different here than they are back home, survival is a prerequisite to any other aspirations we might have. Beyond martyr, of course."

He silenced the song. "Fair enough."

Blot gazed at the pages before her. "Mmm..." she murmured, realization in her tone.

"What is it?"

"I'll tell you later. Just a little something I didn't put together when I took the notes the first time."

Alan stepped into his apartment. Angel, as expected, was waiting for him there. They had a toolbox and a step stool, and had changed back into the white overalls for some reason. They had also turned on all the lights in the apartment and removed all the improvised shades.

"It says something about my life that I'm starting to get used to finding people who don't have keys to my apartment waiting for me when I arrive," Alan said. "At least this time you gave me a heads-up."

"Oh yes. I try not to enter places uninvited."

"Hardly a noble policy, coming from a person who can instruct you to invite them in," Blot jabbed.

"You will be pleased to learn that there was no evidence of a break-in," Angel said with a grin.

"How did *you* get in?" Alan asked.

Angel produced a large key ring. "I had a word with the superintendent. He generously provided duplicates to all the keys in the building."

"Great. Well, do me a favor. Don't mess with the lights. I'm not the only one who lives here, remember."

"Yes, that is right. I do apologize. I spend most of my days reading. Proper illumination is key for me."

Alan dropped his bag and adjusted the lights in the living room yet again.

"Down to business, then. What did you learn in the prison?" Angel said.

He retrieved his equipment from his bag and booted up his laptop. "Take a look for yourself. I've got to get this stuff sent to Cox anyway."

Angel took a seat beside him on the love seat. Blot took advantage of Angel's undivided attention to inspect Angel's toolbox.

"How much you want to bet they warded this thing so I wouldn't be able to look inside..." Blot mused.

Alan didn't waste words. As the photos popped up on screen, he recounted his findings. Angel nodded thoughtfully, eyes on the screen.

"Mmm... I assume *every* one of these inmates has a shade?"

"Yeah."

"There are, by my count, fifty-seven unique faces so far in these images. Correct?" Angel said.

"Sounds right. I was a little too busy fearing for my life to take a census."

"Sixty-two," Blot said. "You didn't get seven of them on camera."

"Blot says sixty-two. She's got a better memory than I do," Alan said.

"There'll be more than that soon," Blot said.

"What?" Alan said, turning to her.

"I didn't say anything," Angel said.

"I wasn't talking to you. Blot said there would be more soon."

"The crime wave is still going, don't forget," Blot continued. "You saw the people in the police station."

"But there weren't really any *shades* in the police station, or we would have noticed."

"No. They're just big, burly, useful grunts. The kind of people who will make for decent hosts for low-level shades like me."

"Have you learned something useful yet?" Angel asked. "I'm afraid I can only follow your end of the conversation."

"I'll summarize for you. Just give me a moment. What were you saying?" Alan said.

The shade flipped her pad out again. "Remember that computer you didn't want me to look at in the police station? I jotted down anything I could remember. And I can remember a lot. But the stuff that stuck out most was stuff I recognized from elsewhere. Specifically, a name. Pretty much *all* the entries that Jessie entered, which were the only ones I could find to open, had the same name under known accomplices. Alicia Coke."

"The mobster lady?"

"That's her."

"So she's loading the cellblock with her crew... Why didn't you bring this up sooner?"

"It's not my fault I can't choose when realization dawns."

Alan turned to Angel, who was pleasantly awaiting an explanation.

"We have reason to believe that a woman named Alicia Coke, who we know is a host to a shade, is having members of her gang incarcerated. So even the people without shades are going to be *working* for the shades, and the shades looking for an upgrade won't just have good hosts to pick from, but *cooperative* hosts to pick from."

"An entire prison of shades," Angel said.

"Not a whole prison. Just a cellblock. So far, anyway," Alan said.

"For our purposes, the distinction is of little consequence." They flipped through their book. "Ah. There. The Roanoke Tactic. This is not a matter of concern." Angel stood. "Thank you for your service. I will certainly ward your home for this new information." Angel grabbed the toolbox and pulled it open.

"Wait, wait, wait," Alan said. "This is not a matter of concern? Are you serious?"

"It is a known tactic. We don't seek to interfere unless things are sub-stantially diverging from expectation."

"But this could be terrible. This could be a *huge* success for the shades at the expense of everyone else."

"It will all balance out," Angel explained. "It's happened before. Shades never work well in cohort when there isn't a focused task at hand. It *is* concerning, having an inaccessible stronghold of shades in the area, par-ticularly this *specific* area, but within a few weeks there will be squabbling, backstabbing. Discipline will flag. Things will crumble, and the status quo will return. No concern at all. It will be a nonissue within a month."

"Within a month, a tour will occur. A bunch of major political figures are going to be showing up for a photo op at the prison that's been so handily pacifying its inmates."

Angel stroked their chin. "I... see." Again, Angel flipped through their book. "So this is the Flanders Tactic then. Agreed. That could be trouble-some."

They slipped the book back in their pocket and turned to the bag. One by one, they removed rolls of clear tape and sheaves of paper slips.

"Well?"

"Well what?" Angel asked without stopping.

"What are we going to do?" he said.

"Mmm? Oh, about the tactic?"

"Yes, about the tactic!"

"Nothing. It's unfortunate, but it still isn't unprecedented. Naturally, I'll pass your findings on to those in a better position to make a final decision, but I doubt their assessment will differ from mine. It's all there in the book. Lives will be lost, certainly. And the entire ordeal will be stretched a bit. But things would have to escalate in unexpected and unwanted directions to a far greater degree for any direct corrective action to be taken."

Angel opened the step stool and set it up in front of Alan's door, then opened it and set about taping a slip to the top.

Alan tried to keep his voice down as he raved, "I can't do this on my own. I need *help*."

"No one is asking, or expecting, you to do anything. It was helpful that you did this bit of research for us, but even that wasn't strictly necessary."

"They threatened my family. We've got my house and my parents' house safe. But what about when they're not at home? And what about the other people?"

"I would certainly suggest you take additional steps to assure the safety of your family."

"I've done everything I know how to do, and it's not doing any good. And while you seem fine knowing that 'people will die,' I'm not fine with that at all. And you people call yourselves angels!"

Angel shut the door and gave him a hard look. "Who said anything about us being angels?"

"The other two are named Gabriel and Dina. I looked them up. Both are angel names. You didn't even *try* for a clever one. You're just Angel. You always dress in white. You just appear whenever I ring a silver bell. The symbolism is about as subtle as a frying pan across the face."

Angel crossed their arms. "I cannot be blamed for the human tendency to find meaning in chaos. And I should know, because as previously stated, I am a human, just like you." They grabbed the stool and marched toward the bedroom. "Since the warding isn't intended to be a secret here, I imagine in private places like your bedroom it would be permissible to affix them out in the open?"

Alan, still aghast, marched after them. "Yeah, fine, whatever. Listen, isn't there some kind of deal we can make for you to give us more help with this?"

"That wouldn't be fair, Alan."

"Fair and right aren't always the same thing," Alan said.

"An astute observation," Angel said. "But I'm afraid I am simply not free to act." They climbed up and applied another strip to the top of his bedroom door. "On the plus side, you have got distraction wards on your entire apartment now. Those who mean you harm will find themselves nearly incapable of remaining focused on their evil intent when they approach your door. You are safe."

Angel paced into the living room and packed away their things. Alan glared at Angel all the way out his own door and across to theirs.

"I wish you luck, Alan. I really do. I wish I could do more."

With that, Angel shut the door to their residence. The number on it faded away and returned to simply the word *Utility*. Alan could feel his mind beginning to discard the knowledge that it had ever been anything different. In moments the number itself was gone from his mind, replaced only with the mild feeling that something about this door wasn't right. Finally, the notion faded completely and he trudged back into his room, completely aware of the conversation he'd had but unaware of where the frustratingly "impartial" person had gone.

"That didn't go as well as I would have hoped," Alan said.

"It went as well as I expected," Blot said.

He rubbed his head. The dull feeling of weariness was stubbornly lingering at the base of his skull.

"We're not much better off now than when we started."

"I don't know. On one hand, you've clearly angered Dun. You've made us a much higher-priority target for Rive, and you've not done much of anything to foil Dun's scheme. On the other hand, if we just keep our heads down and don't leave the apartment much, we'll probably be able to stay alive. And with any luck, we'll be able to move to a better place and fortify that. Or maybe even fortify your car. That'd help."

"How are we supposed to do that? Angel made it clear they're not interested in helping any further."

"Sometimes, you've just got to help yourself," Blot said. She held out a hand and, with a flourish, produced a veritable bouquet of the slips of paper.

"What are those?"

"Wards! I stole them from Angel's toolbox."

"How? Surely they protected it."

"They left it *open*. While you two were in the bedroom, I stretched out here and grabbed any of them that didn't feel like they'd burn a hole through me or go fluttering off when I reached for them."

"That was not a very—"

"Don't lecture me for doing something that'll probably save our lives, Alan," Blot said.

"Fine. So what do they do? I assume there are different sorts of wards."

"I don't know. I can't read them." She eyed one of them a bit more closely. "It seems like they don't *want* to be read. But I'm patient. I'm confident if I have enough time I can figure them out. We could always just stick them on things and experiment. What's the worst that could happen?"

"I don't know. Magic is a relatively recent addition to my life, and I'm not too fond of the sort of impact it's had."

"I'm not too fond of the sort of impact electricity has had on my life, but I understand the value it has."

"Fine. I'll leave that to you. I trust you. But there's still the issue of the prison, and the tour. We've got to stop it."

"We absolutely do not."

"We absolutely do."

"Look, I was all for making the attempt, seeing what we could do..."

"You were against it from the start."

"Oh, I was against *doing* it. But I was fine with you looking into it and figuring out for yourself that we couldn't do anything. Plus, it got us these wards. That was a nice little bonus. Good job. But what's done is done. It's you and me against all of them. You're barely able to keep yourself alive against *one* of the better-trained shades and hosts at a time. I'm nothing special. They were on the cusp of attack when you were just taking pictures and stuff. I would be very surprised if we survived a second visit to that prison regardless of what we had planned when we walked in. But if we showed any hint of actual hostility or motion against them, we'd be done in a blink. We don't have the tools to fight shades, and we don't have any help."

"Tools to fight shades..."

"And I'm not talking about increasingly fancy flashlights, either."

"No, no... You're talking about the stuff the Dawn has."

"Yes."

"I'm calling the Dawn," Alan said, pulling out his phone.

"What? No!" Blot snatched the phone.

"Who else are we going to call?"

"Just stop calling people. Honestly, human beings are the *only* things who don't seem to know when they're beat."

"It's the last option we have!"

"It's not the last option we have. It's not even the *best* option we have. We can run and hide!" She shook the wards. "We just got the tools to make that work!"

"People will die."

"Just keep repeating that, Alan. That's *sure* to convince me," Blot said, vanishing the wards again. "Listen to your own words. It's not 'people might die,' or 'people could die.' It's 'people *will* die.' And you're right. The question is which people will die. Any action we take past this point will only influence *who* dies. I don't know what your priorities are, but here are mine. I want me to survive and I want you to survive, and, if possible, I'd prefer to not be responsible for the wholesale destruction of my own people. If you call the Dawn and we start working with them, I can guarantee at least one of those priorities will not be met."

"My priority is that no one dies."

"Maybe if you clap your hands and make a wish, that'll happen, but here in the real world, we've been outmaneuvered. There's no shame in it. The odds were against us from the start."

"We've seen that the Dawn are reasonable."

"The first time we met them, they tried to stab me. You got your hands on one of their daggers and you *accidentally* stabbed me. They kidnapped us and punched a hole in me. No, they are not reasonable."

"They *can* be reasonable. They agreed to a truce."

"If the most reasonable thing someone can do is agree, for the time being, not to try to kill you specifically, that is not a strong argument in favor of trusting them."

"It's the only thing *you* care about, right?"

"... Fair point. Ah! But they broke in to your house since then. Not very truce-y."

"Fine. Let's look at it another way. The Dawn already knows something is up at the prison, right?"

"Clearly."

"They are already going to do something."

"They're going to try."

"And that something is going to involve killing shades, and as a result, killing the humans they're paired up with."

"They're going to try it anyway."

"If we talk to them, we can find out what they have planned. Maybe there's something we can do that will serve all our purposes. What harm can be done with a chat?"

"A tremendous amount of harm can be done with a chat." Blot sighed. "For one thing, you've gone and persuaded me, *again*, to let you do something paralyzingly stupid."

"I prefer to call it optimistic," Alan said, picking up the phone again.

Blot crossed her arms. "Optimism is just stupidity as a philosophy."

He searched through the lengthy list of contacts they'd stolen from the Dawn. Eventually, he found Brink.

"I want to preemptively say 'I told you so' about this," Blot warned. "Repeatedly. This is the 'so' that I will have told you about the most."

"Granted." He tapped the contact.

"Hello?"

"Mr. Brink?" Alan said.

"Ah. Would this be Mr. Fontaine?" he said.

"Yes. I'd like to have a word with you."

"This wouldn't be about the clash you had with a shifter outside your parents' house, would it?"

"How do you know about that?"

"If you'll recall, I did say we would try to have some of our people on hand."

"So you had Dawn members there to defend my parents?"

"If necessary."

Alan cupped his forehead. "The most heroic thing I've done in my life and it was pointless twice over."

"I'm telling you, with a bit of proper planning, cowardice is a legitimate tactic," Blot said.

"To your credit, they had a glowing account of your clash. Though a bit more discretion would be called for. A figure emerging from the shadows at high speed is liable to draw unwanted attention to you."

"Trust me, I know. It was a bad bit of improv. But that's not what this call is about. As you must *also* know, I've been in and out of the Curran-Fromhold prison."

"And?"

"It's worse than we thought."

"How so?"

"There are dozens of shades, with at least two high-level shades organizing them. They are handpicking the best of a criminal syndicate to build an army of well-trained, well-matched shades."

"That is very close to the worst-case scenario."

"I want to talk to you about what we can do about it. In three days I've got another chance to get into the prison."

"I'll give you an address where we can meet."

"No. You come here."

"Really? You would invite me into your home?"

"Yes. If we talk, we talk over the phone or we talk here. And I'd prefer here."

"You'll excuse me if I suspect a trap. We did not leave under the most pleasant of circumstances."

"We've taken steps to protect my apartment, and since there's a supernatural entity after me, I'd really rather not conduct business with someone they view as an enemy in a place where I can't be sure of my safety."

"You've got a shade, Alan. You can never be sure of your safety."

"If you want to collaborate, we collaborate here, and you come alone."

"… If that's how you want to play it. I'll give you a call when I'm close. I'll have some tools of the trade. But I'll tell you this. If this goes down, it starts with you getting me into the prison. There is no circumstance in which I send you out with Dawn equipment and Dawn know-how but *without* Dawn supervision. I hesitate to think of what would happen if some of our tools ended up in the hands of the enemy."

"If that's what we decide, then that's what we decide."

"Then I'll see you tomorrow, Mr. Fontaine." He hung up.

"Do you really think that man is heroic? He doesn't even have *manners*," Blot said.

Alan leaned back on the couch and rubbed his face. Ever since his clash with Todd, his body had been steadily reporting a growing list of aches and pains. He rolled his neck and rubbed at a bruise he didn't realize he had.

"You should take care of some of those bumps. If things turn out the way I expect, you'll be doing a lot of running."

"They're not that bad." He rubbed his eyes. "The real problem is, I've got this... I don't know... *cloud*. In my mind. It's like I'm tired, but only in my brain."

"What do you expect? You took a trip through the shadows. Went straight across town."

"What's that got to do with anything?"

"You run for a while, you get winded. That's just how physical exertion works. Why would metaphysical exertion be any different?"

"But I didn't *do* anything. It was all you. And you don't seem tired."

She pointed down to his feet, where the band of shadow that connected them met his body. "That connection between us isn't just for looks."

"You were leeching strength from me?" he said.

"Can we avoid terms reserved for parasites? I drew from our common strength pool."

"You could have asked first."

"Oh, I'm sorry. Next time I'll ask you for permission to help you save your parents."

"I don't remember that happening last time. Me getting tired."

"Last time we were pretty fresh as a host-shade duo. Now we're better aligned. Why do you suppose we have to wait so long before we have the strength to take a new host? It's because the safest way to pull it off is to wait until the link is strong enough to borrow what we need for it from our host."

"... And now you've got a strong enough link for that."

"We've got a strong link. Strong enough for that is subjective. I wouldn't really know unless I tried."

Alan pulled himself up and paced into the kitchen. He tugged some canisters from the cabinet and started a pot of coffee.

"Show me how you've been making it so strong," he said.

"Why?"

"Two reasons. One, I've got a lot of work to do and I need to keep my eyes open. Two, I feel like I've got to start pampering you to keep you from testing that whole 'switch hosts' thing."

"Hah! It's about time."

After the events of the day, Alan had some difficulty pulling his mind to the relatively mundane task of prepping his photos for digital delivery to Cox. His focus wandered more than once, and he ended up eating something frozen from the freezer rather than risk leaving his apartment for a supermarket trip or wasting money on takeout.

When evening finally came, Alan passed out the very moment his head hit the pillow. For most people, that would have been the end of his worries until the next day. Alan was not most people.

He was walking down a nondescript street, in the dazed autopilot of the average dream. As he paced along, glancing in storefronts and casually waiting for the dream's plot to commence, he saw a familiar face staring back at him in place of his reflection in a window.

"You know, before tomorrow, I think I should take this opportunity to illustrate my point of view," Blot said.

Alan blinked and felt the weight of full comprehension drop down on him. He shook his head as Blot stepped out of the reflection and hopped down onto the sidewalk beside him. She was in what was as near to her true self as he was ever likely to see. Less than four feet tall, with large white eyes, flowing black hair, and an overall impish appearance.

"You know, there are people who train their whole lives to have lucid dreams from time to time. It's a little weird to have them thrust upon you," Alan said.

"Further evidence that I am a blessing," Blot said. "But as I was saying. My point of view. I understand you've got this hero complex you need to deal with. It leaks into everything you do. You want to take pictures for a living, but you also want to do good, so you tell yourself you want to become a forensic photographer. You see the shades doing their thing, and you believe it is your duty to stop them. You've been a fine host and a decent person to me, recent frustrations not withstanding, but that is probably an extension of your bone-deep desire to be some sort of wonderful white knight."

"Thanks for the psychoanalysis."

"I'm tethered to you all day, every day, and I'm a trained observer. How else am I going to spend my day but analyzing you? My point is, I can't blame you for acting this way. It is your essential nature, and it is the result of a whole life of being you. You may look at me, and the way I behave, and feel the same frustration and dismay at the choices I am making—or, as the case may be, am asking you to make. They seem perfectly natural to me, because I've only ever lived as *I* am."

"You can never really know how the other side lives."

She turned to him. "With your permission, yes you can."

"You want me to turn over the reins to this dream?"

"If you are willing. I think you'll find it educational."

He took a deep breath. "Go ahead."

Alan had shared his dreams with Blot countless times already. He supposed he'd shared every dream he'd had since her arrival with her. But she didn't always step into the spotlight, so to speak. And even more rarely did she ask to run the show. It wasn't as simple as just agreeing to let her do it. It was something deeper and less conscious than that. Relinquishing control of a dream felt a bit like when you've been sitting with your shoulders tensed for many hours and suddenly realize you could simply relax. You don't realize you have control of your dream at all—most people think they don't—but once you know it is there, you simply let it ease away. And so he did.

The effect was immediate. The city street faded, and Alan found himself adrift in a void of blackness. Then a sheet unfurled itself before him. A point of light appeared behind him, casting his shadow onto the sheet along with Blot's. It was strangely disorienting to see a shadow that actually looked like *him* for once. The flashback to the old normal didn't last long, as both his shadow and Blot's started to shift, forming something of a shadow play on the sheet.

"I don't have all the answers," Blot said. "They don't tell us things we don't need to know. So I don't know when or where in your world our other visits have ended up. And I don't know how people who come here come back from your world, but some of them do. Very few. Perhaps one in a thousand who leave our world for yours will find their way back in our world. Sometimes none at all will return from an entire army sent through. It's never someone like me. It's always someone like Dun or Driss. And when they come back, they bring stories."

As Blot spoke, the sheet before them expanded, and the shadows began to illustrate the scenes she described.

"The last stories that came through—stories that came not from the last eclipse but one long before—are what formed my picture of your world. They are how I 'knew' that your world, the world I expected to find on the night of the eclipse, was a simple one. One as simple as mine. It was a place where the fastest way across the sea was a ship with many sails. The fastest way across land was to ride atop an animal. And it was a place where men and women still kept the darkness at bay with torches and lamps.

"Those stories were how I learned about the weapons of the Dawn. The tactics of the Dawn. Those stories are how I learned never, *ever* to trust the Dawn.

"Back then, people weren't so slow to imagine that one's shadow could have a mind of its own. Things that you people call superstitions were common sense. And a group like the Dawn was present in far larger numbers. They had the support of powerful people. But they hadn't anticipated the numbers we would send, so they often lacked the means to find us and combat us directly. They used... other means."

The shadow play became more detailed, their shadows splitting into dozens of figures. They twisted into disturbing tools, implements of torture. Brands sizzled. Struggling figures stretched on racks.

"Your people died at their hands. Far more of yours than ours, honestly. But when they found us, it was so much worse."

By now, the screen had expanded in all directions. It wrapped around them until it wasn't so much a screen as simply the new reality. The black forms became so numerous that the balance seemed to shift, such that it was not black forms cast by white light, but islands of white floating in the sea of black. One such island of white rose up above the rest, like the moon in a black sky. As it rose, it grew brighter. And as it grew brighter, Alan felt an odd sensation. He felt his arms unwilling to cooperate. He felt his legs locked in place. It wasn't like paralysis. It was like there were chains threaded through his body, like his own arms and legs were somehow their own shackles. He tried to fight it, but he couldn't move at all.

"They knew what the light could do to us. They knew it could keep us restrained. But that was never enough. Their command of light wasn't nearly as strong as it is now. But their command of what you would call magic was *much* stronger."

Alan's eyes, the only part of him with full motion, glanced down to find that once more his shadow led forward and was cast in Blot's shape... but something was wrong. It didn't feel that way. It felt as though he was a kite fighting at the end of a string that she held. It felt like *she* was the anchor, not him. He tried to speak, but he found that he couldn't.

One of the other shadowy figures raised something up. It looked like a small clay doll. He cast it down on the shadow that linked Alan and Blot. Then Blot stepped aside. She seemed to fade. When she spoke, it was as a disembodied and distant voice.

"You hear people speak of a cure," she said, chillingly far away. "And maybe those who administered it would call it that. But it was nothing of the sort. The host still died. And the shade? The shade was left attached to this nonliving pile of enchanted clay. Inanimate. Unthinking. Little more than a nail driven into the ground to hold a shade in place."

Figures started to close in around Alan.

"And then they could do as they chose without fear of petty things like a voice they could hear. No host to communicate the pleas for mercy. No host to speak of the screams. Just a shadow, unmoving to their eyes. Just a thing to test. To study. To pick apart."

The figures started to thrust cruel-looking shapes toward him. At first, he felt nothing at all. Just shadows slipping over him. Then he felt feathery, distant sensations. He felt the bizarre and unsettling sensation of something passing through him. Not in a grizzly, surgical sort of way. More like his body was little more than a mist and this thing was curling through it.

"The tales suggest this is how they learned what worked and what didn't. Trial and error. Again and again. So many of them. Over so many years. But you people are persistent."

The piercing white light glinted on an upheld blade. Even before it moved toward him, Alan could feel that there was something different. It felt cold. It *radiated* cold. The closer it came, the more he could feel the icy sting. The shadowy figure held it high, then thrust it down.

Alan gasped in pain and sat bolt upright. He was in his room again, but he could still faintly feel the imagined attack, the way it pierced his stomach. He looked up to find Blot staring down at him from the ceiling.

"Must be nice to be able to wake up from that. When it happens to me, I won't be able to."

Alan took a breath. He knew he had his voice back, but he wasn't certain what to say.

"I just wanted you to see what it's like from my end. I wanted you to see the kind of people you're asking me to trust."

"That's what it was like before. I'm here now. It'll be different. I won't let something like that happen."

"Let's hope not. But do you really think you'll be the one who gets to make that decision?" Blot drifted over to gaze at one of his photographs. "Sleep well, Alan."

He wiped some sweat from his forehead and lay back. He doubted he would get back to sleep, and he *knew* he wouldn't sleep well.

Chapter 8

Alan stepped off the elevator and marched into the lobby. He'd received a phone call from Brink at nine a.m. on the nose, asking to be met in the lobby.

"Fontaine," the imposing man said.

He turned. For someone so sturdily built, Brink did a remarkable job of not sticking out. It wasn't that he'd dressed in a more subdued manner. He seemed to subscribe to the old-school philosophy of combat, choosing to wear a bright and clear indicator of his allegiance in the form of a blue overcoat with polished silver buttons. He nonetheless managed to fade into the background. It was something in the casual way he stood, and the careful selection of a vantage point that gave him a full view of the area without being in anyone's way. Alan wondered if that was the sort of thing that could be taught, or if it was just some sort of instinct.

"Are you ready to start?" Brink asked, hefting a large canvas duffel bag.

"The sooner the better," he said.

Brink marched behind Alan as he led the way back onto the elevator. The whole elevator car bobbed worryingly as Brink stepped on. The doors slid shut, and Blot rose up behind Brink, white eyes glaring down at him as she subtly eased herself to just a bit taller than him.

"You realize that one false move from this one and I'll poke him full of holes," Blot murmured.

Alan gave her a hard look.

"Tell your shade to behave itself," Brink rumbled.

"... Did you hear her just now?" Alan said.

"No. But I'd suggest you never play poker. You telegraph your thoughts all over your face. To call it a tell would be charitable."

"Great." The elevator reached his floor and they stepped off. "Tell me. Do you remember where my apartment is?"

"Of course I do," Brink said.

"Do me a favor and point it out when we get there."

"Why?"

"Call it an experiment."

They continued down the hallway. Alan continued past his own door without missing a step. Brink stopped and pointed.

"This is you here."

Again, he glanced at Blot.

"Okay. So he could find the apartment. It means either he doesn't mean us harm, the ward doesn't work, or Angel was lying about how it worked. Doesn't prove anything."

"Right you are," Alan said. He fought his key into the much-abused lock.

"I notice you haven't upgraded your lock yet," Brink said.

"I've been a little busy."

"You said something about fortifying your apartment. One would think that would *start* with a replacement for your laughably cheap lock."

"Most of the people I have to worry about aren't pick-the-lock types. They're more batter-down-the-door or slide-underneath-it types."

"No excuse for overlooking the simple precautions."

They stepped into the apartment. Out of habit, Brink reached for the nearest lamp to pull its shade.

"Don't," Alan snapped. "You're a guest here."

Brink gave a nod of acknowledgment and marched to the same chair he'd claimed when he was last here. He dropped the duffel bag on the coffee table. "We'll make this quick. If you don't mind, I'll start."

"Go ahead," Alan said. He tried to keep a tough face, but he was his mother's son. Hospitality was dyed in the wool for him. "Do you want a coffee?"

"Tea, if you have it. I never touch coffee," Brink said.

"As if there wasn't *enough* reason to not trust this guy."

"Keep an eye on him," Alan said quietly as he headed into the kitchen.

"Oh, you don't need to tell me twice," Blot said.

"There are procedures within the Dawn for situations such as this."

"So I've been told," Alan said, shuddering at the images from his dream.

"Combating shades in large numbers is very different from one-on-one, particularly this long after their arrival. We have to assume they are all ready to take new hosts. That means that it won't be enough to simply eliminate the current hosts. The shades will simply take a new host. It will come at enormous expense of strength, and thus will make them more difficult to track."

"Just to be clear. When you say 'eliminate the current hosts,' you're talking about murdering people."

"I'm talking about taking necessary steps to curb a supernatural invasion."

"By murdering people."

"If you don't have the stomach for this, then you realize we've lost before we've begun."

"*I* am a 'current host.' Let's just remember that when we're pitching ideas."

"Fine. Regardless. The point here is that we cannot simply do that. In situations such as this, there are only two reasonable ways forward. The first is an all-out assault, matching numbers with numbers. The nature of their stronghold in the prison and the lack of available Dawn operatives makes that impossible. The other is the usage of some more-overtly arcane means. And in any case, a far greater focus of available resources will be necessary."

"That sounds reasonable."

"To that end, you've spoken of Driss and Dun as the two leaders in the prison. Are we certain there aren't any others?"

"None that I recognized," Blot said. "There a few powerful shades and a lot of weak ones, but those were the only ones I recognized."

"Blot says no."

"They will be our primary focus. If nothing else, they must be dealt with. Good leaders are force multipliers. Even if the rest survive, removing them from the equation will be a massive blow."

"Everyone survives," Alan said.

"What?"

"If you expect my help, then we're not going in with a plan that wipes these people out. That's non-negotiable."

"You are tying my hands in a situation that already heavily favors the enemy."

"A good military measures the success of a mission by how few casualties there are."

"How few *civilian* casualties there are. This is a war, Mr. Fontaine. We're talking about enemy troops."

"We're talking about inmates who had no choice in the matter, and shades who, for the most part, didn't have any choice in the matter either."

Brink shook his head. "She's got her claws into you deep."

"Stop wasting my time and start giving me nonlethal options," Alan snapped.

"That's my boy!" Blot said.

When Alan returned with a cup of hot water and a tea bag, he found Brink looking as impassive as ever, though a vein on his neck suggested that was more a result of good self-control than actual composure.

"As it happens, there are still options available to us. I wouldn't call them solutions. All they are doing is delaying disaster."

"Better than nothing."

Alan took a seat on the love seat. Blot stretched up to the ceiling to gaze down into the duffel bag while Brink sifted through it.

"The only way I can think of to preserve the lives of those subverted and prevent them from causing havoc in the public hinges upon the specific stronghold they selected. They are hiding in a prison that may as well be made of paper. We must make it a proper prison."

"How?"

"We must lock the shades to their present hosts and sap the strength of the shades such that they are little more than proper shadows."

"Not possible," Blot said flatly.

"Blot has her doubts."

"She would. It has been some time since a full-scale invasion by her kind. While they may be stuck in the old ways, we have been working hard in the years since."

Brink pulled a small silver case from the bag. Blot narrowed her eyes. He clicked it open.

"By the void..." Blot uttered.

"What? What is it?"

"A Shard of Shadow," said both Blot and Brink at the same time.

"Your shade can enlighten you, I'm sure."

"It's just... it is power. It is life. A Shard of Shadow is the distilled essence of what makes us what we are. I... I can't put it into terms you'd understand. As far as I know, there's nothing in the human world that is even similar to it. They shouldn't even *exist* here. It is... it is..." Her fists tightened. "It is *bait*, isn't it?"

"She says it's bait," Alan said.

"You've got a clever one. It is at that. But it is much more. It is a source of power, and not just any power. It is a source of power that matches their own in kind."

He held up a glass ampule containing what looked like an arrowhead made from pure onyx.

"In the hands of a shade, it is strength. In *our* hands, it is a means to craft items that can influence them. It can tweak their very nature."

Blot was shaking. At first Alan thought it was fury, but it soon became clear there was more to it than that. There was something in her eyes. It was a hungry, feral look. She stretched her shadowy hands down along the floor and up along the table, reaching for the shard. As they drew near, Brink dropped his hand to his belt. In a flash, he had a silver dagger in his hand. He lowered it to the table until its blade threatened to cut Blot's wrist.

"I wouldn't," he said, looking her straight in the eye.

Genuine fear flickered in her eyes, and she pulled her hands back and huddled down behind Alan.

"He can see me! Why can he see me?" she raved.

"I can see you, and hear you, because I hold the shard," Brink said. "It affords me the same insight that a host might have, in addition to some other notable benefits."

He dropped the ampule back into the silver case and clicked it shut. Once the case was sealed, a look of logic and reason returned to Blot's eyes.

"I don't understand. If you can do that, why rely upon those amulets to find shades? Why not just carry a shard and see the shades for what they are?"

"A thousand reasons. The Dawn believes that the touch of a shade is a blight upon the mind and body. We do not seek it. They are also more precious than gold. This is not the only one we have, but there aren't many more. Most importantly, it is more valuable as both the bait and the fuel source for the ritual."

"The ritual?" Alan said.

"We need to get close. And we need time. The ritual's effects will apply in stages. Even without any preparation, once it is revealed, the shard will serve as bait, as suggested. The first stage of the ritual will keep any shades from directly contacting the shard. The next will dwindle their strength until they can have no influence on the physical world. No shifting. No pulling into shadows. No manipulating things via their shadows. None of that. The final stage will make their helplessness permanent."

"My darkness..." Blot said in a hushed voice.

"And that will be that," Brink said. "We will have condemned those prisoners to be at the mercy of their shades, and the shades will be locked away as surely as their hosts."

Blot shuddered. "Trapped."

"But they'll survive. The prisoners and the humans too," Alan said.

"Nothing in the ritual can affect a human," Brink said. "And there is no reason the shades wouldn't survive."

"If you call that surviving," Blot said. "Locked to the same host forever. Tied to the same body for life. Held prisoner by something as simple as iron bars."

"That's the way we all live our lives," Alan said.

"That's *your* problem. It wasn't supposed to be ours."

"It isn't an ideal solution. They may not have any of their more potent powers, but the shades will still have eyes. They'll still have a voice. And many of those prisoners will be released, with the shades still able to spread their influence."

Blot crossed her arms. "I hate it." She turned her head aside. "But I hate it less than the alternatives."

"I think that's it. That's what we'll do. What do I have to do?"

"I'll see to the plan and the materials. On the day, you'll just need to get me inside."

"I'm not sure how I'll do that. The credentials are pretty specific. Can't you just teach me the ritual?"

"No. You won't be able to do it alone, regardless. Never mind how I'll get in. Just be ready to answer the phone and do as I say when the time comes. I'll figure out the rest."

"I just have to trust you'll show up?" Alan said.

"It is a tremendous compromise that I am willing to pursue a non-solution to the problem, Mr. Fontaine. Your end of the compromise comes in you leaving me to perform my tasks." He started to arrange the items in his bag again.

"Wait," Alan said.

Brink glanced up.

"You say that the Dawn has been working on things. Improving things. Researching things."

"Yes. To defeat this enemy, we must understand it."

"And you know that anyone who has a shade has had their shadow torn away."

"Indeed."

"What do you know about what happens to those shadows?"

"Why are you asking this question?" Blot asked. "He's been here long enough."

"We don't know much, beyond the fact that a lot of the same rules apply. Our shadows need to be anchored to something. It's suggested that, this being their world, they aren't destroyed."

"So there would be a way to get them back."

"There *could* be a way to get them back. But to what end?"

"You're asking about this because of what Angel said, aren't you?" Blot said viciously. "You're asking about the cure."

"If you could get the shadow back, couldn't it be restored?" Alan pressed.

"You're welcome to try. We've never succeeded. A man and his shadow are something like a fine vase. Anyone can break it, but once it's been broken, it'll never be the same."

"But, you have that shard. Couldn't it—" Alan was interrupted by his phone ringing. He fumbled for it.

"I have a lot to do to prepare the ritual," Brink said, standing and gathering his bag.

"Wait, I just"—he looked to the phone—"it's Cox. I have to answer this."

"Good. Answer. We're through here." Brink marched out the door, leaving his mostly untouched tea on the table.

Alan answered. "Hello?"

"Fontaine. Cox. I'm looking at these pictures. I want you down here to deliver the goods and discuss matters."

"Uh, yeah. Sure. Are you happy with them? We're still good for the second day, aren't we?"

"Just get in here." He hung up the phone.

"This can only be good news..." Alan said flatly.

He turned to Blot. Her arms were crossed and her expression was stern.

"Why did you ask about the cure, Alan?" she rumbled.

He sighed. "We'll talk about it along the way."

A few minutes later, they were in the car. Blot was seething beside him.

"Why do you *keep* asking about the cure?" she said.

He stopped at a red light and drummed his fingers on the steering wheel.

"I just... it's better to have answers than not have answers, okay?"

"From the Dawn? After what I showed you about how they treat us, and how they treat our hosts?"

"It isn't like I would have subjected myself to them to have some sort of procedure done. I'm just trying to learn. I am at the dead center of a big, terrifying thing that I don't know anything about. And I don't have a whole lot of choices of who to learn *from*. Forgive me, but I don't always get the feeling you're being entirely forthcoming with me."

"What good will it do you to know how to get rid of me? What happens to me then?"

The light changed and he moved on. "If there's a solution for me, there might be a solution for you."

"There is no solution for me. You've got a body and, maybe, you've still got a shadow out there. Both halves of what it takes to survive might exist here for you. I don't have a body here. I never will, unless you've got a bunch of shadowless husks floating around. So what is there for me? Do I go home? Of course not! I'm a traitor! Unless I was the only one from this whole mission to get home, sooner or later news would spread that I turned on my own and that would be it for me. You getting rid of me just means, at best, I end up with someone else. And..." She turned aside. "Forget it."

"Honest, I—"

"I said forget it. It doesn't matter. The facts are, you're never going to find a cure. So we're stuck together unless you get me angry enough at you to abandon you, and then you're dead. Get your head in the game. If you really are going to be heading back into that prison to do this plan, and it's not terribly likely that I'm going to slap some sense into you before it's too late, then we're going to need you to focus."

"But you—"

"I said enough. It's over. It's done. Just drive."

Blot wasn't interested in further conversation, so it wasn't until he was in Cox's office that Alan had to cope with another potentially disastrous verbal exchange. Whatever it was Cox had in mind to discuss, he was excited about it.

Cox shut the office door and sat down in his beaten-up office chair. "Fontaine. These pictures."

"They're just the first set," Alan said, handing over a memory card with the originals. "I promise we'll have better stuff in the next session."

Alan wanted to be quick on the defensive. Regardless of just how strong or weak his plan for the prison was, there was certainly not going to be a chance for it to succeed if Cox pulled the plug on the return trip.

"Most of them are trash. Absolute trash. May as well be in a brochure for the prison. Good framing and all that. Technical stuff is solid. But flavorless. I can sell them. But these aren't award worthy."

"The main focus was the cellblock, sir," Alan said.

"Right," Cox said. "The cellblock." His face lit up with the sort of smile that seemed to be begging to be wrapped around a cigar in a black-and-white movie.

"These!" He turned his monitor to show some of the shots Alan took. "These are what I pay you for. Look at them. Look how sinister they look. Some of them, right down the barrel of the camera. Some of them, just sort of sneakily aside. These... I *love* these. I've got to get legal on it to see if we need releases to use them. I mean, they're prisoners. We can use these however we like, right?"

"I'm not sure, sir."

"Point is, I can see a thousand places for these. You could stitch them together into an essay or whatever artsy idea you had, sure. But these'll sell for all sorts of stuff. I see, I don't know... attack ads eating this stuff up. Look at this rough customer. Glad he's locked up. And if people are looking for the empathy angle, this little guy in the corner looks like a Jack Russell terrier in a kennel with a couple of Rottweilers. Good stuff. I don't know what it is about them, but you can just feel the grit. You feel the *evil* in some of these guys."

Cox flipped through the images, raving about them. Each time he stopped on a close-up to talk up how "you just can't buy" that sort of fear or simmering anger, it was a figure with a pair of glaring eyes peering out from behind him. Evidently, the best way to make someone look haunted was to have them be legitimately haunted.

Blot slid up beside Alan. "Seems like some of the shade makes it through even to the people who can't see them directly," she said.

"Doesn't quite come through in the video, if I'm honest," Cox said, bringing up one of the shots Marie-Anna had taken. "Can't say she did anything wrong. Light's a little low, but it adds to the atmosphere. It just... there's no *intensity* in it. I think we have all the video we need. But I've got some requests for you, when you go back in."

Alan's phone rang. He quickly pulled it from his pocket. It was Jessie. He dismissed the call. "Requests, sir?" he said.

"Yeah. This. More of this. If they try to give you more of that ten-cent-tour stuff, forget it. I want you *in* the cellblock. Hell, I want you in the *cell* if you can manage it. One-on-one. Nothing but you and these killers. Some of this good high-contrast stuff, too. I like the starkness of the flash. And see if you can get some action shots."

"You want action shots," Alan said. "In a prison."

"Yeah. Something vigorous, you know. Something with some impact."

"I'm pretty sure prison guards frown upon vigorous impacts."

He stirred the air with one hand. "You know what I mean. I want more pictures, and whatever you did to get these people squirming like a bag of eels? More of that, too. Big time. Now, as for these shots here..."

Alan's phone rang again. As before, it was Jessie.

"Am I interrupting your busy schedule, Fontaine?" Cox said.

"I'm sorry. I'll get them to stop calling," Alan said. He answered. "Jessie, sorry. I can't talk right now."

"It better be because you're too busy parking."

"Why?"

"Because I'm here in the parking lot behind the precinct, and I'm wondering why you're not."

"Why would I..." Alan trailed off as his eyes locked on the calendar on Cox's desk. It was the fifteenth. He slapped his head. "The forensic photo evaluation."

"Bingo."

"Listen, I'm in my boss's office, I can't—"

"Whoa, whoa, whoa," Cox said. "Don't you turn that down! You get in there and you get that job."

"Mr. Cox, I can't just—"

He leaned across the desk and clenched his teeth. "You know what sort of good it would do for both of our bottom lines if I had someone with an inside line to the police station? You get your ass down there."

"Jessie, I'm on my way there now."

"Great. I'll see if I can get them to move you to the end of the session."

He hung up and stood.

"Wait, my check for the first day," Alan said.

"Check at the end. Call it motivation to finish."

"I've got plenty of motivation, sir. What I'm looking for is rent money."

"Then come back with some more gold and you'll get plenty. Now run along."

The driver's seat was still warm from his last trip when he slipped back inside and started the engine.

"Were you always this harried?" Blot asked as the sun nudged her around the car.

"Gotta keep a lot of plates spinning to stay solvent in the world of the freelance arts." He rubbed his red-rimmed eyes. "I just wish saving the world wasn't one of the spinning plates."

"You're not saving the world. You're swimming against a tide. You and I are basically one soldier in a big battle. And I don't know what sort of stories they tell you here, but back home they make it pretty darn clear that one soldier doesn't win the battle."

"These days we have nuclear weapons, so I'd say one person can make a pretty big dent."

"Do *you* have nuclear weapons?"

"No."

"Then we're not winning any wars." She produced her pad. "What is it going to take for you to get this forensics job?"

"I don't know. I'm technically not done with my certification, and this is my first time doing a mock crime scene."

"But you've read about them?"

"In broad terms. It's just a matter of procedure. Take pictures according to their specifications. Why?"

"I want you to get this job."

"Why?"

"At least then you'd be surrounded by police all the time. Assuming none of them are unfriendly shades, that'd keep us pretty safe. More importantly, you'd have an outlet for your ridiculous hero tendencies." She sneered. "Even if it *did* mean you'd be spending more time with *Jessie*."

"I have coworkers at Cox Media, too."

"It isn't the coworking I'm worried about."

"Then what's the problem?"

"I've watched television. I've watched videos. I know how humans work. First you're working together. Then you're eating lunch together a few times a week. Then you're eating dinner together every night. Then I'm sharing a bed with the two of you. It's crowded enough in there already with just the two of us."

"I think you're overreacting just a bit."

"We'll find out, won't we? Just promise me that if you're going to do some of those silly romantic things you humans do, you'll do the candlelit dinner. I like candlelight. Second only to moonlight in freedom of movement for me."

He chuckled. "If you say so."

Alan arrived at the parking lot where the crime scene was being mocked up. Some threatening gray clouds had rolled in. Combined with a whistling bit of wind, he very much suspected a storm was on the way. He hoped it would be rain. Somehow, performing a potentially lethal operation in a prison while the city was recovering from a late-season snow storm seemed like it would make a bad situation worse.

Jessie flagged him down. "That was quick," she said, leaning down to his window. "You must've... holy moly, you look like hell."

"Been burning the candle at both ends," he said. "Do I just park anywhere?"

"Over there. Behind the SWAT truck. You've got some time. They just started assessing the guy before you."

She paced along beside him and, when he climbed out of the car, gave him a hug. Alan tried to avoid making eye contact with Blot, whom he could feel glaring at him.

215

"Do they just park these things in a regular parking lot?" he asked.

"They've got some training sessions scheduled throughout the day. They'll get back to it once the CSI stuff is wrapped up, according to the supervisor. So what's up? You've been doing the hustle since before college. I've never seen you this run-down."

"I've just got this, plus that prison thing. They've got me frazzled."

"Did something go wrong?" she asked.

"Not exactly. But I've got to go back there in a couple of days."

She slapped him on the back. "That's awesome! You don't get to do something a second time if it didn't work out the first time, right?"

"It's going to be rough. That's all," he said, rubbing his face.

"You'll do great. Just like you'll do great with this. It's a fish in water, right? No one's asking you to do something you aren't already a pro at. It's just using your skills in different ways."

Alan nodded dully. Jessie rocked on her heels a bit. She seemed to be running through something in her head. When she came upon the thought she was searching for, it came tumbling out with the same enthusiasm she applied to seemingly every statement.

"Hey, you ever see inside one of these?" she asked, slapping the side of the SWAT van. "The morning session for the SWAT crew 'less lethal' drills. That's one of the reasons we were able to do some prep-work for the assessment you'll be doing."

"I can't say I've ever seen the inside of one. Except in the movies."

"It's super cool, check it out. If nothing else, it'll get us out of the wind."

She grabbed the door and pulled it open. Without the engine running, the lights inside stayed dim, but that suited Blot just fine, as she slipped up the wall beside Alan and eagerly looked over the endless array of crates, canisters, and cubbies.

"Should we be in here?" Alan asked.

"Probably not," Jessie said with a devilish grin.

"What's all this stuff?" Blot said, awe in her voice.

"You want to know what this stuff is?" Jessie offered.

"You read my mind."

"I actually had to do some training with this stuff. Back away. 'Less lethal' doesn't mean 'less dangerous.'"

He stepped back. The overcast sky meant Blot was easily able to linger inside.

"We've got the assorted Taser-type stuff, but that doesn't get much use in SWAT situations. Over here are flash-bang grenades. Those are serious business. Huge flash of light to blind people, percussive blast to disorient them. I watched the full-scale training last summer, and you can feel these things in your chest from well beyond the so-called safe distance. These are pepper-pellets for the air gun. I actually had to experience these and let me tell you, it'll ruin your day in a hurry..."

She worked her way through the full assortment with the enthusiasm of a kindergartener during show-and-tell. For the life of him, Alan couldn't explain why, but hearing her bubbly, up-beat summary of crowd-control devices was remarkably effective at pushing his worries aside. If someone like Jessie could be so excited about them, they couldn't be all bad, could they?

"I haven't used one of these since the academy." She slid something from a belt holster. "Expandable baton."

She flicked her wrist, and the small black cylinder clacked out to about triple its length. It was simple, just a collapsing steel bar with a knob on the end. It may as well have been an oversize car antenna. But as it whistled through the air, it was easily the most frightening weapon she'd identified for him.

"Easy with that thing," he said with a laugh.

"Not to twist your arm, but if you were to take the test and get on the waiting list for the force, you'd learn how to use one of these babies."

Something inside the van rattled.

"Don't let her look," Blot blurted.

Alan glanced in her direction to discover his shadow was curled down into one of the cubbies, rummaging through it.

"Hey, you mind if I pick your brain on something?" Alan said quickly, before Jessie noticed the sound.

"As long as it doesn't take too long. Looks like you're just about up." She slid the baton into its holster and tossed it into the open cubby.

"Let's say I wanted to carry something to protect myself on my next trip through the prison, what would you recommend? You've clearly got a firm grip on the equipment."

"You won't need to worry about self-defense. They run a tight ship over there."

"Sure, but if I needed to, could I get something like this to have on me, just in case?"

"Not a chance. You don't cross over into a holding area or a cell with something that could be used against other inmates or the staff. It probably took a pile of paperwork to let you bring your camera gear in. I've seen some of those lenses you use. You could lay someone out with one of those, no problem."

"Yeah. That makes sense," he said.

Blot slid out of the van with a smile like a cat who'd just caught a mouse.

"Seems to me like you're pretty sure something bad is going to go down. Do you know something I don't know?"

"You have no idea, Jessie."

"Fontaine? Fontaine!"

"Over here, sir!" Jessie called.

In the distance the gruff Lieutenant Stockton scanned the parking lot and spotted him. "What are you doing in the SWAT van?"

"Just doing an impromptu demonstration of the force's dedication to reduced lethality."

"Get over here. You're up."

The specific assessment method in use wasn't what one might call an industry standard. He'd read up on it, and to his great relief, what he found when the assessment began was pretty much what had been in the book. A series of staged crime scenes had been set up. Before each he was directed to the area's evidence of interest. The equipment was a camera a step or two down the quality scale from his own, but the settings and controls were familiar to him.

As the assessment rolled on, he slipped into a comfortable autopilot. Establishing shots of the entire area. Careful focus and a steady hand for detail shots. Dropping markers for classification and scale. The crime scenes were simple enough. Broken glass here, false blood spatter there. It was like a particularly grim version of the still-life photography he'd been doing for years. All the while, Lieutenant Stockton watched with crossed arms and a sour look on his face. The rest of the hopefuls looked on. They'd been through the whole process already, and from the looks on their faces, they hadn't been terribly enthusiastic about it the first time. If there weren't a half-dozen far more pressing matters for him to worry about, Alan probably would have been anxious that the police would object to an outsider treading on their turf. If that was the case, they were at least professional enough to behave themselves.

After each series of shots, he delivered the camera to Stockton so that he could download and review the images. Like Cox, he didn't so much have a good poker face as a very limited range of expressions. Whereas Cox was some flavor of angry all the time, Lieutenant Stockton was some flavor of impatient.

The last of the scenes had a handful of shell casings scattered about the ground. He worked through it as he had for the first few tests, but after the last photo, he paused.

"You ready to turn in?" Stockton said.

Alan squinted into the wind.

"What are you thinking?" Blot said.

"It's windy. And these shell casings are round."

He murmured quietly. Onlookers would have imagined he was just talking to himself. At any rate, they certainly wouldn't have imagined he was talking to his shadow.

"What about it?" she said.

"I just want to make sure—"

"Make sure none of the casings rolled away. Got it."

She stretched herself as far as the diffused sunlight would allow, weaving between the increasingly antsy police officers while Alan craned his head about.

"Ha! Got it!" Blot called.

Alan turned in her direction.

"Excuse me. I just need to get through here." He worked his way between the police officers and forward another couple of paces to the curb around the edge of the parking lot. Blot was helpfully pointing directly to the shell casing, but Alan made a show of looking around a bit before he crouched beside the casing and treated it like a miniature crime scene of its own. When he was through, he delivered his camera to Lieutenant Stockton one last time.

"What was that about?" he asked as he took the camera.

"It was windy. I figured some of the evidence might have gotten away."

Stockton took a deep breath. Alan squinted, anticipating a gale-force scolding. Instead, when he spoke, it was with quiet intensity.

"First, what you need to know is this. What you did? That job belongs to the detectives, not the photographers." He turned to the other police. "And you? How is it that you are all members of the force and *you* didn't think to see if the evidence had scattered? That casing was there out of the corner of my eye for the entire test, and it took a raw photographer to not only *think* of expanding the area of focus, but to actually *find* it."

He turned back to Alan and gave him a slap on the back that nearly knocked the wind out of him. "Good job. We'll be in touch."

Alan coughed lightly. "Thank you, sir." He looked to the other police and was treated to the angry stares he'd been anticipating when he first showed up.

"That's it. Assessment over," Stockton said.

Alan blinked for a moment.

"Wow," Blot said from his feet. "That was easy. Tell me again why we're not doing this instead of chasing celebrities who don't want their picture taken, or fighting supernatural threats by joining forces with murderous cults."

The police officers filed away. Jessie practically pranced up and delivered another punishing slap to Alan's back. "I knew you'd kill it!" She glanced at her watch. "Listen, I've got to go. I can only stay away from the desk for so long, but before I go, you were worried about the prison thing, right?"

"Yeah."

"Let me ask you this. Would you feel better if I came along?"

"What? No!" he said quickly.

Blot echoed the sentiment. "She better not come."

"Why not? I've got a buddy in the sheriff's office. We work together a lot when doing prisoner transport. I'm sure I can wrangle some cross-department nonsense to get permission to, I don't know, 'oversee' the visit," she said, adding air quotes.

"Jessie, things are going to go down. I just know it, and I don't want you to get hurt."

"Lucky for me 'not getting hurt when things go down' was more or less the entire focus of my training." She gave him a final slap on the back. "And by the way, you've never had to lean on alpha-male machismo before, so let's not start now, hmm? Anyway, I've been wanting to see how you work for a while now. This'll be a good chance."

"But—"

It was too late, Jessie was already trotting away. "See you there!"

"I'm beginning to wonder if either of us has any control over our own lives," Blot muttered from his feet.

"Yeah, I'm beginning to wonder that too," Alan said.

"Well you'd better figure it out, because you getting pushed around pushes me around."

He sighed. "Let's go to the diner. I need to think."

They paced toward his car.

"Hey, what were you doing, rummaging around in the SWAT van?" he asked.

"Don't worry about it."

"No lady friend today?" said the waitress, walking Alan back to the usual booth.

"Nope. Just about as alone as I get these days," he replied. He plopped down in the booth, waited for his coffee, and used a napkin to readjust the lighting for Blot.

"So," Blot said, sipping the coffee. "You need to 'think,' huh?"

"Yes."

"Is there any chance, any at all, that you're going to be thinking about something useful? Or is this just one of those tying-yourself-in-knots sorts of thinking that you enjoy so much?"

"The knots one," he said.

"Of course. Let me guess. You're worried about Jessie."

"How did you know?"

"You're not complicated. You start doing stupid things when people threaten people you care about. People except *me*, of course. They threaten your family, you throw a punch. Now Jessie is butting her nose into things, so you're going to endanger yourself *and* me by worrying about people besides us some more."

"Can you blame me?"

"I can, and do, blame you, yes." She crossed her arms and leaned back. "You have far too many family and friends. They're more trouble than they're worth."

"Since we 'met,' and that's a very generous term for the circumstances of your arrival, you've encountered both my parents and Jessie. That's it. I hardly have an overabundance of friends and family."

"That's already three more friends and family members than *I* have."

"My point is, I can't afford to lose any."

"My point is, you can afford to lose three."

"Stop it. I'm being serious. And you're not scoring any points by being heartless. If I thought like that, where would you be right now?"

"Same place, because you can't get rid of me without dying."

He glared at his shadow.

"Fine, fine," she said. "Point taken. Kindness works out well for other people. But what are you going to do about this?"

224

"I don't know. That's the problem. I don't... I'm not sure I can live with the thought that doing what I feel I have to do is going to keep dragging people into the same mess I'm wading through."

"Do I need to go back and reiterate the points I've made about how being a hero is an inherently terrible thing and is to be avoided?"

He gave her a weary look. "I don't have the patience for 'I told you so' right now, Blot."

She took a deep breath. He braced himself for any of a thousand snide, biting, and potentially well-deserved jabs. Instead, a frustrated sigh followed. She glanced about to ensure she wouldn't be observed, then tugged the mug from the table and slid down beside him, where the shadows were deepest and thus she was most comfortable.

"Do you trust Jessie?"

"Your dad seems like a pretty strong guy," she said.

He gave her a suspicious look. "He is..."

"And judging from her taste in coffee and her hospitality, your mother seems to have a pretty good head on her shoulders and heart in her chest."

"She does."

"Probably where you got those things."

"I guess."

"And Jessie. Irritating as it has been to have to cope with her hanging around all the time, she seems pretty sharp."

"Yes."

"Knows how to get things done."

"Yeah."

"If she's an officer of the law, she's probably got pretty extensive training."

"I'm sure she does."

"And if she hasn't been fired, she's not a total screwup."

"Obviously not."

"Are any of these people fragile? Doddering? Helpless?"

"No."

"Do you have anything about you that makes you special? That makes you better suited to the challenges at hand than they are? Besides *me*, of course."

"I guess the only difference is, I know about the real problem."

"Are we on the same page that if they knew any more than what you told them, it would make them *more* of a target and thus put them in greater danger?"

"Yes."

"Then stop acting like it's your job to protect them."

"I got them into it."

"I'm with you every moment of every day, Alan. I don't think I missed the part where you went and begged your family and friends to step into the line of fire. Despite your best efforts, I'm pretty sure you didn't beg Dun to make them targets either. You don't *nearly* have the control over your life to take responsibility for what happens to them. By the void, Alan, Jessie threw herself into the mix of her own volition. These are adults. They got through an awful lot of life without you. You haven't been anointed by some unseen hand to be their defender. Our time and resources are limited. If you squander everything fretting about what will happen to everyone else, you're going to be charging in unprepared. Your mother and father will lose a son. Jessie will lose a friend. I'll lose a host, and my life. Do us all a favor, and for once in your life, be *selfish* for a second and think about your own survival."

She took a long, slow sip of coffee. "They want you alive, for their own selfish reasons. I *need* you alive, for my own selfish reasons. You can please a lot of people simply by *not dying*. And you can achieve that by worrying about *you* instead of *them*."

Blot handed the mug up just in time for the waitress to come by and refresh it, as well as deliver a split toasted corn muffin that Alan had been craving since he'd seen Jessie eating her pancakes.

"How long have you been planning that speech?" Alan asked.

"Since birth. Enlightened self-interest is my favored philosophy. It sure beats optimism in terms of being prepared for what comes next."

He passed down the refilled mug. "So what comes next?"

"We plan. We pretend Jessie isn't there. We pretend your parents aren't there. We try to imagine every bad thing that might come along, and we figure out how to get out alive if they happen."

He nodded. "I guess we should get started. I don't suppose you have a spare one of those pads and pencils for notes."

She flicked a shadowy hand. Three pristine pads and two pencils popped into three dimensions.

"... Just how many of those did you steal?"

"Enough. Now grab one and let's get started."

CHAPTER 9

The preparations were done. The decisions were made. The plan was unfolding. It felt like the blink of an eye. The time had just vanished. Now, Alan marched through the hallways of the prison, with Brink stalking beside him. The guards were a few paces back, and the guide was a few paces forward. It provided Brink and Alan with a modicum of privacy as they entered Cellblock 33.

"Have that camera ready," Brink warned. "Once it starts, there is going to be pure chaos."

Alan nodded and clutched his camera close. He'd affixed the largest of his flashes and the heftiest of his battery packs to the camera. It had made it unwieldy. Getting good pictures out of it would be difficult. But then, today wasn't about good pictures.

They approached the door to the cellblock. Brink held out a meaty palm, signaling for Alan to wait while the guide droned on for a moment. Alan nodded and turned toward the hallway. It looked terribly long to him. The next time he traveled through this place, he would be at a full sprint, pursued by angry shades. It made every step away from the nearest emergency exit feel like a mile.

"We're good," Brink announced.

Alan turned and slid his thumb across the camera's controls. His nerves were starting to get to him. Fingers that had danced across the controls a hundred times before felt sluggish and clumsy. Words he'd seen written across the screen for hours each day through the last few years suddenly lacked meaning, becoming just jumbles of shapes smeared across a glowing panel. As the door clicked open, he finally got the camera's flash to cooperate. The comforting whine of a beefy capacitor charging up had a wavering depth to it he didn't recognize. Now would *not* be a good time for it to fail on him. But it didn't matter. There was no turning back now.

Brink led the way into the cellblock. It was darker than he remembered. And colder. What little light there was cast sharp, impenetrable shadows inside each of the cells. It looked like the barred doors each sealed off an inky void. Like darkness itself was being held prisoner.

"Where are they?" Alan said.

His throat was tight. His chest was tighter. The rattling of his heart felt like the beginning of a well-earned panic attack.

"They'll be along soon enough," Brink said. He reached into his bag and produced something that looked like a golden egg. "It is going to happen, and it is going to happen fast."

"I'm ready," Alan lied.

Brink nodded once and threw down the egg. It struck the ground and shattered. Pure, piercing light spilled out from within and pooled on the floor like molten iron. He scrambled back a step to avoid the pool, then watched as it cooled into a ring of smoldering runes.

Alan looked up from the ancient, arcane writing. The symbols felt as though they were burned into his eyes.

"What are you waiting for?!" Brink shouted.

He turned to find Brink had dashed for the door. Alan tried to follow. He stumbled and tripped, his legs unwilling to cooperate. All around him, cell doors rattled. Then came a deep, horrible end-of-the-world sort of sound. It was a thumping that Alan felt in his bowels, like the sound of the devil himself slamming a steel door. He turned to see something enormous smash at one of the cell doors on the second level. It was peeled aside like tin foil and sent wheeling through the air. At the peak of its arc, the jagged metal sliced through the overhead light. In a flash of sparks and a tinkle of glass, the whole room went dark.

Silence descended just as quickly as the darkness. Only the glow of Alan's viewfinder offered even a hint of light, and his shaky breathing was the only sound. His mind screamed at him to run, but where? It was pitch-black. He couldn't even tell where the walls were, let alone the door.

A sizzling sound drew his attention. Red light seared across his vision. It was Brink. He'd sparked a standard road flare that cast a tiny circle of red light. Alan's eyes didn't have time to adjust before a blur of something black and twisted struck Brink. He was knocked into the darkness. The flare fell to the ground.

Alan suddenly remembered he had his camera. He raised it and snapped a picture. For a terrifying instant, a tableau of inmates revealed itself to him. Each of them was free from his cell. Each of them had murder in his eyes. And among them, a savage, misshapen behemoth. As the flash recharged, he saw a gaunt foot come down upon the glowing runes. They were snuffed out like a cigarette butt. Alan tried to take another photo, but the camera wouldn't respond. As a last desperate act, he dove for the fallen flare and held it up. It revealed the jagged grin of Todd in his most monstrous form yet staring down at him. Bony fingers wrapped around his throat. Todd hauled him into the air. Alan gasped for breath.

"No hard feelings," Todd said.

He reared back. The claws of his other hand struck Alan's abdomen. He shut his eyes and shuddered...

But there was no pain. When he opened them again, the glow of the flare revealed the same horrid grin. Todd was frozen, unblinking. And sitting on his shoulder was the impish "true" form of Blot.

She leaned on the shifter's head. "Yeah. That's pretty much how I saw it going too."

Todd curled away like so much black smoke, dropping both Alan and Blot to the ground. She landed daintily. Alan did not. He collapsed to the floor.

"This is a dream," Alan said, sitting up on his elbows.

"This time, anyway," Blot said.

"What was this supposed to do, scare me?"

"What are you asking me for? It's *your* dream."

"You didn't do this?"

"I can't do anything of this scope in your dreams without your coop-eration. Do you remember giving me permission?" She leaned back and crossed her arms, a wall suddenly behind her. "This is all your doing. So if the question is 'was this supposed to scare me,' it's probably safe to say no. It isn't supposed to scare you. All of this is your subconscious letting you know you're already good and scared."

She straightened up, then crouched down to lend him a hand in stand-ing. "It's not too late to change your mind. Until things started to get interesting in here, I was looking over those wards I stole. I don't know what most of them do, but a couple of them match the ones on your doors exactly. They've *got* to be more distraction wards. We could apply one to your car and then..."

"We've been through this and through this."

"Well forgive me for trying to talk you into not making this little dream a reality." She snapped her fingers, and the lights in the slowly fading prison of his mind snapped on. "See all those? Those aren't make believe."

She marched up to a particularly burly fellow who was holding a shiv. "See this guy here? He was at the table eating fruit salad when you visited. You've got a picture of him up on your laptop right now. He's real. He's there, waiting for you."

"Someone's got to do something," Alan said.

"It doesn't have to be you."

"It *does*. Because I'm the one who knows it has to be done."

"You aren't a hero, Alan. Not a capital *H* hero. You've done some impressive stuff, but you're not the dashing knight who slays the dragon. They don't exist. The dashing knights I mean. Also, dragons. But mostly heroes. They aren't real."

"I know heroes aren't real, Blot. I know there aren't people waiting in the wings to step in and stop the bad guys from winning. There's just people who see that something needs to be done and decide to do it. That's it. That's the only difference between a hero and a regular person. A hero decides to do the thing that needs to be done. And those people *must* exist. Because this world wasn't conquered by your people the last time they came through, or the time before that. Someone has always come forward and done the job. Maybe they were all like me. Maybe there was a moment like this after every eclipse."

Blot opened her mouth, then pulled back.

"What?" Alan said, expecting more pushback.

"Maybe you're right." She lowered her head. "Maybe there *is* a moment like this after every eclipse. And maybe that is the whole point."

"The whole point of what?"

"The whole point of me. At my level of training, the *main* level of training, they hammer one thing in over and over again. If you can't get your host to play along, then just keep your head down and keep your eyes open. If victory isn't assured, then stay out of the fight. Maybe it's just another way that people like Dun make sure no one interferes. The strong shades step up and do battle. They command the others around. If a weak shade gets isolated? If they start to lose their nerve? They just... infect the hosts with their weakness."

She ran her fingers through her hair. "It isn't like I don't know that keeping you from going into that prison will mean, more likely than not, that Dun and Driss's plan will succeed. By the void, if you weren't *you*, you might even have accused me of still working for them in trying to hold you back."

Blot's jaw tightened. "They cast me out, they tried to kill me. And I'm *still* playing my part. I'm a traitor and they've still got me doing exactly what they need me to do." She stamped her foot. The dream around her wavered.

"You might be giving them a little more credit than they deserve," Alan said.

"You don't know them like I do. Everything is about manipulation. Get better at it. More nuanced. More subtle. And more steps ahead. You have a game here. Chess. We have one at home called preek. It's like chess with little figurines on a board, but there are more of them. Not just little men and monarchs and buildings. There are birds and fish and demons. Seventy-three pieces. The game isn't about capturing pieces, either. It's about maneuvering the other player into playing the piece you want them to play *when* you want them to play it. And the game starts *long* before you set up the board. The game starts before you even challenge someone. The grandmasters become friends with their opponents. They talk to them daily. They watch their moves. And all the while, it's just to try to nudge them unknowingly to make the precise moves you want them to. When the game starts, they write the name of the piece, the move, and the step in the game when it will happen on a card."

Her fists tightened. "Somewhere Dun's got a card that says 'Blot does nothing, just before the big plan.' We are all just pieces... Every shade. Everyone who poured through that portal during the eclipse. We've been on the board since we were born."

She looked up. "We're doing it."

Alan gave her an uncertain look. "Did I persuade you, or did you?"

"What do you care? We're doing it. But I want to make one thing clear. I'm not dying for this. I'll do what it takes to help you, but if push comes to shove and there's just no way forward, I'm *not* dying for this cause, on their side *or* your side. The decision to shake off the shackles is *not* going to be the last decision I make."

He held out his hand. "Sounds good to me."

She shook his hand. "Wake up so we can get started. We need three plans."

"Why three?"

"One for if Brink is really on our side, one for if he isn't, and one for if everything goes wrong."

Alan gripped his steering wheel tight and glanced at the clock on his car's dashboard. It had been a long night and a busy morning. And unlike last time, he remembered every bit of preparation. This was no dream.

"Forty-five minutes to go. Are we sure we've got everything?" he said.

"I've got your backup camera and one of those big flashlights," Blot said.

"I've got my flashlight, my big flash, both of my main cameras, and my film camera." He glanced at the clock again, then back to the road.

"Only one thing missing, then," Blot said.

"Why hasn't he called yet?" Alan said.

"Maybe Todd got to him. Or one of the other shades. He *is* with the Dawn. This isn't the only battle they're fighting today, I'd wager."

Alan stopped at a light. He tugged the phone from his pocket and plopped it on the seat. There were no missed calls. "I think we need to be ready with plan B if he doesn't show."

"I don't like plan B, Alan. Plan B is our weakest plan. It isn't even a plan. It's a notion."

"It's the surest plan we have. Just goad the shades into doing something that gets the Cellblock 33 program shut down and the tour with the bigwigs canceled. It's not perfect. We've still got a prison full of scheming shadows to worry about, but it'll keep them from immediately getting a foothold in a position of power."

"Yes, but the problem is, 'goading the shades into doing something' is more than likely going to mean uncontrolled violence. And with no one else on our side, that isn't going to end well for us."

"Maybe if we just—"

The phone rang. It was Brink.

"Oh thank god!" Alan tapped the speakerphone button. "You didn't leave much time to spare."

"Preparations take time."

"So what's up? What do you need me to do to get you in?"

"It is very simple. The focus is Cellblock 33, correct?"

"Yes."

"I acquired a layout of the prison. There are a handful of staff bathrooms. One of them is near an emergency exit. It will be two hallways before Cellblock 33 assuming you are approaching it from the east."

"You said this was very simple," Alan said.

"Just listen. It will have an automatic alarm that will sound when it is opened. That alarm will be triggered by a small white sensor block on the upper doorframe."

"You can tell he does this sort of thing more often than we do," Blot said, genuine appreciation in her tone.

"You will simply need to pull either of the two wires in the sensor block, then open the door enough that it is no longer latched and prop it there. I'll be along shortly after, in uniform. When you see me, do not react. We don't know each other until we are alone. Your presence should be enough of a disruption that I will be able to avoid being identified as an outsider until after the job is done."

"But how are you going to get as far as that emergency door? It isn't like there are any doors that just lead straight to the outside. And how are you going to know when it's safe to come in? Aren't there cameras that will—"

"I've taken care of everything. Just do your part. Once we are inside, I'll find a defensible position near Cellblock 33 to set up the ritual. If you and your shade want to avoid its effects, you'll need to get at least thirty yards away from where the ritual starts, but we'll cross that line when we come to it."

"Okay. Fine. Blot, have you got all that?"

"Two hallways west of Cellblock 33, a bathroom near a fire exit, pull the wire from the white thing on the door, then the Dawn will come and work a ritual to permanently cripple my brethren," Blot said.

"We've got it," Alan said.

"Then stay focused and this just might succeed. Good luck to us all." Brink hung up without saying goodbye.

"That guy is on the ball. I'm starting to think if he'd had another couple of days, he wouldn't have needed us at all," Alan said.

"Yes." Blot narrowed her eyes. "I'm starting to think that too..."

The phone rang again. This time it was Jessie. Alan tapped the speakerphone.

"Hello?"

"Hey, Alan. Good news! It took some favors, but I managed to get myself assigned as an 'observer' for the prison's new policies. I pitched it to the chief as a way to maybe help out with our holding cell issues what with this influx of suspects and he bought it."

"Jessie, I didn't want you to—"

"Oh, calm down. I know you were nervous about things, and now you've got backup!"

"Ask if she's allowed to bring her gun inside," Blot said.

"She's not going to be able to bring her gun inside," he hissed.

"Who are you talking to?" Jessie asked.

"No one. Listen, you're sure you want to do this?"

"Not only am I sure I want to do this, I'm already at the prison. I called you now because I'm about to hand over my phone to the security folks."

"But—"

"You're on your way, right?"

"Yes, but—"

"Great! See you in a minute. Bye!"

She hung up. Alan slumped in the driver's seat.

"I've now got two of my friends into a life-threatening situation..."

"Two?" Blot said.

"Yeah. You and Jessie."

Blot's lips briefly flashed into a smirk. She wrestled it away and crossed her arms.

"One friend and one soul-bonded partner, Alan. I'm a little higher up on the social ladder than friend." She turned her eyes to the road. "Just remember that, if it comes down to me and her."

Alan stepped into the security-clearance room for the third and, regardless of how things went, the final time. He briefly mused over the worrisome fact that he was now more familiar with the prison and its procedures than he was with the post office. It was an unpleasant indicator for how his life had been going of late. One significant difference this time was a friendly face waiting for him.

"There you are!" Jessie said.

She was hanging out on the "cleared" side of the room. He'd seen her in civilian clothes before, and he'd seen her in her day-to-day uniform, but her outfit was unique today. It wasn't a uniform per se. It was a very specific type of semiformal outfit that somehow screamed law enforcement. It was something about the amount of starch and sharp creases on display. He grinned at the obvious tactics behind such an outfit. This *had* to be some sort of shorthand between police, guards, and deputies to let each other know, *Don't worry, I'm on the team.*

"Wow. You're armed for bear, huh?" Jessie said as Alan stepped up to the flimsy folding table they'd set up beside the metal detector and x-ray machine.

"It's just me today. I've got to handle both photos and video," he said.

It was technically true, but anyone familiar with photography and videography would question the honesty of the statement. He had three cameras on his person, each with some manner of secondary flash attached. The huge camera bag was large enough that it couldn't go through the x-ray machine. A portly, well-kept man was studiously hand-checking the bag when a second guard entered the room. As expected, Alan's flashlight was the first thing to go. His phone was the second. The pile of disallowed tools was growing steadily, but Alan had erred so far on the side of caution that he was confident he'd get through with a reasonable assortment of self-defense tools against the shades.

"Uh-oh..." Blot muttered.

Alan looked up and quickly determined the problem. The new guard wasn't so different from the one going through his bag. His shadow, however, was quite different. A pair of piercing white eyes glared up from it as it slid across the ground.

"We've got one of the guards..." Blot said. "Dun and Driss are making progress."

The shade-afflicted guard tapped his associate on the shoulder. "They want you in there on the monitors. I'll handle this," he said.

"Sure thing," said the first guard, happily handing the job over.

"Remember. Nothing with bright light," croaked his shadow.

"No cameras," the guard said.

"I'm here as a photojournalist. I need my cameras," Alan said. "I got special permission." He slipped the printed-out, signed letter that had gotten him through last time.

The guard took the page and looked it over. "'By special order of the warden'..." he muttered to himself. "Fine. One camera."

"I'm doing photo and video."

"You don't need three cameras for that."

"One for dedicated photo, one for dedicated video, and one for B-roll."

"You can't take three cameras in there."

"Two is the absolute minimum," Alan insisted.

"... Fine. But the bag stays here. Too many metal buckles. Could be hiding contraband."

"I need the bag. Taking proper photos takes a lot of equipment," Alan said.

The guard poked the bag. "Explain the purpose of each. I'll decide if it's necessary."

Alan sighed and started to sift through the contents. Blot, in the meantime, could only glare at her counterpart on the floor beside her.

"So..." seethed the other shade. "You came back."

"It's his job," Blot said simply.

"Don't bother lying to me. You wouldn't let him come back here unless you both had a death wish or you both had a plan. And you're too much of a scrapper to come here expecting to die."

"You have no idea how much of a scrapper I am," she said with a defiant grin. "If I was you, I'd back off."

For nearly a half hour, Alan and the guard engaged in an extended negotiation. Spare batteries? No. The session length didn't warrant it. If his batteries ran low, he could request a spare be fetched. Supplemental flash? Absolutely not. Cellblock 33 has a strict illumination limit as part of the project. The same went for fill lights and other more esoteric lighting systems. By the end, Alan was left with his film camera, one of his DSLRs, and an audio recorder. That was it. He wasn't even allowed to keep his belt.

"Wow," Jessie said as Alan stepped through the metal detector a final time. "They take security even more seriously here than at the station."

Alan nodded as he took the two permissible cameras from the table and hooked them over his neck.

"So, you've been through this once before," Jessie began. "Anything you think I should be looking out for, before the liaison from the prison comes out and talks—"

A bleep from the metal detector interrupted her. Alan was already through the detector, but as Blot was dragged through, helpless against the overhead lights, the machine had weakly pinged.

"She's carrying something," the guard's shade hissed.

Alan and the guard gave each other a hard look. Nothing needed to be said. Both knew that there was nothing *official* the guard and his shade could do about it. It wasn't as though the guard could demand to search his shadow. And even if the shade came along and shook her down, all Blot would have to do was simply let go of a piece of her equipment. Every inch of this place was under surveillance. A flashlight or camera simply appearing, out in the open, with witnesses, was going to raise more questions than Dun would want asked.

"Is he clear?"

The question came from the doorway leading into the prison proper. Reggie, their guide from the first visit, had arrived. From the look on his face, his zeal for potential publicity had not cooled.

"We're having a malfunction with the metal detector. We should hold him here until we get a technician in," the guard suggested.

"Just use the hand wand," Reggie said, reaching into his pocket. "I've got some additional information to share, and I want to be certain we don't run out of time."

He revealed a stack of index cards as the guard reluctantly fetched the handheld metal detector. Alan set down the equipment, and the detector came up clean, thanks mostly to the fact that no reasonable person could justify running a metal detector over a shadow.

"Good. Excellent, let's go," the guide said.

"This seems like awfully strict treatment for someone who is supposed to be doing documentation," Jessie said.

"Prison policy, of course," Reggie assured her. "We are particularly protective of Cellblock 33. It is in many ways something of a social experiment, so there's not just the matter of the safety of the inmates, but the potential contamination of the data. Results like these are not to be taken lightly. As a matter of fact..."

Now that he had a new person to run through his sales pitch with, the guide's attention slid from Alan. This left him walking shoulder to shoulder with the subverted guard. He leaned forward a bit and looked at his name tag.

"Martin. Is that your first or last name?" Alan asked.

"Last," he said.

"How long have you been..." He glanced pointedly at the man's shade. "Part of the team?"

"You're here to take photos, not to talk. Just keep moving and behave yourself. I'm watching you."

Blot was having a similar confrontation with her counterpart, though, as they were unobserved by the guide, they were free to be a bit less subtle.

"You should have stayed away," the rival shade warned. "Dun made himself clear. And Driss has made this place into something far too important to the cause to be left to the whims of a traitor."

"That's the nice thing about being a traitor. I don't have to do what Dun says anymore." She squinted at him. "You're weak. Probably just took this guy as a host a few days ago."

"That's not your concern."

She grinned. "No. It's *yours*."

Blot managed to fight against the influence of the overhead lights just enough to give him a sharp blow to the chest. The shade reeled but snapped quickly back into position and couldn't muster the strength to retaliate.

"New host means two things. You're practically powerless unless you started off with a monumental amount of strength. And somewhere, not too long ago, a human turned up dead."

She glanced up to see that the guard's jaw had tightened somewhat. "I suppose he knows. I suppose that's how you're keeping him in line. 'Do what I say or you die.' I tried that for a bit. There are better ways. You don't *have* to do what Dun says."

"Keep your traitorous mouth shut and you might just live."

Blot fought the influence of the light enough to give him a flick to the nose.

"You're a murderer, and I'm stronger than you. I think I could get behind this heroism thing if it involves pushing around people who deserve it."

Thanks to a full day of prior shooting, their tour was much abbreviated compared with the first one. It was all new to Jessie, though. She consumed the sights and explanations with the same zeal she seemed to treat each new experience with. But thanks to the overlap with her job, much of the information came with knowing nods and simple assertions that turned dense explanations into shorthand.

Alan snapped pictures more as a way to keep up his cover and settle his nerves than to actually get additional coverage. He'd nearly forgotten how easy it was to get an intriguing shot when the camera was being used *only* as a camera and not as a demonic deterrent. There was also some fiendish joy to be had in making sure the rival shade got caught in the flash. Even the relatively weak built-in flash was more than enough to scramble the shade a bit.

"Um, one question," Alan said.

"Of course."

"This is the east wing of the prison, correct?"

"That's right."

"Will we be heading straight into the cellblock from here? This hallway looks familiar."

"We will be heading there shortly. But first, I'm happy to say Dr. Vale has arranged for some of our more successful inmates to be out of their cells for questions, should you require them."

"One of them wouldn't happen to be Leonard Castro, would it?"

"Yes indeed. He is in the library right now. We'll be there in a moment."

"Right, uh, before we go, is there a bathroom this way?" he asked.

"Yes. Right down that hallway there. If you... Oh! Here's Dr. Vale now."

The doctor appeared out of a side hallway. She raised an eyebrow as she approached. Her eyes were set upon Jessie.

"Hello, Mr. Fontaine. Good morning, Mr. Filson." She held out her hand. "You would be Officer Hearst, correct?"

"That's right."

"You are here on very short notice, but I understand you are hoping to observe and potentially adopt some of our new policies, correct?"

"That is the plan. So far it all seems very standard. Well executed and orderly, but standard."

"As I'm sure has been made clear thus far, the cellblock itself contains most of our more revolutionary tactics. But I've taken the liberty of preparing a short demonstration for you, to catch you up on some of the key points in a more law-enforcement-oriented context."

"Oh, I'd intended to tag along with Alan here and watch over his shoulder."

"This will be a far more fruitful lesson, I assure you. Come this way. Mr. Filson, if you'd come along as well. I think your depth of knowledge will come in handy in clarifying some of the finer points."

"If you'd like," he said. "Martin, please escort Mr. Fontaine to the staff bathroom, then take him to the library. We will all meet in Cellblock 33 after you've met with Leonard again."

"I can head to the bathroom on my own," Alan said.

"No, no. I'm afraid you can't be moving about the prison unsupervised. But Martin will respect your privacy."

Before Alan or Jessie could object any further, the woman who was ostensibly there to help set Alan's rattled nerves at ease was walking away with the only non-shade-afflicted members of the tour group in tow. Alan turned to Martin. He took Alan firmly by the upper arm.

"The bathroom is this way," Martin said.

From the way he was looking askance at the guide and Jessie, the comment was more for their benefit than Alan's. He pulled Alan toward the same side hallway Dr. Vale had arrived from.

"I thought the bathroom was that way!" Alan said quickly.

The guide turned. "Martin, please. I realize we have a schedule to keep to, but you were told to escort Mr. Fontaine to the staff bathroom."

"Do it," Martin's shade instructed him. "We'll have him in the library soon enough. Maybe he's planning to take his own life and save us all a lot of trouble."

Martin sullenly tugged Alan in the direction of the bathroom. It wasn't far away. Sure enough, the emergency exit was directly beside it. A bank of light switches on the wall beside the door caught the attention of the guard's shade.

"Are those the switches for these lights?" he asked.

Martin nodded slowly.

"Shut off the lights in the hallway."

"That will look strange on the—"

"*Shut off the lights in the hallway!*" the shade repeated viciously. "We've been out of Cellblock 33 for too long. All this bright light is driving me mad!"

Martin approached the lights and shut them off. The shade rose up to the wall beside Alan.

"You realize there's nothing you can do, don't you? I don't care what sort of plan you think you are going to execute in that bathroom. Things are far too carefully assembled and far too far along for you to do any good."

"Why don't you just shake us down then? Right here? Do Dun and Driss proud and thwart the interlopers now?" Blot pointed a shadowy finger to the blinking red light of a surveillance camera. "Oh, right. Because we are in a prison and anything that camera picks up will ruin your precious plan. You say this thing is unbreakable, but all we have to do is get people asking questions and things will go downhill *real* quick."

She poked her head forward and nudged the shade in the chest. "We're in the position of strength here... whatever your name is."

"Shriff."

Blot's eyes squinted in a half-hidden wince. Clearly, she recognized the name.

"Shriff. You were one of Driss's strong-arms back home."

"That's right. I brought you in for a punishment once. You wouldn't remember me, I'm sure. You had bigger distractions to worry about that day."

Blot steeled herself. "Well you're weakened from a new host, and you can't do anything while the cameras are watching, so we *still* have the power."

Shriff looked to Martin, then to the bathroom door. "Are there cameras in the bathroom, Martin?"

"There are not," Martin said quietly.

The rival shade turned to Alan. "What are you waiting for, Fontaine? Answer the call of nature."

Alan's mind was quick to assemble a terrifying simulation of what sort of plans Martin and Shriff might have for him if he stepped into the bathroom now. Fortunately, the bathroom was never the reason he'd come here.

"You know," Alan said, raising the camera. "The contrast of light and dark in this hallway is really dramatic."

"Don't," Shriff ordered.

Alan depressed the shutter button. The camera released a dazzling burst of flashes. Blot was spared the worst of the light, and didn't need to be told how best to take advantage of the distraction. She fought her way to the door, teased a claw from the shadows just enough to slash the alarm sensor wire, and slid a hand between the door and the jamb until she'd unlatched the door. It barely opened at all. Not even enough to let a sliver of light in around the door. But it was enough that the latch wasn't engaged. She produced one of the endless sequence of pencils she'd stolen from Cox and slipped it between the door and the jamb to keep it from shutting.

Her timing and motion were perfect, as she'd only just finished when Martin angrily grabbed a handful of Alan's shirt and slapped the camera away to dangle at the end of its straps.

"Fontaine," Martin growled.

"If he's more interested in taking pictures than using the bathroom, then he's ready to go to the library. We've been away long enough that they won't suspect anything," Shriff said.

Martin grabbed Alan by the arm again and hauled him forward, leaving the lights off.

Jessie glanced to the door a few times as the guide worked his way through another carefully honed and generally redundant speech about the prison's various policies.

"This is one of three secondary security hubs in the prison," he said. "The primary security room is near administration, and has a complete bank of monitors and camera feeds with motion notification. This secondary security room has only three monitors, but with this panel here, we can pipe any of the feeds to the monitors, providing near-full functionality."

"Right. A good application of fairly standard security methodologies." Jessie glanced to Dr. Vale. "Tell me, does any of this relate to the Cellblock 33 project? I believe that was the focus of this little tour."

"I had thought our surveillance system would be of greater interest to an officer of the law," Dr. Vale said.

"And it's fascinating. But again, these are fairly standard security principles. The mall has a similar setup. It *is* an excellent execution. I'm just curious how it relates to Cellblock 33."

Dr. Vale's lips tightened slightly. For a moment she appeared distracted. When she spoke again, it was slowly. She was taking more care than usual to select her words.

"A considerable focus of the Cellblock 33 project is the improvement of inmate morale. As has been discussed, small quality-of-life improvements are a piece of this puzzle. Softer lighting, more carefully selected cellmates, and so on. But another component is building a degree of trust. We cannot realistically institute an honor system in a prison, but we have made several small strides in that regard. One of them is the promise that video surveillance will be decreased during what we deem to be low-risk portions of the day in low-risk areas. The goal is to afford a modicum of additional privacy and engender a feeling of trust. No single psychology applies to all inmates, but I have carefully interviewed and assessed all prisoners who are a part of the program, and it is my determination that each show certain behavioral markers that indicate they would respond well to such a technique."

Jessie tipped her head. "Keeping *less* of an eye on the prisoners is a technique?"

"It's very experimental," the guide said. "We are a progressive prison. If I can direct your attention to the project brief, which is posted in each of the security hubs, you'll find the list of areas with reduced rotation in the monitoring cycle."

Jessie picked up the laminated card the guide had indicated. It certainly lived up to the word "brief."

"Can you explain? Maybe I'm old-fashioned, but I'd think having a state-of-the-art security system and then choosing not to use it is a strange pair of policies."

"It is a nuanced psychological phenomenon," Dr. Vale said dismissively.

"I *love* psychology. It was almost my major back in college. I'd love to hear the thinking behind this."

Dr. Vale gave Jessie an even but stern look for a moment. "Providing privileges creates an internal pressure to behave in a manner deserving of them."

Jessie looked over the card. "And the library is on the low-surveillance list?"

"Part of the project includes increased access to the library and outside communication to those who have been particularly well-behaved."

"But Alan's headed to the library now, isn't he? He's documenting things. Surely it would be justifiable to bring him up on the feed."

She reached for the keyboard to tap through to the library feed, but Dr. Vale grabbed her hand.

"Officer Hearst, trust is a two-way street. Just as we give them our trust and expect them to earn it, it would be a hollow gesture if we didn't do as we promised."

"... Right..." Jessie said, less than convinced.

Alan was roughly shoved into the prison library. If he had been pressed to produce a list of the places in the world least likely to be sinister and foreboding, a library would have been near the top of it. Even in a prison, he would have thought the library would be the least terrifying place. Dun and his ilk had managed to disabuse him of that notion.

The overhead lights in the room had been shut off. What little light there was came from sturdy lamps bolted to the tables. Aside from Alan and the guard who escorted him, there were only three people in the library. Or at least, there were only three *hosts*. Lenny sat at the table. An additional guard flanked him on either side. Alan didn't have to check the shadows to know that they, too, had shades. There was something in their posture and the look in their eyes. These were men dangling at the ends of choke chains, forced into doing as they were told by dark figures clinging to their souls. The glow of the bulbs illuminating their faces from below cast unpleasant shadows across their expressions. Only Lenny's face was well lit, and his expression was the most chilling of all.

He didn't look frightened or angry. He certainly didn't have the fiendish and smug look of a mastermind. He looked empty, resigned, withdrawn. He didn't make eye contact with Alan as the photographer was roughly

maneuvered into a seat opposite him. He simply sat, head slightly bowed and hands folded on the table. He was a defeated man.

"You were given so many warnings, Alan," Dun rumbled.

The voice came from the ground beneath Lenny, where the light of the lamp cast him. The light wasn't bright enough to force him there, so Alan presumed he was lingering below for a reason.

"You sent Todd after my family. That isn't a warning. That's an assault," Alan said.

"I deployed Rive only because you persisted in meddling in my affairs. And Blot... I really would have thought even a traitor would know better than to permit him to return here."

"I guess you aren't as good a teacher as you thought." Blot glanced at the guards. "Once there's enough slack on the leash, you start to wonder why you don't just make a break for it."

"But you didn't make a break for it. You came right back into my clutches."

"Oh, no," Blot said. "For once, I'm not talking about running away. I'm talking about breaking your hold over me. I'm talking about no longer playing into your plans."

"Evidence, I suppose, that even the finest teacher can be confounded by a particularly unexceptional pupil."

Alan pulled himself out of the grip of his guard and took a step back. "So what is this going to be?" he asked, raising his camera. "Are you just going to repeat the same tired threats?"

"No, no. As established, first come threats, then comes punishment. You are guilty of the crimes I've asked you not to commit. You shall receive the proper sentence. The only thing left for you is to decide if you are going to cooperate in hopes of reducing that sentence to something less than summary execution."

"You can't just kill me. Not here. There are cameras."

"Really. You've seen that we've taken a handful of guards already. Do you really think we haven't taken steps to ensure my privacy when I desire it? Show him."

The final words must have been meant for Lenny himself, as he shuddered, then raised his finger to point to the little black camera node on the ceiling. Elsewhere in the prison, red lights blinked out a constant reminder that the inmates were being watched. Here, the light was dark.

Alan's fingers tightened a bit more around the camera. "So what will you do? Rough me up? Kill me? Do you honestly think the authorities aren't going to ask questions about that?"

"Oh, they'll have their questions. But I very much doubt a medical examiner will conclude that you were killed by having your shadow torn from your body. Your time is more precious than mine, Alan, since it is so very limited. Stop wasting it. I know you lack the fortitude to come back here, knowing what was waiting for you, without some sort of plan. Tell me what you have planned, and I *might* let you leave this place."

"I know about the tour. You're planning on taking the bigwigs as hosts when they come through here. Anything you might be able to do to me would be more than enough to get that tour canceled."

"It would be unfortunate if the tour were canceled, certainly. But I am patient. And we have assembled quite a stronghold here. There will be other opportunities. And this is a prison. Any amount of violence or intrigue could happen here without endangering our cause. The people beyond these walls won't shed a tear or bat an eye. Someone was killed? He was a prisoner, who cares? A *visitor* was killed? Serves him right. He knew what he was getting into. The only thing people will do is lock this place down a little harder, thinking that a few more chains and a few more locks will be all it takes to tuck this problem away forever. Your people lack the tools to defend yourselves. Your own ignorance and delusion will be your downfall."

The words were chilling, but Alan couldn't help but grin. This was evidently not the reaction Dun was hoping for.

"What are you smiling about?" he snapped.

"I never would have thought I'd be on the receiving end of a standard run-of-the-mill supervillain monologue. People don't do this here. Just wax poetic about their evil plan. That's something cartoon characters do. It's making it a little difficult to take you seriously."

Motion drew his eyes to beneath the table. Dun was slowly sliding forward, white eyes smoldering with anger.

"You are trying to rattle me. To coax me into doing something foolish. It is a childish tactic. One of the first lessons we teach when we begin in the art of manipulation."

One of the guards stepped aside, marching past Alan. He split his attention between watching the guard and the advancing shade beneath the table.

"Blot can tell you," Dun continued. "It is a dangerous tactic to use. If it fails, you find yourself facing a foe even more resolutely opposed to you. And if it succeeds, you had best hope you have the capacity to endure whatever actions your foe may pursue to illustrate precisely why he must be taken *very* seriously."

The lamp behind Alan snapped on. It wasn't strong enough to pin Blot where she was, but it was enough to nudge her forward and into the range of the cobra-strike of Dun's claws.

"No!" she shrieked as she was hauled under the table.

Alan dove forward, but the guard behind him grabbed him and held him back. Another guard stepped forward and tried to strip him of the pair of cameras he wore, but the way his arms were pinned, the camera's strap was pinned as well.

"Get off! *Get off!* Help!" Alan shouted.

A rough hand was clasped over his mouth.

"Shut your mouth and stay put, or I'll hold Blot and I'll have my men haul you away until she is torn free," Dun ordered. "And you, Blot. I won't be fooled again."

Blot fought against the claws of her former instructor, but there was little she could do. She'd been taken by surprise. Unlike the shades of the guards, who were weakened by taking a new host so recently, Dun had recovered as much as she had in their time here. He was stronger to start, thus he was stronger than her now.

He shook her violently and raked at her. Perhaps it was the violence of the motion, or some twist of his will fighting with hers, but she began to lose a grip on the equipment she'd hidden in the shadows with her. A camera popped into three dimensions and rattled to the floor. A few scattered pads with the Cox Media logo on them flopped to the floor.

A hefty black flashlight dropped down. Then, a small canister with a dangling ring attached to it bounced free. In a desperate lurch, Blot heaved herself up out of the shadows. She didn't bother trying to twist herself into her frightening combat form. There wasn't time. As little more than a silhouette separated from the floor, she scrambled for the canister and slipped her finger through the ring.

"Back off!" she shouted as Dun tried to drag her back into the shadows. "Do you know what this is?"

Dun hesitated just long enough for her to pull free. She rose up where all could see, finger firmly curled around the ring as though it were the trigger of a gun.

"This is a flash... a flash..." Blot began, fumbling for the words.

"Oh, jeez, where did she get a flash-bang?" shouted one of the guards.

"Right! Yes! A flash-bang." She shot a quick glance at each of the shades in the room. "He knows enough to fear it. But for the rest of you, let me make it clear. We all know the humans have a mastery over light that can make the lives of us shades terrible. But you don't know the half of it. Their mastery of light is such that they've made light weapons so powerful they can be used against other humans! If I pull this pin, there will be a light so powerful it could *blind* a normal human. Imagine what it will do to you or me."

"Is it's true what she says..." Dun asked warily.

One of the guards nodded. "Yeah. We've got flash-bangs here, for riots. They're bad news."

Dun focused more intently on Blot. "You wouldn't dare use it. It would do the same to you as it would do to the rest of us."

"You are trying to kill me and Alan. If it comes down to letting you kill us, or killing *all* of us, you'd best believe I will gladly take you all with me. And remember, there's a *bang* too. Loud enough to bring people running." She grinned. "Loud enough to be the signal for our troops to strike."

"What troops? You came with one woman, and she is unarmed and under the supervision of Driss."

"You said it yourself, Dun. We wouldn't have come back here without a plan. We knew what we were getting into when we came here. We knew the sort of numbers we'd be up against. And we planned accordingly. There are only two ways this happens now. Either you let Alan go and we talk about this as equals, or I pull this pin and the chaos begins."

Dun rose slowly out of the shadows as well. Unlike Blot, he chose to twist and contort himself into the gangling, dagger-clawed combat form. "You are terrible at bluffing, Blot," he hissed.

She furrowed her brow and curled her lips into a cruel smile. "You're right. I am."

She pulled the pin and rolled the canister across the floor. For a very crowded few moments, absolute madness reigned. Lenny finally showed some life, jumping to his feet and dashing for the cover of the shelves. Alan did the same. Blot raked her arms across the floor as she was dragged after him, desperately trying to gather the things that had been pulled free from her.

Then the grenade went off. Alan expected something loud, something violent. Instead, there was an instant of noise, like a thunderclap cut short, then silence. The sound hit him like a blow to the ears, dizzying him such that if he'd not been huddled against a shelf, he would have fallen to the floor. Even in the shadow of the bookcase, the light was so bright Alan could see it through his tightly shut eyelids as it bounced off the walls and ceiling.

He blinked his eyes open and found his vision swimming with purple and blue blotches. The silence gave way to a dull hiss and then, Blot's voice.

"Alan. Come on. Get up, we've got to go," she said.

Her voice was clear as a bell despite his ailing hearing. Perhaps it was because he didn't truly *hear* the things that Blot said. Not with his ears at least. But there was no time to puzzle after that now. Her voice was pained and labored.

"I can barely see!" Alan replied. Though he'd shouted, he couldn't hear his own voice. He could *only* hear *her*.

"Never mind that," she said between hissing winces. "I'll guide you."

"Are you okay?" he said, stumbling to his feet.

"Remind me, if we ever use one of those again, to make sure you get *much* farther away. I feel like I've bruised my whole body."

He stumbled and reeled through the library. Behind him, a second voice began barking vicious orders.

"After him. After him, you idiots," Dun ordered.

The guards were down, and Lenny was still fighting to climb to his feet against the dizziness, so Dun's orders went unheeded. Alan made his way shakily into the hallway.

"People are shouting. I think guards are coming. Nonshade guards. Let's get out of here. This is good enough, isn't it? Good enough for plan B. This'll upset his plans for a while. We just need to get out of here. Turn left. We're going for the emergency exit."

Alan did as he was told, as his vision and balance weren't up to the task of navigating without her help, let alone improvising a better solution. She mostly trailed along as his shadow, but now and again, when he teetered or stumbled, she forced herself up against the bright light in the hall just enough to steady him and nudge him along.

"We're not going to be able to just run away," Alan said. "And what about Jessie? We have to—"

"Dodge!" she shouted.

He felt her hand hook his leg and yank it out from under him. He fell hard against the wall, but the swinging claw of Dun whistled through the air where his head had been.

Alan spun his back against the wall. His fumbling hands found their way to the sturdy old film camera still dangling about his neck and raised it. The flash was wimpy, but a few rapid shots dazzled the weakened Dun. Lenny, eyes wide and crazed, rammed into Alan and pinned him against the wall. Blot rose up and heaved him aside, and the two hosts and shades squared off against their counterparts.

Still suffering from the effects of the flash-bang as they were, it was a less than heroic battle. Both humans were half-blind and could only hear the shades, teetering and stumbling as their balance sluggishly returned. Blot and Dun were tender from the intense light. The lightest slash or impact caused them to hiss and recoil in pain. Alan, through sheer force of will, managed to get himself together enough to gain the upper hand on Lenny. He swept the inmate's legs out from under him and shakily kept him pinned with a foot to the chest.

Alas, while Blot was doing her best, Dun was too powerful, and recovering too quickly. He smacked her aside and swept onto the wall behind

Alan. A twisted claw emerged from the shadows and pulled tight across his neck. When Blot did this, it pulled Alan into the shadows. Dun had no interest in that. The grip pinched off his throat. He fought for breath.

Blot surged forward, but the still-shadowy form of Dun lashed out and caught her by the neck, holding her at bay.

"There won't be any question marks on the prison medic's chart today, Alan," Dun hissed into his ear. "Asphyxiation by a crazed inmate. Just a dead photographer who should have known better."

Alan fought for breath and snatched at his cameras, but Lenny threw himself against him.

"Hand on his throat, idiot. Over mine," Dun ordered. "The light is too bright for me to fight its influence for long. And quickly. Guards are coming. They aren't any of ours."

Lenny nodded dully and clamped his free hand over Alan's throat, hiding Dun's inky claws until one could imagine they were simply the starkness of his own shadow. He leaned close.

"You could have stayed away, Alan," Lenny said.

His words weren't vicious or vengeful. They were weary, the words of a man who had lost his final battle long ago. He almost sounded disappointed that another person had fallen into the same pit he found himself in.

Alan gasped for breath. Blot could see the light fading from his eyes, but she simply lacked the strength to save him. Fear, anger, and desperation caused her mind to spin, but beneath it all she felt a familiar sensation. An unsettling feeling of being watched.

Not a moment too soon, a burly figure bashed into Lenny and sent him sprawling. Dun held his ground as best he could, determined to wring the last bit of life out of Alan before being torn free, but a flash of silver and a flick of motion conjured a screech of pain. The evil shade retreated, his claws releasing both Blot and Alan. Blot spared a look at their savior.

It was a guard. Or at least, one could be excused for believing it was a guard. He was dressed in the proper uniform, but the rugged face was unmistakable. He carried a heavy duffel, and in his hand, a silver dagger that should never have made it this far into the prison. This was Brink.

"The Dawn..." Dun growled. "You brought *the Dawn*? *Here?!* Does your treachery know no end?"

Brink took a step forward, eyes not quite on target for Dun. He couldn't see the shade himself, only the illusory shadow the rest of the world saw. Nonetheless, the bright light of the hallway meant Dun wasn't far from it, and thus the dagger would strike its target. Lenny and Dun retreated rather than risking its bite.

"Cellblock 33. We need to move. Now," he barked. "We won't have much time for the ritual."

"What? I can't—" Alan began, still trying to catch his breath.

"He wants to go start the ritual, but I think we need to get out of here before—"

"No... we need to get this done. This way," Alan said.

He started to lead the way toward Cellblock 33. Blot shuddered angrily. This had already gone far worse than she would have hoped. The wise thing to do would be to back away. Damage had been done to Dun's plan already. But if she'd already earned the undying ire of a powerful shade such as him, it was just as suicidal to leave him in a position of power as to take him on. She may as well go through with the madness. Now that they had Brink with them, maybe they could actually make it in and out again without putting their lives any *more* on the line.

As though the thought of victory was too much for fate to bear, the very moment it passed through Blot's head, the overhead lights flickered and failed.

"What the hell was that?" Jessie demanded, eyes scrutinizing the bank of screens.

She had been nodding through the latest in a stretch of explanations for the last few minutes. The good doctor and Reggie the guide had been taking turns tooting their own horn. Dr. Vale's mastery of psychology, or at least of certain elements and jargon associated with psychology, was genuinely impressive. And to be perfectly honest, listening to her thoughts and theories had been fascinating. But in the last few minutes, her speech had begun to cover old ground in a way that a suspicious mind might label as stalling for time. The bright, interested officer's focus had started to waver. As a result, she found herself gazing directly at one of the handful of monitors actually trained upon Cellblock 33 and its surrounding areas when the flash-bang grenade had gone off. The feed hadn't been on the library itself, but the thump of a not-so-distant explosion had visibly startled the prisoners on the feed. They were still scrambling for answers when the screen went dark.

It didn't go *black*, as the emergency signs and what little licks of light made it through the shades could still be seen. It was merely the lighting itself that had dropped away.

"I am sure there has simply been a malfunction in a transformer nearby that is affecting the power in the facility," Dr. Vale speculated.

The guard currently charged with operating the monitors had a different opinion on the matter. His radio was already squawking with guards attempting to deploy to the site of the disturbance. A matching radio on Reggie's belt distractingly broadcast his message on a quarter-second delay.

"I need verification on the feed from CC-CB-33-1." The tech's forced calm moderated his tone as he clicked through a sequence of other feeds. With each new darkened view, his training-enforced calmness wavered. "Also CC-CB-33-2 through 6. And CB-30-6. And…"

The peal of an alarm split the air. Jessie's hand instinctively went to her belt, where her pistol would have been if she were in full uniform.

"This can't be a power outage. *Our* lights are still on," Jessie said.

"The prison draws from two separate grids and has backup generators," Reggie said, quoting the prison's bullet points. "To lose lighting in just one cellblock would be a circuit issue. A maintenance team will be—"

"Where is Alan?" Jessie said, addressing the security tech directly.

"Officer Hearst, I assure you—" Dr. Vale began.

"You've got policies. Keeping track of visitors is one of those policies. Where is Alan, right now?" she demanded. "And if the answer isn't 'on his way to a more secure location,' then you and I are going to have a long policy talk *after* we find him and get him."

"He should be in the library."

The guard clicked through to the feed. What he saw was a barely visible scene of overturned chairs, shredded paper, and slowly recovering guards. Jessie was out the door before either Reggie or Dr. Vale could attempt to set her mind at ease.

CHAPTER 10

The soft, lingering hiss that had swallowed Alan's hearing after the detonation of the flash-bang was just beginning to recede as they quickened their pace through a darkened prison hallway. Thus, the first sounds he could hear with any clarity were the distant wail of warning sirens, the urgent shouts of prison staff, and a thousand little rattles and scrapes of shades helping their hosts to escape.

Alan held a camera in each hand. The DSLR was in video mode, with its attached light casting a reasonable pool of illumination. His other hand snapped hastily framed film photos whenever he caught a glimpse of motion. It was a tribute to his consumer research that both cameras still functioned after the jostling they'd received. The flashlight Blot was smuggling probably would have been a more reliable defense, but the photographer in Alan couldn't let the concept of being the only lens on the ground at a prison riot go by without putting his skills to work. And if there was one thing he'd learned in his dealings with the shades, it was that a sudden flash packed a heck of a wallop on an unsuspecting shadow.

"Why aren't they mobbing us?" Alan asked. "It's been minutes since the lights went out. I know these bars are meaningless to them now. Why have we only seen glimpses of inmates?"

"I suspect it has something to do with the fact that we've not encountered any guards either," Brink said. "They're shoring up their defenses. Ensuring any outside interference is locked down or locked out. It's what I would do. They know that an enemy has breached the prison; they are closing off avenues of escape."

"How far do we have to go?" Blot asked. "What are we aiming for?"

"Blot wants to know where we're heading and what we're doing."

"I need to ensure that every shade falls within a ninety-foot radius of the position of the ritual."

An inmate who had been lurking around a corner charged toward them. Brink didn't so much as flinch. A stiff forearm to the chin knocked the man back into a wall, and, while he was dazed, a slash of Brink's blade made the shade think twice about following.

As though the brief encounter was of little concern, he continued without skipping a beat. "We'll need someplace fairly defensible, as the first stage of the ritual will take all my attention for a time. Once it has begun, you'll be free to escape. Which you will want to do, as I have no way of excluding you and your shade from the ritual's effects."

They reached the security checkpoint outside Cellblock 33. To the right was the very room where Alan had filmed the interview with Lenny. The guard's vestibule stood on the other side. It wasn't much bigger than a closet. The guard was nowhere to be seen. Alan could only hope it was because he was one of the subverted ones and was planning an ambush. The alternative was that an innocent person had been disposed of already.

"Cellblock 33 is through here," Alan said.

"Near enough to fall within the radius?" Brink asked.

"I'm not a great judge of distance. Especially not indoors."

"This is fine, then." He dropped the duffel in the guard's area.

"Isn't the interview room easier to defend?"

"If you don't know the distance, I'll need every inch I can get. This is a few yards closer." He pulled out a familiar silver case. "In a moment, every shade in the area is going to be drawn to us like moths to a flame."

"That is a ridiculous metaphor," Blot snapped. "We would specifically avoid flame."

Next, Brink pulled out the beefiest flashlight Alan had ever seen. It looked like someone had pulled the headlight and battery out of a car and duct-taped them together.

"Block the doorway. Keep us safe. Stun with the light, stab with the dagger," Brink instructed him.

"Don't you dare take that blade from him," Blot growled. "The last time you held one of those, you ended up stabbing a hole through me."

Alan took the flashlight. "I'm not going to be killing any shades. You know that."

"The blade has to penetrate to kill, and we're surrounded by tile and cement. The worst you'll do is sting them." He clicked open the silver case. "And I don't have time to argue."

Blot became visibly rigid as the case hinged open. The raw, unfiltered aura of the shard was clearly difficult for her to resist.

"Focus, Blot," Alan said.

"I don't know if I can..." she said. "You don't understand... it's... *calling* to me."

Brink placed the crystal on the ground and produced a piece of chalk. It wasn't standard schoolyard chalk. The substance was more rustic than that, more akin to a lump of coal, only white. He traced a circle out on the ground and carefully drew out some simple, precise shapes within it. After the final stroke of the final shape, he smashed the vial that contained the crystal shard. The circle and symbols alike were illuminated with a unique glow. It wasn't brilliant. Indeed, it wasn't even clear to Alan if it was truly a glow at all. The light shimmered and eluded his gaze, a slice of the spectrum just beyond what human eyes were meant to see.

Blot's senses seemed to return a bit as the spell took effect. She was still distracted, still quite aware of the prize that lay so very near, but she no longer had to physically restrain herself from reaching out for it. The half-seen glow nudged her gently aside. Her roiling hair shifted away from it, as if blown by a powerful wind. Her desire for the crystal was simply stunted by the knowledge that she could no longer reach it, thanks to the spell that had activated.

"These are our spells," Blot said, her eyes locked upon Brink. "He's casting *our* spells."

Alan switched on the flashlight and squinted at its glare off the opposite wall. "We don't have magic of our own," Alan said. "Or at least... I don't think we do. Where else would they learn magic?"

Blot looked down to the shapes he was inscribing. "I don't know. But it burns me that he knows what these shapes mean and *I* don't..."

She reluctantly took her eyes from Brink's work as the rattling of doors and thundering of feet echoed louder along the hallway. Most of the sound came from the cellblock side of the door, which was mercifully still locked, but piercing white eyes cut through the darkness in the hallway. Shades surged along with their hosts. Alan shifted the light toward them. The sheer power of the beam shoved the black shapes back. Two guards shielded their eyes. Ghostly, windy voices demanded they continue forward.

"Alan!" Blot shouted.

He turned to find jagged silhouetted claws sliding beneath the door to the cellblock. Blot contorted her own shadowy form into something more formidable and clashed with them. Alan turned and slashed at the claws with the dagger. The door rattled and started to ease open, impossibly thin fingers easily manipulating the workings of the lock and latch. He threw himself against it and did his best to split his attention between the guards and the door. It was a horrid game of whack-a-mole. He couldn't just leave the light trained on either potential source of attack, or the other would overtake him. Whenever the light was trained in one direction, Blot made certain to turn her attention in the other to hold them at bay. She stretched out and rose up, inky black hands tugging, shoving, and tripping the guards. Then she swung back to snake her fingers into the door to foul their attempts to open it.

The fight was desperate and chaotic. Against all odds, they seemed to be managing. The combination of light and the dagger was enough to keep the shades at a distance, and to make those who got too close regret it. The guards were a constant threat, but Blot had them handled. Indeed, it wasn't until the inmates and guards halted their assault that genuine concern crept past the frenzy of activity.

"Why are they stopping..." Alan said, hand tight around the grip of the dagger.

"Do you hear that? What's that sound?" Blot said.

It wasn't a threatening sound. Certainly not compared to the angry chorus of human and shade voices that had filled the hallway until now. Instead, it was a barely audible, distant crunch. It began within the cellblock. A second matching crackle joined it from farther along the hallway.

Then came a single, startling clatter as something lofted across the hallway and struck the door they'd fought so hard to secure. Alan shifted the light to reveal a twisted wad of shattered plastic and metal.

"It's a camera. They're backing away, and they're taking out the cameras," Alan said.

"They're planning something big..." Blot said.

Silence reigned for a few moments. The only sound was the grind and click of the chalk on the ground as Brink continued his work. "I'm nearly through," he said.

Now there was a new sound. A rhythmic, fleshy slap that grew steadily closer.

"Oh god... I know that sound," Alan said.

"Round three, son," slurred a familiar voice from down the hall.

"Todd." Blot shuddered.

"Just a little longer," Brink said.

Alan shifted the light. The figure stalked into view at the end of the hallway. Rive had outdone himself this time. Every scrap of mass the drunkard's body could spare had been sculpted into something worthy of folklore. His face was a long, snarling muzzle. Eyes were sunken and fierce. His filthy clothes were barely holding to him; iron-hard muscles wrapped in sinewy bands around a spindly nightmare of limbs. Alan stepped as far away from it as he could manage without abandoning his post as Brink's defender. His back was against the door. It shook, the center of it denting outward with clearly defined knuckles and claws as emboldened shades on the other side attempted to break through.

"Been waiting for this one," Todd said, twisting his neck to produce a chorus of crackles. "I keep saying no hard feelings, but you take enough lumps from the same guy and you start looking forward to returning the favor."

"Hold him at bay," Brink said.

"I don't know what you expect me to do about this, but I'm not going to be able to do it," Alan said, eyes wide. "Trust me. It's been tried. This guy doesn't stay down."

Another blow caused the door to buckle behind him. Todd leaned low, his bony knuckles resting on the ground in a gorilla-like stance. "I thought it'd be hard to get in here, but the door was open," he said. His little eyes narrowed. "Now hold still for once, will you?"

"Enough! Run!" Blot demanded. "If you think I'm going to be able to stop that thing, think again!"

Todd ground his contorted foot against the wall behind him, like a sprinter dropping into position.

"Brink!" Alan raved.

"Fine," Brink uttered, standing up from his task. "You finish this."

"But I don't know how!" Alan said.

Todd leaped forward, traveling in bounding, pouncing leaps. Two of them covered the entire hallway. A third delivered him to his prey. Brink barely moved in response. A tiny shift in his stance. The simplest angling of his shoulder. When Todd struck, he was met with a shoulder to the gut. Brink stood and pivoted, lifting the hulking but still quite human-weighted abomination from the ground. Every bit of Todd's momentum went from a targeted attack to a flailing tumble. His body struck the abused door and sheared it from its hinges. A tangle of contorted limbs, hammered metal, and complaining inmates slid into Cellblock 33. Brink turned back to Alan.

"It is all a matter of timing. You start here, you end there, and you don't cross any lines except for the circles. Imagine you are drawing a fuse. Give yourself enough length to have time to get away, because as soon as you finish the connection, the ritual begins, and it won't end until the shard is used up or removed."

He tossed Alan the chalk. The clash hadn't even crushed it in his grip. He took the dagger in return, then paced through the doorway of the cellblock, straight into the lion's den. Out of habit, Alan snapped a few pictures, then set down the DSLR on video mode.

Alan could only see the first few moments of the brawl that followed. Brink's motion was fluid and precise, his bulky body falling back as his free hand grabbed the jumpsuit of a charging inmate. He rolled back and caused the brute to overbalance and thump into three of his fellow rioters. The battle was easily the most awe-inspiring sight Alan had ever beheld. Brink and Todd traded blows like they'd been born to battle each other. Alan prayed the beating his cameras had been taking hadn't broken them too badly to catch the highlights. It was a joke of fate that after spending so much time looking for interesting, fascinating, or exciting things to snap pictures of, the most astounding of them all came at the precise moment he had something far more pressing to deal with.

He turned his attention to what Brink had drawn. It was a series of three concentric circles. They were littered with intricate runes following the curve. There *was* space for an additional line to be traced, but it wasn't a generous amount by any means. He saw where he should start on the innermost circle, and he saw where he should end on the outermost, if there was an intended way to connect them, he couldn't see it.

"Drawing a fuse. Drawing a fuse..." he repeated.

"Just start drawing. And make it long. I don't want this spell hitting us," Blot instructed him.

Alan started tracing a line, and the reason for the fuse analogy became clear. The half-seen illumination of the gem and the inner circle slowly traced along the line as he drew it. As the line grew longer, the relationship between length and time became clear, and knowing how far he had to go to get out of this place, even without difficulties, he was going to need a *lot* of length.

Growls, slaps, slices, and thumps filled his ears as he crouched over the arcane shapes. The battle between Brink and Todd was raging on, and it had seized the attention of the rest of the inmates. From the sound of it, more than a dozen had joined in the fray. That it hadn't ended meant Brink was holding his own somehow.

"That way! There's more room that way," Blot said, peering over his shoulder.

"I can't go that way, I'd have to cross the line there."

"Oh, right. Then this way. And then up, and then around that way."

"*Just let me think!*" Alan said. "This is already like trying to solve a maze during an air raid. I don't need a backseat driver too."

He looped and wove his way through the first circle and continued to the next. Squealing, inhuman howls suggested Brink was scoring some worthwhile blows. Alan added as much length as he could to the next ring before finally connecting it to the smoldering endpoint.

"Finished!" he proclaimed.

He snatched up his camera and snapped a picture of the shape. When he raised his head, he saw Brink thump into view. The battle had taken its toll on him, but not nearly as much of a toll as it had taken on Todd. The Dawn member dragged the bruised and bloodied shifter into the doorway. He left Todd sprawled on the ground, his form blocking the doorway alongside two other incapacitated inmates as in improvised barricade.

"Go. Move!" he ordered.

"What about you?"

"I've got to protect the ritual. Shades can't reach the shard, but humans can."

"But what happens to you?"

"*Go!*" both Blot and Brink barked.

"Right! Okay! Let's go!"

Alan sprinted through the halls of the prison. The voice of good sense told him it would be wise to take things slowly. Danger lurked around every corner. If he encountered another shifter, the likelihood of besting it—or even escaping it—was practically nil. Unfortunately, that very sane and reasonable voice was handily drowned out by another voice screeching in his ear.

"Faster, faster!" Blot screamed.

Only once before had he heard such fear and desperation in her voice, and it was when he'd accidentally dropped a dagger into her shortly after they'd met.

"By the void, I can feel it. It's terrible. You've got to get away. You've just *got* to."

All around him, to greater or lesser degrees, Alan could hear very different demands being made of the other inmates, but with similar intensity.
Some were still trying to heed whatever command had alerted them to the
arrival of a member of the Dawn. Others could feel the presence of the
Shard of Shadow and rushed to it like a shark after a bucket of chum.
Others were becoming aware of the same enchantment that had Blot on
edge and were uncertain of what it meant. And there were other things
too. Small, darting forms. Startling cackles and crows. Bestial sounds that
Alan couldn't identify and Blot was too frightened to address.

It was chaos. Dozens of voices shouted conflicting orders. Some inmates
stumbled and tripped over each other in their attempts to obey this command or that. Other inmates were huddled on the ground trembling at
the supernatural madness. Alan's hands worked on autopilot, snapping
pictures while making his way through hallways. Alan was one of the only
ones fully aware of the situation. He'd been *expecting* it. That left him with
just enough of his wits to be able to dodge or bowl over what few inmates
had the presence of mind to try to stop him.

He'd been through these very same halls just minutes before, but somehow they were entirely different now. Dun must have had the shades
well trained, each with a part to play, should the Dawn infiltrate. Barri-
cades filled some hallways. Some doors were wrenched open. Others were
wedged shut, their locks damaged beyond usefulness. There was no sign of
any guards. Alan didn't want to think about how they'd been cleared away
so quickly and effectively. He didn't want to think about how so many of
the shades had gotten clear of Cellblock 33 while the door was still intact.
He didn't want to think about *anything* except getting away.

"Faster, farther. We're not clear yet!" Blot shouted.

Alan could hear thumping up ahead. It wasn't the massive, terrifying slam of a shifter breaking a door down. It was more rhythmic, more coordinated. A square of light was visible at the end of the hall, what little he could see of a still-lit hallway through the reinforced glass of the door. As he got closer, he could see people working to get the door open. He slid to a stop and slapped at the window.

"Quick! Quick!" Blot begged, her hands tearing at her hair.

"Get me out of here!" Alan cried to the people on the other side.

All of them shouted back to him at once, and three were guards. One looked to be of a higher rank. After a few seconds of confusion, someone fought her way through to the window.

"Alan!" Jessie said. "The door's wrecked. Stand by. We're trying to get it open. The whole wing got sealed off."

"We're still too close, Alan. We're still too close," Blot raved.

"Just stay put. Tools are on the way. We're going to get this thing open and get you out of there."

"Time's running out," Blot fretted. "By the void, don't let the spell catch us. I can... I can feel a draft. That way!"

Alan turned. Blot's fingers were pointing not just back, but up. He'd become quite accustomed to differentiating Blot's darker form from the darkness around him, so he could see *that* she was pointing, but he couldn't see precisely what she was pointing *at*. Realization dawned after a few seconds. There were vents. There *had* to be. They wouldn't be large enough for a human to crawl through, but that wouldn't stop Blot.

"I've... I've got to go," Alan shouted to Jessie through the window. "I know what to do!"

"Alan, stay where we can see you!" Jessie called to him.

"Don't worry about me!" he shouted back to her as he dashed into the darkness.

The very moment he slipped from the tiny pool of light cast by the window, he felt the cold grip of Blot's fingers about his leg. Other times, she'd pulled him into the shadows with a gentle, reassuring embrace. She had neither the time nor the inclination to do that now. Her grip pulled him hard. His foot sank into the shadows as though he'd stepped into a mud puddle. It caused him to lose his balance and tumble forward. Blot lurched up behind him as he fell, threw her arms around him, and *tackled* him into the shadows.

Too often, Alan's trips through the shadows had been at the mercy of light, at least for a few fleeting moments here or there. In the blackness of the darkened prison, it was an entirely new experience. The difference was like night and day, or perhaps more accurately, like day and night. Gone was the constant gale force, the light that shoved against them. They were free to slide up the walls, to curl through the grates. In other circumstances, he might even have called it *fun*. In the context of a race against the clock amid a prison riot, it served instead as a precious moment of calm and control amid a sea of chaos.

Now that he'd joined her in the shadows, he could understand what had Blot and the other shades so wound up. There were two very different sensations rushing from the same place. One was a sort of pleasant warmth that instantly put him in the same state of mind as a freezing hiker discovering a nice, toasty campfire. All he wanted was to get closer to it. This must have been the shard. The second sensation was more subtle. An acrid tinge to the atmosphere, as though someone had tossed something into the aforementioned fire that they shouldn't have. Something poisonous. The spell. Both sensations were fading fast, each twist and turn Blot was taking took her away from it.

The toxic sensation was all but gone now. Alan's chest was beginning to heave from his body's insistence that it hadn't taken a breath in far too long. Blot spilled out of the vents and allowed Alan to pop unceremoniously back to three dimensions.

He gasped for breath. "Where... where are we?"

"We're safe. That's good enough for me," Blot said.

It was still dark, suggesting they were still in the shade-controlled section of the prison. The sounds of chaos were distant, however. She produced the flashlight for him and slid aside while he cast a beam on their surroundings. It was a small room filled with assorted innocuous supplies, some sort of utility closet.

"That was close... That was too close..." Blot said. "I can feel the spell just about to lock into place."

Alan took another deep breath and leaned against the wall. "I can't even remember what this spell was supposed to be."

"It weakens us. It's going to keep them tied to their current hosts and powerless. I can feel the shape of it now. Probably they all can too. But it's too late." She shut her white eyes and trembled lightly as something rushed over the prison that she could feel but he could not.

"It's done. They're crippled. And now the next spell is starting."

"This one's supposed to make it permanent, right?"

Blot's eyes were shut, her head tipped slightly aside. From the furrow of her brow and the tightness of her lips, she was working at some sort of riddle. "No..." she murmured. "That's not what this is... This is..."

Her eyes opened. "By the darkness, that *monster*."

The distant sounds of chaos were slowly growing louder. It wasn't that the riot was getting closer to where they were, it was that they were getting more agitated. And the cries had the distinct tinge of fear.

"I'd know that feeling anywhere. That's the feeling of Driss's office. That's the burning light."

"But it's still dark."

Blot gritted her teeth. "I know. But this is the way it *felt*. That spell is doing the same thing to them that *Driss* used to do. He's making the light not just a force, but a *flame*."

"I don't understand how—"

"When that spell is completed, light won't just shove us around, it'll *kill* us."

"No. That wasn't the plan. He was supposed to just make it a proper prison."

"I *told* you we couldn't trust him. He's with the *Dawn*. All they ever wanted to do was kill us. I'm surprised he kept the promise of making sure *we* could get away. In a couple of minutes, this isn't going to be a prison. It's going to be *tomb*."

Jessie marched down the still-lit hallway, headed toward Cellblock 33. Normally, a nonemployee walking the hallways of her own accord would have been nipped in the bud instantly by the staff, but at the moment, the staff had far more important things to worry about. Thus, Dr. Vale and

Reggie were the only people attempting to keep Jessie from taking matters into her own hands.

"What do we need to do to get him out of there?" Jessie asked.

"Miss Hearst, this is a prison matter. We will handle this," Dr. Vale said.

"*Officer* Hearst, and like hell you will." She didn't stop walking, or even look Dr. Vale in the eye as she spoke. "Unless I'm mistaken, electronic locks default to *locked* in a power failure, and something coordinated is going on for all the doors providing access to that cellblock to have been disabled so quickly. There are innocent people in there with inmates running amok. There are *guilty* people who sure didn't deserve to be pummeled by their *more* guilty cellmates while the guards are distracted. More importantly, my friend is in there. So what do we need to do to get him out?"

"You need to come to your senses and—"

"Do I sound like I'm in a tizzy, Doctor?" She held out her hand. "Reggie, give me your radio."

"We don't need an untrained voice confusing matters further."

She took a deep breath and presented her hand. "If you don't like my discipline, you can talk to my superiors. Until then, give me your radio."

The raw authority and certainty in her voice must have triggered something in Reggie's brain, because he quickly handed it to her. With a skill that betrayed a great deal of experience in navigating a crowded communication channel, she inserted two quick questions and received two quick answers.

"Do we have eyes on the photographer, Alan Fontaine?"

They did not.

"Do we have a crew in the utility room for Cellblock 33 and surrounding areas?"

They would, momentarily.

Jessie handed the radio back to Reggie. "Which way is the utility room? And don't waste your breath telling me to leave it to them."

Reggie's mouth hung open for a moment, and when he spoke, it was only to comply. "This way."

Blot had her eyes cast upon the far wall, squinted in either deep thought or intense focus. Alan had been rummaging through the various items in the room in search of something that might help him. In a place that seemed to be primarily a storage room for cleaning supplies, he found a single adjustable wrench in a forgotten tool kit.

"What have you come up with?" Alan asked, slapping the wrench against his palm to test its heft.

"It's not going to be pleasant, especially if you insist on breathing, but I think I can get us outside without crossing through the influence of the spell."

"You're not thinking of escaping are you?"

"Of course I am! What's left to be done?"

"People are going to die in there, and it's my fault!"

"I know, Alan. I was being kind enough not to point it out. If it sets your mind at ease at all, most of the shades were going to die anyway, and the humans are all criminals. So no one innocent got hurt. Unless they've killed some guards. But then, if the guards are already dead—"

"We have to save them."

"Oh, spare me, Alan. What's done is done. Your conscience will only burn for a little while. Before you know it, it'll just be a dull ache that haunts you when it's too quiet. Take it from someone who knows."

"I won't leave them to die."

"If we take more than a dozen steps toward the center of this little ritual bomb, I'll be sizzling at the slightest touch of light, just like the rest of my kind are right now. I'll die before we make it there. Then that'll be another death on your conscience, only you won't have to worry about living with it, because you'll die a few minutes later."

Alan's eyes flicked downward. A desperate, terrible thought simmered in the back of his mind. In the absence of better alternatives, and with time running out, he dredged it up. "How many minutes?"

"We aren't going out there," Blot said through clenched teeth. "I'm not dying for this. I told you that."

"How many minutes?" Alan repeated, an edge in his tone.

"Maybe five. *Maybe*. It's tough to say. By the time it happens, we're supposed to move on."

"You're ready for a new host, aren't you?" he asked.

"Stop," Blot snapped. "We've been through this. You should know better than to ask."

"Right. Because I know the answer. If there are some of these shades who have taken new hosts, then you *must* be ready for one. Go. Get out of here."

"Don't be an idiot. If you're afraid of being dragged through the vents all that way, then we can just wait here. We'll have some questions to answer but—"

"All I have to do is pull the shard out of the ceremony circle before the spell finishes. That's why Brink was defending it, right?" He turned to the door and tested it. It was locked from the outside. "I'll need you to get this door open."

"No. Your plan is stupid. You'll still have to *get* to the shard."

"The lights are out here. That means we're in the shade-controlled part of the prison. The locked doors are to keep other people out. I'm willing to bet the rest of the doors are all open, just like this one would be if it had been between a shade and the shard."

"The doors are open so the inmates can track you down and murder you."

"The inmates have their hands full dealing with shades shrieking about the burning light."

"And what about Brink? This is his doing. He's defending the circle. And he took out a full-fledged shifter. I hate to tell you this, but if he can do that to one of them, he's sure not going to have any trouble slicing your guts out with a dull silver knife."

"I've won a couple of fights against a shifter."

"With my *help*."

"Then let's hope I learned from you."

"Alan—"

"We don't have time to argue! Just go. Find yourself a new host. I'd like to believe you'll continue to do the right thing, or at least continue to show the world there are shades out there worth saving. Because you've sure shown me that."

She gave him a sour look. "Don't you hang this suicide on me. You know there's no going back from this, right? If you get cold feet, if you change your mind, you'll be too far inside that spell for me to get to you."

"I know. I've got to do it. One life is a small price to pay for dozens. Shades and criminals or not."

She gritted her teeth. A single, gleaming tear ran down her inky cheek. Her hand closed into an angry fist. Her body stretched and contorted into its fearsome combat form and slid into solidity. With a single, vicious blow she knocked the comparatively flimsy utility room door from its hinges. When she slipped back into two dimensions and eased back into her proper form, she reached her shadowy fingers out to the walls of the room and clutched them tightly.

"I'm never going to find a host nearly as nice as you, even if you *are* an idiot. You realize that."

"I think the human race will surprise you, Blot. There's a lot of nice idiots out there." He took a steadying breath. "Now... let go."

She shut her eyes and tugged hard. He tried to take another breath, but a chilling sensation caused it to freeze in his chest. He'd felt this once before. The horrible, icy, numbing emptiness creeping up in him. The feeling of no longer belonging in the world. He could feel Blot's presence sliding out of him. His body felt hollower with every strenuous tug of her shadowy form. When she tugged entirely free, his very being felt like a husk, already beginning to shrivel.

Blot gave him one final, pained look before flitting into the vent and away.

The utility room responsible for the blackout in Cellblock 33 was, it turned out, quite far from Cellblock 33. The lights in the hallway were still on, and thanks to its distance from the riot happening deeper in the facility, there were only three guards on hand trying to get in.

"What's going on?" Jessie said, trotting up to them. "Why aren't we in?"

Two of the guards were heaving their shoulders against the door, trying to break it down. A third red-faced guard was recovering from his turn at doing so.

"It's wedged," he explained. "Or braced or something."

"Definitely braced. There must be five guys in there," countered one of the other guards, backing away and rubbing his shoulder. "Look at the hinges. The latches. The whole door's practically ready to fall off, but it still won't budge. Someone's holding us out."

Jessie assessed the situation. It was true that the abused doorway was on the verge of collapse. Now and again a shudder from within suggested someone was leaning against it. She scanned the hallway for a solution. Her eyes set upon a large fire extinguisher in a wall-mounted cabinet. She dashed to it.

"Don't! An alarm will sound!" shouted one of the guards.

"What's one more alarm?" she replied.

Jessie wrenched open the extinguisher cabinet and added a fire alarm to the general din of the building. She tugged the heavy red canister from within.

"Clear out," she said, hurrying back.

"Wait... Do you even work here?"

She ignored the question. A good sharp blow with the canister caused the door latch to give. A second one shattered it entirely. The door lurched inward, then outward again as whoever was inside pushed it back into place and held it firm.

Jessie narrowed her eyes at the door. Dozens of kicks and shoulders had hammered countless dents into it. It was made from thin sheet metal, no match for the reinforced doors elsewhere in the prison. Another idea flitted through her mind. She reared back and hammered the canister down again. This time she aimed for one of the corners of the door. Two hits folded a corner back that no amount of bracing could restore. Rather than working it any farther, she pulled the pin for the fire extinguisher, stuck the nozzle in the damaged bit of the door, and pulled the lever.

A startled, angry, frightened cry rang out from within. She pulled back.

"Hit it, boys!" she said.

Two guards charged in and took full advantage of the lapse in bracing. Their combined effort knocked the whole door from its hinges. The light flooded into the darkened utility room to reveal the person or persons responsible for holding off three guards for so long.

"You've got to be kidding me..." Jessie said.

Inside was a single inmate. He couldn't have been more than a hundred pounds, with the paper-thin physique of a life-long addict. Nothing had been piled against the door. Somehow this one person was solely responsible for holding them off for so long. The guards didn't stop to consider the impossibility. They simply hauled the prisoner out. Jessie slipped inside and started restoring the switched breakers.

Mist from the extinguisher still hung in the air, making it difficult to breathe, but this wouldn't take long. The current state of the breakers wasn't the haphazard work of someone randomly throwing switches. The selections were deliberate and specific. It stank of premeditation. Training.

She felt an odd prickling sensation against her skin as she snapped the next few switches in place. It must have been the chemicals from the extinguisher making her skin crawl, but it felt like needles grazing across her skin. She threw the last switch and charged out of the utility room to take a deep breath of fresh air. Rubbing her watery eyes, she set her mind to her next task.

The lights flickered on as Alan hurried through the hallways. After rushing about in the dark for so long, he was almost disoriented by the light. More disorienting was what he saw once the lights were restored. The dozens of inmates from Cellblock 33 were free. Every hallway Alan dashed through was crowded with them. Rather than hunting for Alan, they seemed to be grappling with the terrible effects the Dawn's enchantment had on their shades. Hardened criminals had their hands clamped over their ears, trying to shut out the screams of their shadows. Others were desperately seeking darkness to shield their shades. Men assaulted overhead lights, trying to shatter them. Madness was the only word for what reigned in his place. Without Blot, Alan saw them as everyone else would. Raving lunatics shouting at and begging with people that weren't there. Their shadows were simple silhouettes of their bodies, no hint that they might have minds and agendas of their own.

Alan clamped his eyes shut and steadied himself against a wall. One hand held the grip of his camera. It was recording video. He faintly remembered making the decision to record what would likely be his last moments. Better to die doing what he did best. Stripped of his shadow, and free of the shade who had replaced it, a roiling panic and unease was making it difficult to think. Though he knew his hand was resting against the cold stone of the cement wall, it felt far away. The world was gray, and growing grayer. His sensations were echoes of what they had once been, more like memories than reality.

He turned the corner leading to Cellblock 33. Broken glass crunched like potato chips beneath his feet. The lights here weren't just broken, they were torn from their fixtures. The wall felt sticky against his hand. He took it away and found it smeared with blood. There was a figure crouched in the doorway of the side room that held the ritual. As Alan approached, the figure stood. It pulled itself to its full height, which wasn't nearly the towering size of Brink. As Alan stepped closer, he recognized the man blocking the doorway.

"Lenny," Alan said, his own voice sounding tinny in his ears.

"Just get away, Alan," he said, hoarse and haggard.

"Where is Brink?"

"Where do you think? You brought that man into the meat grinder Dun had set up. He wasn't getting out of here. No one who crosses Dun gets away. Not alive."

"Listen. That ritual there, we have to take the shard away from it."

"Just get away," Lenny repeated.

"Lenny, people are going to die. All of these people."

"It's better this way, Alan." He raised a hand shakily. "Is that recording?"

"Just get out of the way!" he demanded, staggering forward.

Lenny addressed the camera directly. "I'm sorry. I did my best. I didn't know."

Alan tried to shove past him as the unhinged former intern confessed to the camera. Lenny caught Alan by the shoulder and shoved him back. The shove lacked any real strength. He felt no jagged claws tugging at him. But holding to the ragged ends of his mind and body as he was, Alan nearly toppled at Lenny's weak assault. He gathered himself and fought back.

The battle that followed was an awkward, fumbling one. Something deep in Alan's mind rebelled at the indignity of the fact that this battle, one that held the lives of dozens of humans and shades in the balance, was playing out with all the grace of a drunken tussle. He heaved Lenny aside and crawled for the ritual. Shaking hands grabbed his legs and tugged him back. Alan almost couldn't feel their grip. His mind was shrinking further into itself, crumpling up and flaking away like a sheet of paper too near an open flame. He reached for the etched shapes on the ground. He couldn't see the unholy light, but the supernatural nature of the ritual was evident. Shapes drawn with simple chalk refused to be wiped away as he dragged himself over them. His extended hand approached the chip of crystal sitting in the center. Though the incoherent growls of Lenny may as well have been echoing from the bottom of a well, and the clawing fingers on his legs were little more than a half-forgotten notion, something very real and very potent seared his fingers. The unseen light and power of the shard managed to assert itself as the one part of Alan's world that was still real.

"No!" Lenny shouted. "N-no..."

The grip on Alan's leg weakened. He heaved himself free and slapped his hand down over the shard. When it touched his flesh, his ears suddenly filled with the horrid screeches of dozens of shades sizzling under the prison's lights. He pulled the shard from the ritual circle. It felt like he was clutching a hot coal, but as soon as it was free of the chalk figure, the screeches and cries started to die down. The influence of the final stage of the spell eased away, unable to complete itself and become permanent as the first few stages had.

He clasped the shard tight in both hands, holding it close to his chest as he curled up on the ground. There wasn't much time left, and the shard was the one thing left that felt real. He held it tight and focused on it. A single candle in a sea of oblivion.

Blot wove through the vents. Her mind felt like it was on fire, and not merely because she was disconnected from her host and badly in need of a new one. Through her training, one of the most crucial parts of her education had been aimed at assuring her that the humans wanted nothing more than to exterminate the dark and everything it hid. Though she'd learned that much of her training had been false, its roots reached deep into her. She still believed, with plenty of evidence, that humanity as a whole had only hatred in its heart for things like her. All of Alan's actions had managed to convince her only of the fact that he specifically might be an exception. Knowing that she'd left him to die had awakened the conscience that her superiors had so strenuously tried to train away.

She emerged from a rattling grate into the shadow of the building. Ahead lay the parking lot. It was crowded with vehicles that hadn't been there when they'd arrived. A news crew was already setting up. They had a camera Alan probably would have killed for trained on a woman with immaculate blond hair and perfect diction speculating into a microphone. Some distance away, the SWAT van she recognized from the police lot belched fumes as officers in heavy armor equipped themselves.

Other bits of her training surfaced, measuring each of the people she saw for their potential value as a host. The newscaster would have significant influence over the thoughts and minds of others. People on television tended to have a lot of money too. But right now money was second to safety. The SWAT officers had training and access to much better equipment to defend themselves. People like them usually had fairly strong wills. She would have to lay low for a long time and gently ease herself into their awareness. If she chose one of them, she would be safe, but she might be little more than a shadow, eyes closed and form matching theirs for months. No watching videos. No drinking coffee. No talking. No sharing dreams. No *life*.

Blot's memories of the last few weeks flicked across her mind. The only thing that should have mattered was staying alive. Every second that ticked by without a host to anchor her was another step closer to fading away forever. The parking lot was *filled* with fine hosts. She was spoiled for choice, and even if such hadn't been the case, *any* host was better than squandering her rapidly dwindling strength deliberating over one of them. But she couldn't shake the feeling that all those little things she'd be giving up were worth so much more than the things she'd been taught to desire. And the sort of person who could provide them was so much harder to find than someone who was merely influential or powerful.

Her thoughts were getting muddy. Desperation for something solid to hold on to started to compete with anger, doubt, confusion, and shame. She had to stay sharp. She had to act fast. This was important. There were a dozen correct choices she could make.

But there was only one choice that was *right*...

Jessie rushed through the halls. With the power on, and thus full surveillance active again, something resembling order and organization was being restored to the emergency response team. At some point the more logical part of her mind came to embrace the fact that things had progressed to the point that she would only be in the way if she attempted to lend a hand.

One of the more frustrating things that police officers had to deal with on a daily basis was the utter inability for the average person to stay out of the way when better-prepared, clearer-headed trained professionals were trying to do their jobs. Now that she had skin in the game, in the form of a dear friend buried somewhere deep in the middle of still-simmering prison unrest, she found it took every ounce of her self-control to keep from shoving guards and paramedics out of the way to get to the heart of Cellblock 33 first.

As she ran, falling mere steps behind men in riot gear, she couldn't help but dwell upon the fact that Alan had seemed to know this very disaster was going to happen. Learning the source of his premonition joined several thousand other reasons for why she was determined to find and save him. Until then, though, she could only watch, wait, and try to rub away the lingering prickling sensation in her shoulder from standing in a cloud of fire suppressant.

Alan didn't know if he was alone. He felt alone, insomuch as he felt anything at all. Even the searing sensation of the Shard of Shadow tight in his grip was fading away. Though his eyes were open, the images that reached his brain were tiny and sapped of color. He felt cold. It was the same sort of cold he felt when he was tugged into the shadows. This time, there was nothing guiding him. There was no control. The long, slow slide from reality started to accelerate. Until now, he'd been floating atop the icy lake of nothingness. Now he'd started to sink below the surface. He wasn't sure if he was breathing anymore. It didn't matter. Nothing mattered. His last task was done. The world was done with him. It was time to go.

He dipped below the surface of consciousness. It wasn't sleep. It was far beyond that. Far below it. And he was slipping further. Dropping. Adrift. Unmoored.

Then, a single, precious point of reality asserted itself. Small, strong fingers laced between his. They held firm to his hand. Color and sensation started to weave its way up his arm. A fresh flame stoked in his mind. One by one, his senses awoke. The last of them was his vision, which gradually faded from blackness to reveal two piercing, soulful eyes staring deep into his.

"I'm here, Alan," Blot said.

A world started to knit itself out of the nothingness. Downy soft grass, still a muted gray, spread out beneath him. A paler gray sky pooled into existence above. The impish form of Blot helped him to his feet.

"Where am I?" he asked.

"You're out cold. This is a dream," she said.

"You came back for me," he said.

"Try not to flatter yourself too much," she said. "I didn't want to have to break in another host. With my luck, I'd end up paired with someone who drinks decaf."

"Did I do it? Are they alive?"

"I wouldn't have made it here if you didn't stop the spell. How'd you get past Brink?"

"I didn't. He wasn't there. Just Lenny. Do you know what's going on out there?"

Blot shut her eyes, as though it was necessary to look upon the waking world.

"A wave of guards and police and the like are heading this way. The inmates are jabbering like fools, and they aren't putting up a fight. Some medical people are picking through, separating off the people who need treatment." Her expression soured a bit. "And Jessie is headed this way. Looks like you're going to have an escort to the hospital."

Alan nodded and took a breath, testing the renewed senses. "So... what made you decide to come back? And skip the coffee jokes."

She raised her nose haughtily. "I never joke about coffee."

"Come on."

"The truth?" she asked.

"Yes."

"There are a lot of reasons, Alan. Don't get me wrong. You're still pretty subpar as hosts go. There were some *real* gems out there." She gazed upward dreamily. "Oh, what I could have done with some of those SWAT officers. But you taught me there is more to a host than what they can do for you, and what you can do with them. There's the biggest part. There's *being* with them. And there's how you feel about yourself when you're around them. Maybe I could whip one of those guys into something tolerable. But it would never be the same. I think, maybe, right now at least, I don't want a host. I want a *home*. And I have that with you."

"Blot, I'm touched."

"Don't be. I'm not done." She raised her hand and produced an unmistakable fragment of gemstone. "I *also* came back because you were holding *this*."

"The Shard of Shadow."

"That's right. It's pretty depleted right now from fueling such a big set of spells, but I can still feel the power inside it. And it's returning bit by bit. This is going to help us keep ourselves nice and safe, once I work out how to use it, and how to hide it."

"Okay, that's fair."

"And *third*, don't think I don't know that me coming back to save your life means you owe me *big time*. So if you want to show your gratitude, I expect some changes. Starting now. First and foremost, you've got to stop being so trusting and optimistic. That Brink guy was *exactly* who I warned you he was."

"Yeah, I know…"

"From now on, if I tell you someone is no good, I *mean* it. Things are only going to get harder. It's one thing for me to be a traitor. We just launched a huge, very successful attack on my people. Sapped them of their power. Left them helpless and imprisoned. That's an act of war."

"But I ran in and stopped the spell that would have killed them. Surely that counts for something."

She crossed her arms. "You've met a fair number of my people by now, Alan. Do we strike you as the forgiving type? And you don't really get any bonus points for saving their lives when it was your fault the lives were endangered to begin with."

"Alan!"

The voice echoed through his head. It wasn't Blot, but it *was* a woman. And a very worried one.

"Alan, wake up!" the voice insisted.

It was Jessie.

"Time to wake up, then," Blot said. "You're going to have a lot of questions to answer. Listen closely to me. I'll help you lie like a seasoned veteran."

She vanished like the Cheshire cat, only her eyes and mouth remaining as the dream started to fall apart around her. "Oh, and when you wake up, remember these words. I told you so."

Alan's eyes shot open. He tried to gasp, but something was blocking his mouth. The blockage cleared, and, for the second time since he'd passed out, he found a pair of concerned eyes staring into his. The leaden curtain of unconsciousness was only just beginning to lift. Having been rendered incomplete by Blot's departure hadn't done his brain any favors either. As a result, it took several seconds to realize that the thing that had been blocking his breathing a moment ago was Jessie's lips. She'd been giving him CPR.

"He's coming around," she shouted. "What day is it?"

"I'm a freelancer, Jessie," he said sluggishly. "I can barely keep track of that when I *don't* have a concussion."

She released a relieved laugh and turned to the source of some sort of commotion beside him. "How's he coming along?" she shouted.

Alan turned his head dizzily to find paramedics feverishly pounding someone's chest and applying a mobile defibrillator.

Assorted medical terms Alan knew exclusively from police procedurals barked out of the cluster of emergency workers.

"Unresponsive. Pupils fixed and dilated. Complete cardiac arrest. Respiration negative."

A stretcher rolled through the hall, and Alan caught a glimpse of Lenny as he was loaded onto it.

Alan tried to get up.

"Oh, no. You're not going anywhere without a stretcher," she insisted. "You just lie there."

Alan blinked and turned aside. Now that his wits were returning and the adrenaline was fading, his body was loudly complaining about the accumulation of injuries. Along with too many bumps and bruises to mention, rolling around on the floor while it was covered with glass from the overhead fixtures had poked enough holes in him to bloody his hands and arms.

"That's some intuition you've got, Alan. You were sure something was going to go down, and boy, did you call it," she said.

"Yeah, there's a little voice in my head these days who seems to know what's going to happen."

He turned his head aside. Blot stared back from the wall beside him.

"Lips, locked. First opportunity," the shade stated.

"Are you okay? Did you get hurt? Inmates were running amok," Alan said, turning back to Jessie.

"I'm fine. By the time we got the lights on, something had spooked the inmates good. Most of them have been herded out into the exercise yard. But I'll tell you this. Once the smoke clears, something tells me you're going to have a *lot* of questions to answer."

Epilogue

"I'm fine, Mom. They feed you here, remember?" Alan said.

It had been two days since the event at the prison, and Alan was sitting up in the hospital bed with a laptop on his lap. He'd assured all involved that he was fine, but it turned out that if you've lived through a prison riot, you're not going home until you've had a fair bit of nebulously defined "observation." On the medical side, that meant a couple of stitches and a few electrodes affixed with adhesive that were likely to take a plug of his hair with them when the time came to remove them. On the psychological side, that meant a lot of questions with unclear motivation, and no less than seventy-two hours in a place where they could be confident you wouldn't do any harm to yourself.

His parents had worn out their welcome during visiting hours, but they'd managed to leave approximately twenty thousand calories of junk food and homemade goodies. Three hours seldom went by without a call from one or the other.

"Yes. Yes, I gave them my insurance information. We went over this yesterday. ... Well, of course it's still going to be expensive. This is America. Land of the free, home of medical debt. Do me a favor and worry about

your own finances. I'll worry about mine. ... I'll see you when I get out."
He slumped. "Yes I have underwear, Mom. ... Okay, bye. Love you." He
hung up and found the end of his charger to plug the phone in.

"It's too bright in here, Alan," Blot said. "I swear to the darkness itself
that if you don't get us out of here and into someplace nice and dim, I am
going to start yanking wires out of the wall."

"Yeah, I know. I'm sorry."

The fluorescent lights of the hospital had her pinned roughly beside
him, as though she were trying to whisper in his ear. The adjustable bed
at least meant that she could stare at the screen as he worked.

A quiet chime indicated the arrival of an email with entirely too many
exclamation marks. Cox was, to put it lightly, pleased with the footage
Alan had been able to recover from his battered cameras. It had taken a
considerable amount of persuasion for the hospital staff to allow him to
get any work done, but he'd clipped out some sizable chunks of the shaky,
poorly lit recordings and photos he'd taken and uploaded them to Cox.
The prison wouldn't be happy the footage was going out, but at this point
Alan had stopped keeping track of how many people were unhappy with
him.

The riot footage was easily some of the worst output he'd produced in
his professional career, but Cox was raving about how "raw" they were. He
promised a massive payday. If Alan was lucky, it would cover enough of his
hospital bill to not put him into years-long debt.

Alan finished answering the email and watched the last few percent of
the latest upload fight their way through the hospital's Wi-Fi. He switched
to a new browser tab and brought up a streaming app and started an
episode of *The Great British Bake Off*. A satisfied smile curled Blot's lips.

"Lemon curd..." Blot said. "I think I could make a lemon curd. It looks like it's just like brill pudding. Only more yellow. And probably you don't have brills here." She subtly revealed her pad and pencil, tucked behind Alan, and started jotting down notes.

"Knock, knock!"

Alan looked to the curtain to find Jessie, in full uniform, standing there.

"Of course," Blot muttered, vanishing her pad again.

"I guess swish, swish would have made more sense," she said, nudging the curtain aside. "I'm surprised they don't have you in a room yet."

"I've only got another half a day and then I can get out of here, so I'm not going to hold my breath for it."

"Fair enough. I brought you some stuff." She took a seat in the visitor's chair and set down a plastic bag. "Your mom wanted me to bring you some soup."

"I should have known she'd recruit you to smuggle more food in here."

"Broccoli cheddar," she said, reaching into the bag. "And I got these back for you. I didn't even know there were still places that developed film."

He took a paper envelope from her and eagerly flipped it open. "There are still places that make musket balls. Technology never completely goes away." He flipped through the pictures from the film camera. "Wow. Some of these actually came out."

"Was there any doubt?"

"Film is more temperamental than digital. Particularly with my old camera."

He started sorting the pictures into piles of good and bad on the keyboard of the laptop. The good pile was very small. By the time he'd been using the film camera, he'd been more interested in using the flash to keep himself alive than getting a good shot, and it showed.

The sound of Jessie grumbling drew his attention from the cards. She'd slipped a hand into the collar of her shirt to scratch at the back of her neck.

"Something wrong?" he said.

"Oh, don't mind me. I think I had an allergic reaction to something I got on me in the prison. I keep getting this weird itch. It comes and goes, but today I can't seem to shake it."

She finished her scratching and picked up the "bad" stack of photos. "This is like something from a horror movie." She flicked through. "All blurry and stark. This one's pretty good. Except for the shadow."

He glanced at the one she was indicating. It was a shot of a random inmate, and by Alan's standards it wasn't even *approaching* good. The framing was crooked, and there wasn't anything resembling proper composition. But the image was at least sharp. He shuddered slightly as he gazed at the shadow. The flimsy flash hadn't been enough to completely push the shade behind the man casting it, so a twisted form still peered around him, white eyes burning with anger.

Alan's expression became more stern. "What's wrong with the shadow?" he asked, keeping his tone as even as possible.

"It's all twisty. And there are those two spots there. What's *that* all about?" she said.

Blot huddled down a bit farther behind Alan. "What did she say?" she whispered warily.

"Spots." Alan tapped the photo. "These spots here?"

"Yeah. They kind of look like eyes. What causes that? Is that lens flare?"

"Yes." Alan said woodenly as he took the photo from her. "Lens flare." He gathered up both piles and dropped them beside Blot.

"She doesn't have a shade. I'd know if she had a shade. Why can she see the eyes, Alan? *Why can she see the eyes?!*" Blot raved in a near-silent hiss directly into Alan's ear. "I don't like when the rules change. People without shades aren't supposed to see us. You've taken photos of us before, and no one could see but you."

"I guess things come out differently on film versus digital sometimes," Alan stated, hoping that the statement would serve equally well for both members of his audience.

"You'd know better than me," Jessie said. She glanced out the curtain, then casually closed it to provide some additional privacy. "Believe it or not, I'm not just here as a delivery girl. I have a semiprofessional purpose for the visit."

"What's up?" Alan asked, trying to force the buzzing of the recent revelation from his mind, or at least keep it from his expression.

"There's a big investigation going on back at the prison. As you might imagine, when something like this goes down, they take it very seriously. You're going to be questioned."

"I'm surprised I haven't been already."

"It's coming. And it's going to be intense. I can't get too deep into specifics, but that whole Cellblock 33 project weakened surveillance *just* enough for there to be a whole lot of question marks regarding what happened and when. The precision with which camera footage was unavailable was downright surgical in some instances. Too precise to be an accident. So the question isn't if someone was pulling strings, but how many people. Dr. Vale is already under intense scrutiny. But you're going to have a spotlight on you too. You were present. Right at the epicenter of it. Guilty or innocent, you're going to be on the record."

He nodded. "That's fine."

Normally, the thought of being questioned on such a matter would have been terrifying to Alan, but recent events had served to recalibrate his threshold for terror. It helped that the truth of what he was doing and why was steeped in the supernatural, which no sane prosecutor or investigator would consider reasonable to suspect of him.

"I'm not in on the investigation, you understand. I'm too close to it. Conflict of interest, and questions of my own to answer. So what I'm about to ask you, I ask as your friend Jessie, not Officer Hearst."

"Okay," he said. "If you're trying to set my mind at ease, you're not doing a great job."

"I saw you for a second, remember? Through the door?"

"Oh, I remember that vividly."

"How, and why, did you end up all the way back to the doorway of Cellblock 33?"

"It was dark, you were panicked," Blot said quickly.

Alan relayed the answer to Jessie.

"I've seen panic, Alan. I've seen fear and confusion. And you had it all over your face. But it wasn't prison-riot-level panic. You were moving like a man with a plan. Like a man with something to do. Now you don't have to answer. But if you do, I expect the truth. Did you have *any* solid evidence that something was going to happen."

"Of course not. You wouldn't have gone in there if you'd known something that bad would happen," Blot instructed him.

Alan sat silently for a moment.

"Fast, fast, fast!" Blot said. "When someone asks you a question like that and you pause, that's just a quiet way of saying you're lying."

"I didn't know what would happen. I was hoping nothing would happen. But that first trip through that place..." Alan paused again.

"This is a bad start, Alan. Are we going to have to run drills for the proper way to lie?" Blot said.

"You saw the pictures from the first trip," Alan said. "There was something wrong in that place. I felt like if I didn't go back there, things would have been even worse."

Jessie gave him a measuring look. "That voice in your head again."

"Yes."

"Don't blame me for this!" Blot snapped.

"Do me a couple of quick favors, would you?" Jessie said.

"What?"

"If you do end up giving a deposition about this, maybe don't mention the voices in your head. Also, possibly don't do what the voices in your head tell you to do anymore."

"Hey!" Blot objected.

"But, if it's any consolation, maybe your intuition is onto something. Considering the scope of that riot, it's downright miraculous that only one person died."

"One person... So Lenny didn't make it?" he said gravely.

"Afraid not. Pronounced dead on arrival at the hospital."

"I didn't... it wasn't *me* that did it, right? We had an encounter."

"Pff. No, unless you reached into his chest and stopped his heart and lungs."

"... Another one of those?" Alan said.

"Yeah. We had three more in the neighborhood of the prison over the course of the last few weeks. If this keeps up, we're going to have the CDC down here."

A figure approached the curtain and tugged it aside. Alan's eyes widened.

"I'm terribly sorry, ma'am, but I need to have a word with this patient," said Angel.

They were, as always, dressed in white from head to toe. This time it was a setting-appropriate lab coat, which blended perfectly with the staff.

"Oh, right. I should be running along anyway." Jessie gave him a slap to his shoulder. "Let me know if you need a ride home. Oh! And watch your email. Final choices are going to be made for the forensic position."

Jessie slipped out. Angel shut the curtain and cleared their throat.

"I did make it clear that it was important that this little assignment goes well for me, did I not?" they asked.

"I did what I had to do."

"You didn't have to do anything! I told you, this was charted territory. There were already *names* for the two most likely outcomes. But you... you recruited the Dawn. You trapped shades in an insubstantial state. A *Shard of Shadow* was revealed and utilized. And you... I don't even want to tell you what else you did. I know you think this went well, Alan. This did *not* go well. If it wasn't for the fact that Stigma is up north doing things that are potentially even more disruptive, you'd be getting a very stern talking to from Dina and Gabriel, and I think you can imagine what sort of an effect that would have on you."

"What do you mean? What went wrong?"

"Blot *must* have told you about the level at which manipulators like Dun play. You gave him..." They raised their hands. "I don't even want to say. It is a problem that will need to be addressed. And rest assured, you will have a role in it. Until then, the shard."

"What? No," Blot said. "I stole that fair and square. I have *plans* for that shard."

"Why should we give you the shard?" Alan asked.

"Because if we are going to use you for future tasks, you need to *survive*. You've already got targets drawn on you from three different angles. As that shard recovers, you will find things crawling out of the depths that you haven't even imagined. And more to the point, you don't have a choice."

Angel took a deep breath. When they spoke again, it was with a width and breadth that defied the limits of mere sound. It punched through to the core of the mind.

"You, Alan Fontaine, and you, Blot, shall present the Shard of Shadow. Now."

Blot's hand rose up. It trembled lightly as she tried to resist, but she was no match for whatever power Angel possessed. Her fingers uncurled and the fragment of crystal popped into three dimensions. Alan picked it up and held it out. Angel slipped on what might have been a welding glove. They plucked the gem from Alan's hand and retrieved a small silver locket from another pocket. They clicked the gem into the locket and held it out.

Alan took it. "Wait... you're giving it back to us?"

"For reasons that you'll hopefully work out eventually, we certainly can't just give it back to the Dawn, and intriguing though it might be to work with it, I really don't want to be responsible. But this, at least, should keep you from gathering any more attention."

Blot snatched the locket out of his hand and vanished it. "It's still mine," she asserted.

"So what happens now?" Alan asked.

Angel turned to leave.

"That's not for me to say. But if I were you, I'd keep my head low. Sooner or later Dina and Gabriel will be after you to clean up your mess." They hung their head. "And oh, what a mess you've made."

From The Author

Thank you for reading! If you liked this story, or perhaps if you found it lacking, I'd love to hear from you. You can find me online at my website, bookofdeacon.com. For **free stories** and important updates, join my newsletter.

Discover other titles by Joseph R. Lallo

The Book of Deacon – an Epic Fantasy Series:

Book 1: *The Book of Deacon*

Book 2: *The Great Convergence*

Book 3: *The Battle of Verril*

Book 4: *The D'Karon Apprentice*

Book 5: *The Crescents*

Book 6: *The Coin of Kenvard*

Book of Deacon Anthology: Volume 1

Book of Deacon Anthology: Volume 2

Other stories in the same setting:

The Rise of the Red Shadow

The Story of Sorrel

Entwell Origins: Anya
The Redemption of Desmeres
The Adventures of Rustle and Eddy
Jade
Halifax
The Stump and the Spire

The Big Sigma Series — a Sci-fi/Space Opera Series:

Book 1: *Bypass Gemini*
Book 2: *Unstable Prototypes*
Book 3: *Artificial Evolution*
Book 4: *Temporal Contingency*
Book 5: *Indra Station*
Book 6: *Nova Igniter*
Book 7: *Quantum Shift*
Beta Testers
Big Sigma Collection: Volume 1
Big Sigma Collection: Volume 2

The Free-Wrench — Steampunk Adventure Series:

Book 1: *Free-Wrench*
Book 2: *Skykeep*
Book 3: *Ichor Well*
Book 4: *The Calderan Problem*
Book 5: *Cipher Hill*
Book 6: *Contaminant Six*